Steamscape

D. Dalton

Author: D. Dalton
Editor: Nia Shay
Cover Art: Dennis Saputra

First Edition, published July 2013

Chapter One

"Where is that girl?" Jing Li turned on his steam-powered leg, all metal and gears from the thigh down. The mechanical knee whirred and clicked as it twisted at an inhuman angle when he moved. The heavy heel clanked down on the wooden floor.

Across the teeming taproom, Drina de Avila cupped her slender hands around her mouth and called, "Where is she?" But the noise of the crowd swallowed her voice.

Jing held up his hands uselessly. She shook her head in frustration and shoved past the people between them, her black silken mane flying out like a banner behind her.

She wore a coquettish brown corset over her white blouse, with clockwork keys instead of lace to keep it tight. However, she was too skinny to be considered pretty by most of the men in this place. She paused to put on a smile as she neared Jing.

"Where's our boss?" He stamped toward her on his habitual limp.

"I never know where she is." Drina's brown eyes probed the throng. Her focus whipped to the few mops of red hair in the crowd, but none of them belonged to their employer. Instead, they were all hungry customers. And she was the only cook.

The gaslights were glowing against the polished counters, and someone was playing a fiddle somewhere in the crowd, although only a few hints of any musical notes managed to tread above the noise. Towering over the mob was the late owner's massive grandfather clock, a wonder of glass and metal sheeting with its whirling gears shining in the lamplight. Jing buffed up the copper exterior twice a month.

He pushed his way through the crowd. His size helped, being that he was easily over six feet and barrel-chested. Drina fell into step behind him. She fired a look through the window to the twin railroad tracks. Another approaching whistle sounded.

The wood beneath their feet vibrated as the northbound engine rolled into the station, pulling up for a meal for its passengers and to refill its water tank. They'd built the Pitchstone Waystation with a pullout so that the north and southbound trains could pass each other. This was the only place in the mountains with dual tracks, and it wasn't uncommon for one train to be stuck for hours until the other finally slid by.

Passengers from the train on the pullout track could only exit to the west, and then climb through the other train. To the east was a two-thousand foot drop into the absolutely scenic valley below.

The waystation perched halfway up an ancient volcano on a rocky shelf in the Riverrock Mountains between Codic, the capital of Eliponesia, and Valhasse, the nation's current industrial heart.

The second train slowed to a full stop on the parallel track. Off to the side of the waystation, the lone dirigible's crew hauled their sandbags over the ship's railing as they lifted away from the Pitchstone's tiny air-dock, trying to outrun the oncoming storm.

Overhead, the aether bands in the sky shone in all the colors of the prism. The fifth element, aether, only became visible when in contact with one of the material four, and then only in large concentrations. High up in the atmosphere, higher than airships could venture, bands of the element twisted together in their mix of ever-changing colors.

Above them, the two moons coasted in the daylight as the clouds rolled in. One was a cold, dead world, but the other was pure diamond, determined by spectral analysis from Industrial Future University's best scientists. They'd said it was a failed star that had turned to precious stone.

Back inside, Drina nodded her head in the direction of the kitchen. "All these people need feeding." The pressure cookers were hissing under the stress and she could see them wobbling against the countertop. "Not to mention managed, but where's our manager?"

***

In the closet, where the noise of the world dimmed, a single candle flickered and made ghostly reflections in the steamy air. Solindra Canon, seventeen-years-old, poured some more water on the coals. A cloud puffed up like an angry retort.

The steam curled around her like mist. She held out her hand and watched it cross her palm, twisting as it coasted across her hand like a ballerina. Deep blue and purple blossoms surrounded her where she had packed them around herself. The steamflowers only opened in the presence of steam.

She closed her eyes and rocked back. "Father, I hope you can hear me."

"Unfortunately–"

Solindra gasped and jumped, accidentally knocking the candle into the water pitcher. The light in the room immediately darkened to only the simmering glow of the coals.

"—He can't."

"Drina!" Solindra grabbed her chest as if trying to push her heart back down inside her suddenly-heaving torso. The cook had slipped into the room without a sound, without even disturbing the steam floating about the space. Solindra, so deep in concentration, hadn't even noticed the light changing.

The young woman yanked the candle out of the water and struck a match. Then she glared at Drina with eyes as silver as the steam surrounding them. She sat back, hovering in front of the huge stack of travelers' abandoned magazines that she hoarded with the same care as a collection of rubies.

Drina's gaze softened and she brushed Solindra's fiery red hair away from the girl's face.

"We all miss him." The cook looked down at the coals and sighed. "But what are you doing?"

Solindra dropped her gaze and muttered something.

"What was that?" Drina asked, an edge glistening somewhere in her voice.

"Ghosts in the steam."

The woman bit down against a second sigh. "Cylinder, the steam isn't full of everyone who has died. It's just a story."

"So then how does the steam power everything?"

Drina inhaled sharply. "Because the aether that is dissolved in the water only reacts, or comes alive if you will, in the steam and the mechanical force of the steam itself. I know you know this because I taught you."

"I still don't know how you got a microscope up here," Solindra mumbled.

"You've had a better education than most kids in the cities. Your father—"

"No!" The girl pushed her away. "Drina, I can do it. I can talk to the ghosts in the steam. I know it. I can find my father."

"Everyone who lives in the Steamscape countries has tried, Cylinder. It's just a myth." Her chocolate eyes unfocused. "I remember the day your father brought you home to our makeshift family. Said you'd been abandoned." Drina tugged Solindra's blouse straight. "But he's gone and you're the proprietor of Pitchstone now. He left it to you."

"Right." The girl squeezed the creases back into her blouse again.

"And it's overrun with customers. Jing and I need you."

Solindra's face bloomed as red as the sizzling coals. "Maybe I don't want to bother with customers anymore. I'd like to meet real people someday."

Drina rolled her eyes and pushed open the door. Lights and sounds flooded the closet. "You meet new people every day."

"Not the ones who I want to meet. I read about airship-jumping players. Or maybe even Steam Princess Adri."

Drina's mouth twisted further down. "Whose father, Boras Saturni, owner of Steampower, *started* this civil war. And there are worse than him out there, too."

"What? Like crypters?"

Drina scowled. "Even crypters can be explained by science. If they're real."

"Or the Hex?"

"That's enough, Cylinder."

The teenager folded her arms. "But the war isn't *here*."

The cook gently pushed her shoulder, guiding her through the crowd. "That is fine with us, little Cylinder."

Solindra growled. "Drina, I'm not little anymore!" She stomped off, or at least she tried to, but got stuck in the wall of people. Drina waved at Jing, who started toward them.

A group of soldiers slouching in front of the fireplace stopped the large mechanic's progress. The gray and gold flag of Eliponesia hung on nails above the fire. The soldiers splashed their beers together and leaned back in their salutes to it so much that they looked as if they would fall over.

Drina pushed through them, with Solindra trailing further behind.

"Hey!" the cook yelped as one of the soldiers yanked on her long hair. Her thin fist smacked him in a roundhouse punch with all the momentum of her spin. Her short skirt flared out around her.

The man staggered back, his backside dangerously close to the flames. He shrieked and grabbed his ass. The other soldiers' faces immediately darkened.

Jing loomed over the offender, cutting between Drina and the soldier. Solindra slipped right behind him, staring in fascination. The men coalesced into a wall of six warriors.

Drina held up her fists and tossed a flashing smile at the growling men. "Your choice, lads."

"Men, stand to!"

Jing, Solindra and Drina whirled. An Eliponesian major shoved through the crowd toward the soldiers. His fierce scowl knocked the bravado from the privates. "Get back to the train. Now!"

The troops dropped their gazes. "Yes, sir," they mumbled, and then shuffled past the waystation employees without looking back.

The major brought his blue eyes up to the pair and then looked directly at Jing. "My apologies. They just can't seem to recognize a veteran."

"What?" Jing forced out a laugh. "Oh, no. I was never a military man."

The officer raised an eyebrow, causing his mustache to shift upward like the rising double moons. His gaze traveled over to the practiced and comfortable way Drina still held her fists. She slammed them down to her sides and glared.

"Any news of the war?" Jing asked quickly, sliding in front of Drina.

The major answered after a long moment, "No." He clicked his heels and dipped his head. "If you'll excuse me, I'm sure you must be busy."

"Oh yes!" Solindra squeaked and whipped her gaze back toward the overcrowded taproom.

When he had gone, she turned around and blew her nose at the flag. "That's my respect!"

"Cyl, no." Jing sighed and glanced at the pipes along the ceiling overhead. Steam was leaking at the joints again, but he couldn't help it. The hot springs, heated up by the volcano, provided all the steam to the waystation. He had constructed the piping system to bring that natural heat and water down in order to power the waystation, as well as provide train water and hot baths. And it worked perfectly. Most days. Some days, anyway.

The mechanic stretched his hands near to the leaden pipes, feeling the heat. "I'd just like a little place of my own where the steam is constant, you know?"

Drina chuckled. "I'd like a boss that I don't have to boss around."

"Hey!" Solindra said.

"Alright, I didn't mean it, Cyl." The cook thumped on the steampipe. "Something wrong with the springs again?"

Jing raised an eyebrow. "Do you think I can fix the volcano by banging my wrench against it?"

She shrugged. "Sometimes, I really think you can."

Drina and Jing exchanged a look before turning back to the crowd. Solindra was watching the two of them for cues. The mechanic ran a hand through his hair. "The conductor said that the south train needs some work on its cattle-catch."

But Solindra didn't hear him. She was watching the crowd. A man in black drifted in front of them, seemingly at ease in the forest of people. He wore a bowler hat and carried a slender glass cane underneath his arm.

Solindra's gray, almost silver, eyes followed him for a moment before the swell of the throng overwhelmed her. She could see the two different cities in the taproom. The women from Codic wore shorter, ruffled skirts and thick, high stockings that were the newest fashions. Meanwhile, the women from Valhasse wore dirty shirts and trousers. Soot stains smudged their faces and they tended to shuffle away from the capital's women, who conveniently twirled their parasols between themselves and the working folk.

The men from the capital wore creased, crisp vests and jackets, as if there were no war. The men from Valhasse looked as if they'd just come off the factory line. Their eyes were sunken and outlined by dark circles.

A nearby man, obviously from Codic, checked his gleaming pocket watch, attached to his vest by a golden chain. It bore a scene of a hunting stag on its cover. Despite the war, intricate artistry was still coveted.

The Pitchstone didn't have much art, just the grandfather clock and a couple of antique gears on the wall as decoration. All the other gears were at work, either pulling in steam from the hot springs, turning the waystation's conveyor belt that Jing had rigged up for faster dinner delivery, or one of a hundred other everyday things.

Drina nudged Solindra, bringing the young woman's focus back to the moment. "Any ideas?"

Jing shook his head, trying to squeeze a few drops of grease out from the corner of his shirt. "I think we'll be overrun like this for a while, especially since the capital has to rely on Valhasse now."

Drina nodded. "Steampower provided everything to Codic."

Solindra frowned, her brow furrowing. "Why would the company that makes nearly everything for everyone want to take over the government?"

Drina and Jing exchanged a glance. The mechanic shrugged. "I guess they got sick of paying taxes?"

"News!" The Pitchstone's telegrapher shouldered his way through the throng. He was a neat, elderly gentleman with his vest tucked into his trousers. His white hair was cropped close to his temples and nonexistent on the dome of his skull, but he wore his waxed mustache like a badge. He waved at Jing and Drina, ignoring Solindra.

"I have news." When he reached them, he paused to straighten his vest. "I've just gotten word. A boulder has taken out part of the track between here and Valhasse. The south train is stuck here until it's repaired. Can't get anything on the radio either, but you know how unreliable those things are up here. Telephone would be down too, *if* we had one."

"What? What do we do?" Solindra backed up until she was pressed up against the wall.

Drina nudged Jing. "I could mix some opium into everyone's food, have them all pass out."

"Hm. I'll leave that one up to the boss." He looked down.

"Uh, what?" Solindra looked back up at him, wide-eyed. She started chewing on her lower lip and shook her head, causing her hair to wave like fire. "There are over two hundred people here."

"Right, I don't have enough opium," the cook remarked. "I mean, headache medicine."

"But you have belladonna," Solindra shot back. "Does that work?"

Jing rolled his eyes. "Only if you don't want them to wake back up."

Drina kicked him in his metal ankle. "Not in very tiny measurements. Then it's just sleeping poison. I mean, sleeping medicine."

"Do what you want." The telegrapher growled. "I am not sleeping on the roof again. It's freezing, even in summer. And last time you let someone use my quarters they stole my charcoal pencils."

"Sorry, John." Jing shrugged.

"I'm Calvin!" the telegrapher interrupted. "John was your *last* master of messages!" He jerked his vest again. "I can see why he left! Over two hundred people here and four people to handle them." He snapped up his chin and strode away into the crowd.

"But we only have two rooms to rent!" Solindra protested.

"One room."

Solindra turned to see the man in black. He doffed his bowler hat to the women and tapped the butt of his glass cane on the floor. "Cooper Smith, Esquire." He proffered a couple of gold coins of Eliponesia, and the gaslight reflected from the wreaths and gears embossed on the money.

Drina smiled tightly and took the coins. "Of course, Mr. Smith. Let me show you to your room."

He swung his cane between her and himself. "A moment, please." His dark eyes slid over to Solindra.

Jing stepped between Smith and the girl. "Excuse us, sir, but we're already busy, as you can see. So Drina will just show you–"

Smith raised his cane toward the mechanic. "Just a moment please, sir. I am a paying customer." He looked back at the proprietor. "You have the most amazing, otherworldly eyes."

Solindra blushed. "Thank you, Mr. Smith." She glanced back to her guardians, looking for a cue.

The man in black reached into his inner jacket pocket and removed a puzzle device. It was a wheel decorated with crowded etchings of pastoral scenery – the kind extolled by the transcendental literature so popular in the cities at the moment. She had many examples in her trove of abandoned magazines. This one boasted rows of letters and teeth like a typewriter's circled around a central dial. The numerals and foreign letters were raised in gold.

"Are you any good with puzzles, my dear? I've been trying to solve–"

Drina pushed Smith's hand and box away. "I'm sorry, sir, but we are just far too busy."

Meanwhile, Jing tugged on Solindra's shoulder. "I need you to run to the back and fetch me my tools. Now."

"But, Jing–"

The mechanic's grip was like a crushing vice. "Now, Cylinder."

Smith sidestepped Drina and materialized in front of the teenager. He smiled stiffly and held out the circular puzzle box. "Please."

"Don't." Drina's hand shot out, trying to intercept.

But the girl had already reached out. She lifted the stunning puzzle into her fingertips.

It disintegrated into its individual cogs and springs. Gears shot up past her nose and ears, and the numerals clanged loudly as they bounced off the floor.

"Oh!" Solindra cried, but stopped short of an apology. She stared at what had been left behind, glowing on her fingertips.

Smith chuckled, instantly chilling Solindra's wonder. The man in black smirked and then erupted into a neighing laugh. "A vessel!"

Chapter Two

"In all of Steamscape…" Solindra lifted up the glowing blue device that had fallen from the puzzle box to eye level. It took the form of a pre-civilization thunder deity's hammer, but it looked to the girl like a double-bended fishing hook. Patterns and endless knots swirled with an inner light deep inside the hammer, and they sparkled and moved whenever she tilted the device.

"A vessel!" Smith's neighing laugh didn't quit. "How long has it been?"

Solindra dropped the glowing device in surprise. It chimed like a bell when it crashed on the floor.

"Cyl!" Jing jerked her away and they plunged into the crowd. "Drina!"

The cook nodded. She jumped up and over the bar counter and jerked on a hidden lever underneath it. Holes snapped open throughout the steampipes across the ceiling, releasing a cloud of vapor into the room. Smith disappeared into the sizzling mist.

Solindra reflexively ducked underneath the descending steam. It was hot, but not scalding by the time it descended closer to the floor.

"What's going on?" she screamed. Other surprised shouts exploded around them and she clapped her hands over her ears.

The mechanic guided her out the door. He pointed up the mountain to the thin trail that led to the little pocket they had nicknamed the Garden. He swung wide to his workshop and came back out with two shovels. "Go!"

Overhead, lightning flashed. Thunder bounced around the mountain peaks.

Solindra tripped over her skirt on the narrow steps worn into the mountain. Her hands caught her fall. The stone gashed her palms as she rebounded off the granite. "Jing?"

"Go, child!"

She hitched up her dress with her free hand and kept climbing. They wound their way up through the trail's narrow turns. As they ascended, the sounds of the Pitchstone's chaos began to fade.

They rounded the final turn into the Garden, a natural bowl filled with a clump of aspen. It also contained a trickling stream lined with smooth stones, some radiantly green grass and Mark Canon's grave. On top of it, Jing had let out a small pipe to breathe steam continuously over Mark's special steamflowers. Their petals remained open almost all spring and summer on the grave.

Jing had made the tombstone from an old engine's steam whistle marked with Canon's favorite saying, *veritas temporalis est*. Truth is temporary.

The mechanic stopped in front of the marker and bowed his head. "I'm sorry, old friend."

He handed Solindra a shovel.

She let it fall to the ground without closing her fingers around it. Her face paled as she looked between the shovel and the grave. "I... I don't understand."

Jing sighed and looked away. "Sorry, Cylinder, but these are your old man's instructions."

"To, to..." She backed into the granite wall. She looked everywhere: the trees, the storm clouds flashing, the walls of the garden – everywhere but the grave.

The mechanic scooped up her shovel and held it out to her again. "He well and truly wanted to be buried with this secret."

"But why? Why now?"

He closed his eyes. "He said that if either of us ever saw such a puzzle box again that we would all have to know."

"Again? But I've never seen one before!"

"He kept this away from you all your life." He thrust the head of his shovel deep into the dirt. "Now dig."

Solindra, trembling with fear and rage, slammed her eyes closed against the sight of the flying shovel. "No!" She gritted her teeth and covered her ears again, trying to block out the sound of moving soil. Thunder boomed, causing the freshly loosened dirt to slide toward her boots.

"Solindra Canon!"

She flinched. She'd never heard Jing snap before, nor could she remember the last time he'd used her given name. She rubbed her eyes. She didn't know what to do.

Numbly, she curled her fingers around the handle of her shovel and followed Jing's lead. She had always followed the three of Dad, Drina and Jing.

She remembered when she, Drina and Jing had buried her father. She didn't know if she'd been crying harder then or now. Only the lightning illuminated their actions.

"We've all had to do things that we hated ourselves for doing," she recalled her father saying one morning as she sat on his lap. Mark had been supervising her as she had transcribed the telegraph. She had learned the dots and dashes when she'd learned her letters. It had been the first time he'd let her transcribe one by herself.

"We each had to do things, but it was for the highest good." A scowl weighed down on his brow, causing his brown eyes to narrow and his dark hair to slide forward across his forehead. "Or so we were told." A new smile washed away the brief darkness. "Little Cylinder, we always have to face what we don't want to. Face it, and it will have no hold on you."

"I don't understand," she had said, so long ago.

Solindra tossed a shovelful of dirt behind her. Her tears blurred her vision too much for her to see what she was doing. Time also blurred. She knew she was moving down and was soon working in a hole. The shovel's edge cracked against wood, jarring her back to attention as it thudded to a stop against the coffin's lid.

"No!" She yanked up on the handle.

Jing set his shovel aside and offered a hand to help her climb out of the hole. Then he turned his back and smashed the shovel through the lid, splintering the wood.

Solindra kneeled at the edge of the hole, helplessly staring. The mechanic reached down and removed the large fragments of wood.

She covered her eyes, but she'd seen enough. Two years of burial had not been kind to Mark Canon. The only father Solindra had ever known was well into becoming part of the earth again. The bottom of the coffin had rotted away.

She slammed her eyelids down, but the scent knocked her back. It wasn't strong, not after two years, but the echo of the smell of decayed meat was still there, clawing its way up her nose. But through the nasal cacophony there was just a hint of what Mark had smelled like when he had been alive.

Jing reached down and wrestled an identical puzzle box from his friend's skeletal hand. He bowed his head. "I'm sorry that it came to this. I know that you had expected to be here."

"Daddy…" Solindra whispered.

Jing brushed the accumulated dirt from the box's raised, typeset numerals and ancient letters. He passed it to Solindra and when it touched her fingers, it cracked apart like Smith's had before. It released another stylized hammer, this one red and glowing.

Jing leaned against his shovel. "It's called a sancta, if I remember eavesdropped conversations correctly. Put it in your pocket, that's right. Now let's cover him up, Cyl."

She nodded, trying but failing to gasp out something. The shovel seemed to float on its own accord as she pushed the dirt back into place. The tears dripped off her nose to mix into the soil, just as they had done two years prior.

They were just patting down the grave down when Drina, breathless, rounded the corner into the Garden. "I lost Smith in the crowd."

"Doesn't matter," Jing replied. "We got it."

Drina nodded. "Good." She looked back to the rusting steam whistle poking up out of the ground. "Goodbye, old friend." She looked up at Jing and Solindra. "It's ready. I've got all the cargo, including our weapons and even our old uniforms."

"Weapons? Uniforms?" Solindra started shaking her head. "But my father wasn't a soldier. He worked on ships his whole life before he settled down to build the waystation. He told me that, so he couldn't have been a soldier."

Drina and Jing both hesitated.

The teenager repeated louder, "My father wasn't a soldier!"

Jing started to limp toward the path. "No time, Cylinder."

Drina grabbed the girl's shoulders and steered her away from their secret garden. "Everything soon, Cyl, I promise. Even the secrets your father had buried with him. But for there to be time in which to explain everything, we have to leave."

"What? Leave? Leave the mountain?"

"Isn't that what you've always wanted?" The cook pulled her toward the trail.

"Not like this!" Solindra bounced off the rock wall, stinging her shoulder.

"Too bad."

"Drina," Jing sighed.

They hustled down the thin steps around the mountainside toward the air-dock. A small engine pumped hydrogen into the waystation's emergency air-dinghy. The sky-boat had only been used a couple of times that Solindra could recall and she'd never been on it no matter how much she'd pleaded.

Jing ran his fingers over their emergency airboat's little coal-fired engine props on the dinghy's tail. He had built the engine and the boilerbox too. He had made them so they recycled the water of the steam that powered the propellers so the boat wasn't weighed down with excess water.

Jing's boots pounded on the wood as he approached the air-dinghy, barely big enough for four people. The pliable bubble hissed as its sides bloated. A cargo box had been latched to the bottom of the craft.

Solindra eyed the dials on the hydrogen tanks' gauges. Those were Pitchstone's most expensive possessions, since they were the hardest to replace in the mountains.

"We can't leave." She backed up toward the edge of the dock. "We can't leave."

Jing and Drina glanced at her, but the cook went over to the hydrogen tanks and Jing tossed another bag into the dinghy.

"All my things are in my room!" When they didn't respond, she waved her hand at the lightning and clouds. "And we can't fly in this!"

"Yes, we will," Drina replied coolly.

Jing paused at a large lever on the edge of the platform. The ornate brass-and-copper handle seemed out of place, away in its own little corner of the dock.

"Drina, it's fifteen years old, but I know my work."

The cook's chocolate eyes widened briefly. Then she shrugged. "There are lots of travelers in there, but okay."

"Never stopped us before." But his fingers slackened and he pulled them away from the untouched handle. "But we can't blame it on orders anymore."

"What?" Solindra stared at the dinghy as she watched the dirigible's bubble bloat. She looked back down to the lights of her home. "Wait! Where's Calvin?"

"He'll be fine." Drina pushed the girl toward the airboat. Jing fired up the propeller.

The cook helped the younger woman sit near the stern. Solindra gripped the side with white knuckles. The craft wobbled as Jing hacked clean the ropes. The hose broke free from the balloon, hissing and writhing against the platform since no one was there to shut off the tanks. The balloon's valve closed, and they hovered in the storm's darkness over the waystation.

"But where can we go?" Solindra gulped.

Drina pointed. "Valhasse. We'll get some information and supplies, and then we'll head for the frontier. Maybe beyond Steamscape itself."

"Barbarian lands?" Jing grinned. "Been a while."

Solindra squeezed her knees together and bit her lip. She peeked over the side. Lightning lit up the walls of the mountain, throwing blinding whiteness and deep shadows across her vision. She scrunched her eyes closed and huddled down against the deck, staring at the cook's boots. "Drina, I think I hate sky-sailing."

⚓

Chapter Three

"Crypter! Yer a crypter!" The greasy little man hauled on Theo's wrist, trying to spin him about. Theo just stiffened and planted his feet.

"What? No! Piss off, old-timer!" The nineteen-year-old set his teeth and shook his arm. His hair was a light brown, but the grease had stained it darker, so that it matched the color of his eyes. He eyed the constables down the street, but they hadn't seemed to notice. Then again, even if they did, he wondered if they'd care. Two dirty workers fighting in the street was nothing rare in Valhasse, especially since the start of the mass conscriptions.

He glared down at the street dweller. Then again, the constables might yell at them just to prove what scum they thought the workers were. Let the machines break their limbs instead, he'd overheard last night in the guardhouse.

Exactly where he wasn't supposed to be, and now he was attracting exactly the eyes he wanted to avoid.

"Crypter! Crypter!" The old man danced in place, roaring. He pointed at Theo's chest and cackled in triumph.

"Just a bricoleur." Theo turned and marched away.

"Bricoleurs are crypters!" the man snapped like a whip.

And it stung because there was truth in that. Almost all of the tribes of itinerant machinists and smiths did boast fortune-telling powers through the ghosts in the steam. So-called polite people ostracized them for it, but their bricolage arts made them useful, and they could make just about anything from whatever scrap happened to be littering the floor.

Theo's gloved hand went to his chest, where he'd felt the swing of a tiny counterweight. His old necklace had slipped out. It was only an old brass coin he'd drilled a hole through. It was worthless, but it was the only thing of home that had survived the fires.

It certainly wasn't a cipher medallion like the crypters were always hunting, whatever those things were. How did those fringe fanatics expect to communicate with the ghosts in the steam through jewelry anyway? Not to mention their secret order, the Priory or whatever it was called, that supposedly ruled them all. He yawned before he finished the thought.

He spat, "I'm just another man pounding out drums for the war machine."

The old man tugged at his gloves. "Then why ain't you–?"

"Shove off!" Theo swung away and walked down the next block, rounded a corner and took off sprinting down an alley.

He pulled around another corner and pressed his back against the wall, listening. No hasty footsteps echoed off the brick walls anywhere near him.

A steam whistle screamed from the nearby train yards. Theo flinched and wished he didn't know what those calls meant. He breathed, trying to slow his heart. Maybe it wasn't *that* train. After all, Valhasse's traffic had increased tenfold since the start of the war. Maybe it was just a regular cattle car or something.

He shaded his eyes from the blackened ash that choked the entire city. Smokestacks and boiler towers had been thrown up against any old warehouse-cum-factory now. He coughed out some of the ash into his glove.

Turning up his collar, Theo walked out of the alley into the droves of people floating down the avenue. Everyone wore black or brown, or rather, all their clothes had been stained black and brown, and they let themselves be dragged along by the crowd.

That icy, calculating part of Theo's mind pointed out that it was possible to slip by unnoticed as he focused on his target. He ground his back teeth. He hated when his inner voice spoke that way, but it did make life easier…

Before the war, Codic had paid Steampower to do almost all of its manufacturing, so now they were hurting to learn to bend metal again. The capital owned thousands of war machines on paper, but Steampower had stopped deliveries well before they launched their attack.

That meant that these poor bastards lost their limbs and lives churning out weapons and machines.

Another day, another atrocity.

Well, today some workers might get a break. Theo smirked to himself as he sauntered toward the boiler tower. He didn't dare raise his eyes to it, though.

This boiler had been constructed inside the decaying remnants of an ancient castle. Only the keep had remained after the centuries, and even that was half crumbled. The shiny, newer tower rose up through it in stark contrast, resting thirty feet higher than the old stones. This boiler was one of a dozen around the city's industrial zone, now in operation all day and night.

If the city was a body, these points would be various hearts, pumping out the lifeblood to all of the factories and driving their conveyor belts and machines. Of course, smaller heating sub-stations were everywhere, but those were really just fires to keep the steam active, and the ghosts happy.

Theo leaned his back against the old castle wall. He rubbed his shoulders between the blocks. They felt smooth and worn by the ages. He pulled on his cap and slid seamlessly into a line of downcast workers dragging their feet into the boiler tower for their perilous shift.

He kept his eyes pointed at the floor and shuffled inside. A soldier shoved his shoulder with a rifle butt, but Theo just rolled with it and kept on walking.

While the men trudged on toward the furnace, Theo slipped out of line and started to circle alongside the central pillar of the boiler. He hopped onto a thin metal line of stairs and moved up to a catwalk.

With his back pressed against the stones, he put his boots against the metal central pillar and started to walk his feet horizontally up the wall.

After a couple of minutes, he could feel the heat through the soles of his boots. He'd coated them with ceramic plating, rubber and thick leather too. He tried not to imagine the thousands of boiling gallons on the other side of the metal. His protections might not be enough.

Theo wiped his sweaty forehead, and it dripped freely off his glove. He frowned at the steel plate in front of him. Some worker had drawn the Hexagon before this panel had been placed. Theo guessed he must've been scared of something.

The artist had even drawn in each warrior's individual symbol at the points of the shape. It had been common –was still common – for the last thirty years to make the mark of the Hex.

Theo's mother had often charmed all the clan's kids with tales of the Hex's heroics in the border rebellions. But she also chided the youths that the Hex would come and steal them away if the kids didn't learn to pick pockets better. He had grown up with those stories just like everyone else, in total awe of invisible, fearsome soldiers.

People drew the Hexagon for protection, to ward off intruders, and even as a charm against evil spirits or as a curse on someone. The Hex. Elite warriors trained by Steampower for Codic's pleasures. Theo wondered which side they'd fight for now.

His eyes traced the symbols surrounding the shape. The Death Spinner – a soundless assassin, marked by a silhouette of a spider. Flame – Theo squeezed his eyes closed at his fiery stamp. Parrot – who was said to be anyone he chose to be, represented by a winking bird. Ghost – as close to a crypter as one could be – whose symbol was only a white circle. Silvermark – the leader, with his silver shooting star. And the Steam Slayer – the warrior depicted by claws.

The young man breathed in the coal-laced air and reopened his eyes. "Ghost, if you're out there, lend me your ability today." He had grown up believing that Ghost could just talk to the machines and make them fail. Of course he knew better *now*, and felt instantly stupid.

Talking to the ghosts in the steam. Ridiculous. The crypters claimed that they could send messages without a telegraph or radio, and even scry distant lands through the steam.

Theo scowled and re-secured his footing. He climbed a few more feet between the pillar and the tower wall. Glancing overhead, he saw he was running out of the old castle's wall to the place where the boiler continued up on its own. He hoped he was high enough.

He dug out a device from his pocket. He'd spent three months building this contraption to do two minutes of work. It was a heavy cylinder with a large, hollow screw in the center. He jammed it up against the boiler tower and waited for the coating of heat-sensitive glue to melt it into place.

Then again, this thing was hot enough it just might melt the glue entirely. Theo lifted his other hand to the handle rising out of the other side of the tool. He gripped it, squeezing his fingers as tightly as he could.

But he could not turn it.

Theo's breath came in gasps and he ground his teeth against it. The tool wavered in his vision and fires rose up in front of his eyes.

His boots splashed up the mud as he sprinted through the downpour. They knew by the look on his face. His mother had buried his face in her stomach and held him tightly. It had been the first embrace from her that he could remember.

She hustled him into the smuggling compartment of the wagon with several other children. He'd curled up toward the front, his hair sticking to the top of the false floorboards.

It was raining, but that hadn't stopped the fires.

Flame...

Theo gasped as he slipped down the wall. He scrambled to stop himself from falling. He felt one drop of sweat slide down his cheek, linger for a moment, and then fall toward the catwalk below.

He cursed himself. This was not fire. This was only steam.

But it could still burn, a traitorous thought flared.

He cranked the handle with all the force of his internal anger. The auger chewed through the deep wall of the boiler. It wasn't a large hole, but it didn't have to be.

Theo reached toward the base of the tool and pushed the valve closed. No steam seemed to be escaping. He unscrewed the handle from the tool and replaced it with a plunger. He dug back down into his pocket and pulled out a handful of small capsules.

Each capsule was comprised of thick, hard gelatin which would melt soon after exposure to moisture and heat. He shook one of the pills, listening to the waxy blocks rattle inside.

White phosphorous. It was so expensive during this war that he'd had to break into a mansion and steal someone's collection of sapphires.

The powder was incredibly flammable, and even better yet, pyrophoric. It would ignite upon contact with air once the thick gelatin melted far enough down the steampipes – and then it would also turn into phosphoric acid, causing even further damage.

Even more sweat ran down his cheeks. It was already so hot here, and the sweat made it dangerously slick. He glanced down at the capsules in his gloved hand.

He froze. Two more men passed below. These carried wrenches and their shoulders slouched forward as they walked. They weren't soldiers.

Theo mouthed, "Get out of here!"

His hand started to punch down the plunger, but then he paused. He wondered who he would really be hurting – Codic or those conscripted workers?

He shook his head and steeled his eyes. His inner, dark voice said, *the only thing you owe is your anger*. Besides, if the machines stopped turning, the slaves wouldn't have to work.

"They say the ghosts in the steam love fire. Well, here ya go, boys."

He tipped the capsules into the tube and closed it up with the plunger. Then he breathed deeply, opened the valve and slammed the plunger down, hurling the capsules into the steam-stream. He pumped the second dose into the tower.

He almost breathed out when he heard from below. "Hey, up there!"

***

Solindra lifted her skirt to step over a puddle of what she could only hope was muddy water topped with rainbow sheens of oil. She wrinkled her nose – it smelled like the privy.

Valhasse stank. She'd always dreamed of visiting a city, but now she was dreaming that she could just go home and return to pretending what a city should be. It wasn't supposed to be noisome, clogged with ash, or so downright dreary.

She'd always pictured people laughing in front of flower shops. There was supposed to be color and light! Instead there was fog, coal-scented air and herds of people like animals.

Jing, limping along behind her, tapped her shoulder. "Remember, your name is Marissa Clifton and you're from Codic."

Solindra bunched her skirts. "I've seen how those women dress, and I don't look like them."

"Smart. Okay, you're from Chimney Rock. It's a frontier town."

She gasped indignantly. "The border?"

Jing frowned and started walking again.

"Okay, okay." She pointed at a large, tall structure with pipes coming in and out of it at all angles. "Jing, what's that?" It looked like it had been constructed out of a rotted castle's core.

He blew out a sigh. "Boiler tower. Helps propel steam around the city."

They kept walking through the down-facing droves of people.

"Where's Drina?" she asked.

"Behind you."

Solindra whirled. There was Drina, standing there with a bag of bread and cheese in her hands.

"You always do that!" The girl's face glowed red.

Jing chuckled while Drina tore off a piece of bread and held it out. But the mechanic's expression quickly darkened. "Dinghy can't carry enough coal for a long journey."

Drina shrugged. "Sell it for a couple of horses then."

He shifted his weight onto his metal leg. "I don't like horses. But I suppose I'm game if it gets us out of the country."

"Remember why Mark didn't do that seventeen years ago?"

"The borders can't possibly be as well guarded now with the war on. Besides, nobody's looking for teenagers."

"What does that me—"

A steam whistle blasted four short notes and a long from the nearby train yard, halting Solindra's question. The ground underneath their feet shook at the weight of the rolling cars. Solindra's expert ears picked up that this was a fully loaded passenger train slowing to a stop.

"Four and a long?" she asked. "Haven't heard that combination before." She smiled. "Why don't we catch a train?"

"Not that one," Jing said darkly. "I read John's– Calvin's reports. We're not going into that yard."

The girl finished chewing on the bread. "Then why not a stagecoach? I've always wanted to ride in one. Even one of those that are pulled by horses."

The mechanic mused, "Buying a cheap farm cart might do it. Couple of draft horses. We'd be just another family of refugees."

Drina shrugged. "We'll probably have to bribe our way out of the city if we leave by road."

Jing sighed. "And neither one of us were the best at that."

The cook curled a hooked smile. "There's always my way."

"As if that wouldn't raise the alarm?"

"Not at all." Drina smoothed her short skirt. "They'd just blame it on Steampower, and us with the vessel–"

"What is a vessel?" Solindra pulled out the red sancta from a skirt pocket.

"It's nothing," Drina and Jing replied in unison.

The girl frowned. "This may be my first time off that blasted mountain, but it's not nothing."

Drina smiled sadly and folded the sancta down lower in Solindra's hands, out of view. "A vessel, is, ah, a rare person who both Steampower and Codic used to be after."

"Why?"

"Different reasons. They tried to ma—bree—*train* infants to be crypters. Real ones."

Solindra jerked the sancta free and jumped back. "I am not one of those freaks! How could the capital or Steampower give credit to those crazy ideas?"

Drina frowned. "So says the girl in the closet trying to find her father in the steam."

"It didn't work now, did it?" the young woman snapped. She gasped and lifted up the device. "This sancta-thing is a cipher medallion, isn't it? No. No! My dad was *not* one of those occultists!"

"No, he wasn't." Jing shook his head. "He was unfortunate enough to know the truth."

Solindra crossed her arms. "Which was?"

"He never said, Cyl. He wanted you to live a good life."

She tossed the device up in her hand and caught it again. "I say let's destroy the damned thing. Ain't worth nothing to me."

Drina caught it on the next toss. "Not right now. Mark thought you would need it if events came to pass, like the puzzle box. And since it probably *is* a cipher medallion, I'd suggest keeping it out of sight, young lady."

Solindra grumbled, but tucked the sancta back into her pocket. She jumped at the four-short-extra-long whistle combination again, blasting off right behind her. She turned and gazed through the tall, barbed fence between them and the train yard.

And then she saw a thousand or so people crammed into cattle cars. Only dullness splashed across their faces as they stared at the ground through the slats in the cars. Soldiers surrounded the train, sometimes even pointing their rifles directly at the people, who didn't seem to react to the threat.

Drina rubbed the girl's shoulder and Jing limped to stand between them and the fence. Solindra started heaving for air. "What is that?"

"It's called the Killing Train," Drina said. The woman paused; she and Jing exchanged a glance. "Some guilty, but most probably just happened to live on the wrong side of the new border dividing the country. Codic's clawing its territory back, you see? Steampower's got the better weapons, but Codic's got the men."

Solindra continued to gasp. "Killing Train? But those are people. They're *people*."

"They're just numbers to Steampower and to the capital."

"They're people." Her face had faded to a shade of old porcelain, and she started to sway like wheat in the wind.

Drina steered her ward away from the fence by her shoulders. "Nothing we can do, Cylinder. I'm so sorry."

"But they're people!"

"We can't help them." Jing stepped in way of her view. "I'm sorry."

A couple of patrolling soldiers drifted past on the other side of the fence. Solindra flinched at them, blinking back tears in her gray eyes.

Drina rubbed her shoulders, pushing the girl away from the train yard. Jing followed, his metal leg thumping against the brick street.

The mechanic stopped, raising his nose into the air. "Do you smell burnt garlic?" His expression changed to wide-eyed comprehension just as the first explosion rattled the street. Metal squealed briefly as the blast shredded the roof of a nearby factory. Its steampipes ripped open in a blossom of flame.

Fire consumed the nearest boiler tower from inside. A second, smaller explosion erupted from the top of the dome. The ancient masonry of the castle started to crumble away like a snake shedding its skin to reveal the body of the burning boiler. People streamed out of the collapsing building, not even yelling and instead saving all their concentration for escaping.

Solindra crashed down onto her knees, her cries lost in the sudden roar and stampede of the crowd. More explosions tore apart the steampipes leading from the nearest boiler in buildings on either side of them.

Drina wrapped her arms around Solindra and forced them to squat. Jing leaned over and shielded both of them. They backed up to the train yard's fence, having no avenue of escape.

Jing wiped the sweat from his forehead. "Chalk that one up to Steampower saboteurs."

"We're being attacked?" Solindra covered her ears with her palms.

"Eh, not so much," Drina replied, a treacherous grin on her face. "Maybe it's just an accident."

The mechanic groaned underneath his breath. "Either way, we'd better get out of here fast."

Drina eased her grip on Solindra. The girl gripped the fence, shaking so hard that she could hardly stand up on her own. Scents of burnt garlic and oil rolled over them, adding to the falling ash from the sky.

"Garlic?" Solindra frowned.

"Strange. Phosphorus, likely." Jing nodded almost approvingly. "Started fires in half a dozen warehouses I bet, and look at the boiler. It'll be so hot it will melt its own metal. They can't put that out any time soon. Not bad."

Solindra pulled herself up on the fence to stand, still shaking visibly. "I want to go home."

Shouts and shots arose from around a corner. A young man was sprinting ahead of several soldiers. A guard leveled his rifle and fired, but the runner had already weaved before the rifleman had squeezed the trigger.

The shot pinged off the fence above Solindra's skull.

She crouched down and tried to yelp, but the scream froze in her throat. She'd never been on the wrong side of a bullet at Pitchstone!

And now the world was filled with soldiers guarding the Killing Train and a city that didn't seem to have the heart to care. Its men were shooting on a crowded street!

Another shot rang on the fence further down from them.

"Just breathe, Cyl," Drina said, watching the runner and soldiers with eagle eyes. "This moment will pass."

Solindra wanted to scream at the older woman's calm voice. How could *anyone* be so unruffled right now? A third shot ricocheted off the brick street and back toward them, narrowly missing her thumb. She heard the bullet clink against the fence.

Solindra kept her hands pressed to her ears and watched as the fleeing boy, near enough to her own age, gazed at her for just a moment, before speeding back up.

She looked back between the herd of people bound for the Killing Train and this young man. She stood. "We have to help him!" She jumped forward and nearly careened into the fugitive. Terror lent her enough strength to almost catch up.

"Cyl! No!" Jing leapt after her, but his metal leg weighed him down. Steam hissed out of its joints at the sudden movement.

"Cylinder!" Drina spun around to face the oncoming soldiers instead of giving chase.

A soldier slammed the lever on his rifle home, reloading the chamber, and leveled at the runners. He started to exhale and his finger slowly increased pressure on the trigger. He never saw the piece of brick flying through the air aimed for his head.

***

"What are you...?" Theo couldn't finish, he had to breathe instead. He stared in amazement at this flame-haired girl.

That hateful part of him prompted him to think, why don't you trip her up? They'll stop chasing you.

"Shut up! Shut up!"

"What?" Solindra glanced behind them. "I'm here to help you. We need to hide."

"Help me?" He blinked in confusion.

She sprinted ahead, her gaze buried deep into the back of an alley. "There!"

They charged ahead into the darkness. Their footsteps suddenly surrounded them, echoing off the high walls.

Another backstreet corkscrewed away in the middle of this alley. Theo grabbed the girl's shoulder and tugged. She burped a yelp of panic.

"Don't! I guess I'm saving you instead." He stuck his finger in her face. She went cross-eyed, and he felt himself tipping forward into the silver orbs. He had never seen eyes like that before. For just an instant, their grayness brightened and he saw all the colors of the prism, just like the aether bands in the sky.

He shook himself free and yanked her down the curving, ever narrowing alley. "Just don't."

After two corners, they came to a thick, iron gate. He crouched down. Unlike most things that had been made before the war, this one wasn't all curving patterns and stained glass. It was a simple gate, meant to bar unsolicited passage.

She knelt beside him, shivering like a beggar in a blizzard.

The thundering of boots echoed around the curving corners. The girl flinched. Theo did too, and immediately started brushing off his soot-stained sleeves to hide the action. The footsteps didn't grow any louder.

After a moment, he exhaled. He cocked a seamless salesman's smile at her. "What crime did you commit?"

She just shook her head and replaced her hands over her ears.

He held up his hands and widened his smile. "I won't squeal, I promise."

"Home," the girl muttered. "I was trying to do the right thing, but I want to go home. But Dad's not there, so it hasn't been home in a while."

"What? Where are you from?"

"The mountain."

"Which mountain? There are hundreds between here and Codic alone."

She shook her head and rolled against the wall.

Theo sighed and leaned back against the gate. He rubbed his face with his dirty hands, only smearing the sweat and grime.

"Ah ha! Trying to escape, eh? Well, you should have kept running!"

Theo and Solindra whirled.

Five soldiers pointed their rifles at them from behind the gate. The one in front smirked.

The chubby trooper waved his gun at them. "How the hell did they get over it?"

Another one fumbled with his keys and then yanked open the gate. Theo jumped to run, but the leader of the soldiers slammed his shoulder with the butt of his rifle.

He smashed face first into a wall. Two more guards grabbed his arms. Another seized Solindra. "Jing! Drina! *Jing! Drina!*"

Her legs went limp, but the soldier just dragged her along as the guards hauled them both into the train yard.

After a few minutes, the engine began to chug and wheels started to roll. The whistle hissed its four-one note pattern as the train started to roll out of town.

***

The glass cane clicked over the cooling remains of masonry strewn about the street. Cooper Smith, Esquire twiddled his mustache. His gaze quickly passed over the bucket chain and hoses attacking the smoldering lump of metal that had once been a boiler tower.

He stepped over a corpse of a guard, kept warm by the nearby fire.

The man in black frowned and turned at the sound of an engine's steam whistle. The glass cane clicked over the brick street as he strolled toward the train yard.

Chapter Four

"Where is that girl?" Jing shaded his eyes against the glaring sunlight, reflecting off all the rails and boxcars in the train yard. The brightness had all but diluted the aether bands to nothing but twirling shadows in the sky.

Drina, bent low in the shadow of the alley, straightened. "Not here, that's for certain."

"I thought her voice came from this way." He clenched his jaw and glared at the conspicuously empty train track. "You don't think…"

The cook smoothed out her skirt. "Of course I do. And so do you." She nodded toward the alley. "And now we'd better get out of sight before—"

"Hey! Trespassers!"

"*Before* we're seen," Drina growled. Her hands disappeared inside her front pockets as she and Jing backed away into the darkness of the corkscrew alley.

Three Codic soldiers, coming from the street, brought their rifles to their shoulders and stalked into the alleyway. The shadow of the buildings closed over them and their eyes slowly started to adjust. They rounded another corner. No one there.

The first one called, "Come out! Hands up!"

Nothing stirred in the shadows.

The smallest man, barely two inches over five feet, started to back toward a wall. "I bet they skedaddled already. But where?"

"Hands up!" the first one yelled again.

"Have you ever been caught in a web?" a woman's voice whispered from behind his ear. He felt the heat from her breath on his skin.

A cord tightened around his throat. He'd never even felt it slide around his neck.

The third soldier spun and fired. He hit his choking comrade in the chest. The bullet passed right through his body, but Drina had been twisted enough to the side that it bounced harmlessly off the brick building behind her.

Jing slid a large, flat knife into the spine of the short soldier from behind. He sagged forward, eyes widening in surprise.

The remaining soldier swung his rifle at Jing and heaved on the lever-action. The new bullet slipped into the chamber just as he stumbled forward, pushed by Drina's unseen hand behind him. His entire body clenched at a sudden cold sensation. He squeezed the trigger and fired off into the sky.

A heavy hand helped his collapsing body faster to the ground, and then Jing slammed his metal leg down onto the soldier's skull and all the way down to the brick paving below. The skull popped apart with several splintering cracks.

Jing sighed and scraped his bloody and brain-splattered heel against the ground.

Drina pushed her long hair back behind her shoulders. "That was clumsy of us."

"We've gotten old." Jing exhaled and held his metal leg up as high as he could. After a moment, he let it smash back to the ground. His single metallic footstep reverberated around the twists of the alley.

"Out of practice," she corrected, deftly replacing her silk cord back into her pocket. "I haven't had the chance to kill too many people up on the mountain."

He frowned. "Too many?" He wiped his knife clean on a soldier's trousers and replaced it into the metal casing of his artificial limb.

The cook shrugged indifferently.

He blew out a sigh. "I hope they were worth it."

"It was to keep the peace. And if you noticed, no one was ever murdered or raped at the Pitchstone."

"No one was murdered," he repeated deliberately.

She lifted her chin. "No one that I didn't approve of."

"Oh right, because that makes *all* the difference. Did Mark know?"

She shrugged. "He never asked."

Jing pressed his back to the wall and glanced around the yard again. "She's on that train, you know."

"Likely, but…"

"We're not certain, I'm aware. If we choose wrongly, we'll have failed in our orders to protect her."

She pressed her lips together. "The others, they didn't—"

"Don't you dare finish that! Don't you dare." His gaze softened. "And besides, I like the kid, orders or no."

"I know." She jerked up a hand for silence and pointed.

Strolling across the train yard as if on a walk in a sunny park, Cooper Smith, Esquire chatted casually with the soldiers. His glass cane clinked against the iron rails.

"I want to know who he works for," she whispered, drawing back toward the shadows.

"I want to know his leads," Jing countered. "How could he have guessed we'd come here?"

Drina raised her eyebrows. "I think we can learn both." She tapped the warehouse wall behind her and looked through the iron gate. She stabbed the ancient lock with a very thin knife she'd pulled from a casing on her wrist. It fell away. Then they eased their way quietly through.

Ahead by the rails, Smith strolled on beyond the warehouse. The two soldiers accompanying him saluted and then hastily jogged back the way they had come. Smith ambled on alone, his cane clicking continuously against the metal walkway.

Jing and Drina hustled, albeit not quickly with the mechanic's perpetual limp, alongside the building to the corner. The soldiers were congregating up on the other end of the train yard, shouting orders ahead, waiting on the arrival of the next train.

The pair slipped around the corner of the warehouse, where Smith's cane had been echoing. But the man in black was gone like a ghost into the mist. Behind them, the ground rumbled as the next Killing Train rolled into the station.

***

The train cars rumbled along the tracks. Solindra swayed with the alien seesaw motion. Despite having lived her life next to trains, she'd never been on a moving one.

Nor had she ever seen people packed in as livestock. She'd rarely seen any livestock cars roll through Pitchstone to stop for water, but she'd always remembered the stench of terrified cattle.

It was the same here. Everyone tried to crowd to the center of the car. No one dared touch the door or the tiny, high vents. A scalding steampipe barred each opening to discourage any escape attempt. There was often a cry from someone pushed into the heated pipes by the sheer weight of the people.

Solindra traced the trail to the front of the car where the master pipe connected to a coal boilerbox built on the outside of the car.

She couldn't see the box itself, but she knew exactly how it worked.

She inhaled again. The air was too laden with the stench to breathe. Her hair seemed to be the only color in the room. Over in the far corner stood a knot of Steampower soldiers, gazes broken and shoulders slumping forward. Their black uniforms bore fresh tears and stains.

"You have very strange eyes."

She whirled to Theo, almost slapping him. So, he'd made his way back over to her. How dare he! It was his fault she was here.

He grinned, despite the hopelessness around him. "What's your name?"

She licked her lips. "Marissa Clifton?"

"Right." He rolled his dark eyes. "And I'm Boras Indecent Saturni."

She sighed. "I'm Cylinder."

He barked a laugh, raising a few faces directly around them.

She blushed as red as her hair. "No, Solindra! Solindra Canon."

His grin curled toward the side of his face. "Well, Ms. Solindra Canon, we are going to die. I hear that when we arrive, they stick brush and logs underneath the cars and light them on fire. We burn alive in our very own oven."

Solindra jerked her face away. "Shows how little you know. That would warp the axles, and more. The cars would be useless afterward, and Codic is already reusing boxcars that should've been retired five years ago. I saw them at the yard."

He rocked back half a step and raised his eyebrows. "Who are you?"

"Who are you?" she asked back.

"Just another bricoleur." He winked.

"One of those traveling thieves? My father taught me about you."

"Itinerant tinsmith," he corrected with that devilish grin. He glanced around. There were other bricoleurs on the train, too. They weren't part of the war; it was just an excuse to get rid of them.

The train rocked. Theo went with the motion and crashed into her. Solindra stared at him directly in the eyes.

He held up the faintly glowing red medallion in his gloved fingers. "What the hell is this?"

The girl went for her skirt pocket. It was empty of its now-familiar weight. "Give me back the sancta!"

"The what?" He squinted at it and held it up to his nose. Around them, the train's other unwilling occupants stared at the walls or the floor, taking an intentional disinterest.

His dark eyes widened. "This is a cipher medallion! Why do you...?"

His internal voice cut in and demanded, *Steal it! It's worth a fortune to those old, crusty cooks!*

"Some collector will buy this," he murmured. "I wonder if the Priory really exists."

Solindra grabbed at the sancta. "Give it back!" She wrapped her hands around his and jerked. "And I want no truck with stupid secret sects that don't exist! The Priory isn't real."

Theo had to mentally acknowledge the point. They probably didn't exist, but persistent stories like that one often had flakes of truth in them. He bet there really were men who sat around in candlelight and heavy robes pretending to talk to the steam. The mysterious "they" even claimed that the Priory owned all of Codic's higher-ups, including President LaBier.

He stared hard at the cipher medallion. It seemed to expand in his hand, driving out the noise and smells of the car, pulsing in time with his rising heartbeat. His grip loosened on the device.

He narrowed his gaze, letting it fall deeper inside the glowing hammer. There was something further down there, hiding in the center. Some image floated like a lily pad. Something bright. Something burning.

Theo screamed from the back of his throat, the yell bursting up from the pit of his stomach. He tried to shake away the medallion, but the thing seemed glued to his hand. He opened his fingers and hurled it, but it didn't move.

"Fire! Fire!" He leaped back, barreling over several people behind him. His free hand flailed at the invisible flames lighting up his body and clothes.

"What?" Solindra jumped after him, her hand going again for the sancta. "There's no fire, you idiot."

"Fire!" Theo started to tear at his shirt with his gloved hands. He could smell his clothes and flesh, and he knew very well what he smelled like on fire. It had been seared into his memory that day Flame had come to town.

He heard his mother howling as she died all over again.

A flash of silver interrupted him.

Solindra smacked him in the jaw and kneed him in the crotch, just like Drina had taught her to do.

Theo managed to focus on a pair of silver eyes in the middle of the burning wagons, hanging there in the sky.

A face faded into view, her red hair mixing with the flames. Then the memory released its hold. The motion of the train rocked him back to the present. He suddenly lurched forward in pain, realizing that he'd been struck.

Solindra glanced at the scars all across the young man's torso underneath his torn clothing, but then focused back on the sancta. "Give it back!"

Theo started to raise his hand to throw the thing clear across the boxcar. The hated part of himself wrapped his fingers even tighter. It whispered, *It's worth money!*

Solindra clawed at his glove. "It's mine!"

Theo grunted. "Not right now it isn't."

She didn't let go and stared in concentration at the red device. She let her own gaze fall toward the center of it. Now she was back in the closet, letting the steam rise and dance all around her. She knew she could do it then. "It's mine."

"It's mine now."

"No, it's *not*!" The rivets mounting the steampipes popped free from the walls. The pipes crackled like old newspaper, and they danced in the air like snakes on fire. People screamed, trying to stampede away from the steam, but there was nowhere to run.

The Killing Train's boxcar exploded into a riot.

"Kill the crypter!" A woman in a faded bonnet leveled a finger at Solindra's nose from less than a foot away. "Kill her!"

Solindra stared, all the words she wanted to say dying in the back of her throat.

From the corner, the Steampower soldiers shoved their way through the crowd. Solindra cried aloud as someone behind ripped out a length of her hair. Many more hands pawed at her clothing.

"Stay back!" Theo roared, putting the cipher medallion into Solindra's hand and raising her arm. "Stay back or she'll turn the steam on you!"

He kicked the nearest person in the face. The press of people around them lessened slightly as everyone in the car watched the glowing sancta.

"What are you doing?" Solindra hissed.

"Saving you so you can save me. Think you can burst the boxcar door open?" He dropped his grip on the medallion, brought up his gloved fists and eased into a fighting stance. "Now would be good." People tightened around them again.

She stared at the sancta in her hand. "But I don't know how!"

Chapter Five

The sagebrush scratched against Jing's metal leg as he knelt in front of the tracks. He couldn't feel it.

His fingers, however, could sense the slightest vibrations across the sandy surface. He didn't even need to touch the track to know the train would soon be in view.

He fingered the hose leading away from his prosthesis and into the Pitchstone's escape dinghy. "Time to hurry." He pulled out the welding torch's head from his leg.

Drina nodded and dropped more coal into the box. "We were lucky to get ahead." She reached down into the dinghy and retrieved a hatchet. She'd swapped out her skirt for her old uniform trousers and braided her hair into a crown on top of her head.

With barely a footprint left behind her, she walked to the nearest telegraph and telephone pole in a line of thousands that followed the railway, where the words effortlessly streamed across the vast desert. The entire wooden pole shuddered at the hatchet's bite. Drina struck again.

Jing attached the fuel tube from the dinghy to the welding torch from his leg.

The hatchet hammered and, after a while, Drina kicked the shredding wood over. The pole sagged forward on a broken back toward the tracks, tethered by the wires.

"Drina!"

"I know," she called back, marching intently to the next pole.

On the horizon, a pillar of smoke was beginning to come into focus. Jing laid a hand on the track and felt the vibrations travel up his fingers and his arm.

With a thundering crack, Drina dropped the second pole. The first pole crashed down onto the steel rails. Jing lit the torch and knelt over the telegraph and telephone wires and the tracks.

Sweat beads immediately crowded his forehead. He straightened the wires to the track and welded them into place along a good foot-long section, with them still attached to their poles.

He slammed the torch against the sand to extinguish it and limped away from the track. With his free hand, he wiped his forehead. "Should cause trouble."

Drina frowned. "But not derail it. Just enough to make them to stop."

He grinned. "Probably. I know if I were the engineer of that thing what I would do." He knelt back down to replace the tools inside their casing.

"You'd speed up, expecting a trap."

"Hey now." He stood up and shaded his eyes at the oncoming steam engine. "Just be safe, Cylinder."

***

"Kill the crypter!"

Solindra stared at the sancta. Someone knocked it out of her hand. Others grabbed at her skirt and ripped at her hair. Fingernails dug deep and yanked back layers of skin.

The shouts became so solid that her ears simply shut down. She tried to push back toward Theo, but too many hands pulled her the other way. Helpless, she was dragged like a fish caught in a riptide.

Daylight suddenly brightened the room from above. Gunfire outshouted the screams of the captives.

Solindra froze, her heart stopping for a second as the woman trying to pull her arm out of its socket died. Hot blood splashed her face from the gunshot wound. The woman's body sagged and collapsed.

The vessel craned her neck. Codic soldiers had popped open a hatch on the roof. More rifle barrels poked through the portal and more gunshots resounded.

Solindra covered her head and ducked. More people went down, some clutching arms and legs. Others were gone before they fell.

Theo slid sideways and tucked the cipher medallion in between his gloved fingers, avoiding looking at it again. He gasped as a ricochet bounced off the back of his leather jacket.

The gunmen stepped back and other soldiers leaned in over the hatch.

One of them slid on massive thermal gloves, and then tossed a handful of burning coal down into the boxcar from the boilerbox.

"Fire!" Theo covered his face with his hands, heaving for air.

Solindra slammed her hand over her nose. She still could not hear anything. She could smell it, though. The smells of burning clothes and hair instantly overwhelmed her.

The train shuddered beneath their feet, and she bobbled for balance. "We're braking!"

Theo grabbed her shoulders. He shoved the sancta into her hand. "Get the door open!"

She cupped the medallion in both hands. "I can't! There's no steam!"

"What?" He turned his back to the hatch and spun in front of Solindra just as the soldiers tossed more coal and it bounced off his back.

Her boot slipped on an ember. "I think this thing only works on steam!"

Theo cursed under his breath. The train shuddered again. His eyes flashed back up to the open hatch. The soldiers were pointing to the front of the train and shading their eyes against the desert sun.

The train's whistle screamed in sharp bleats. In response, the soldiers shouldered their rifles and moved out of sight.

Theo shoved several moaning people out of his way and pushed Solindra ahead of him. He interlocked his fingers on his knee. "Go!"

Solindra stared at him and then looked up. "But…"

"Now!" He eyed the Steampower soldiers marching forward, shoving bystanders aside.

She placed her boot into his gloves and then she was flying up toward daylight. Her knuckles banged against the hatch's edge, but managed to grip the sides. Theo pushed; she pulled. Suddenly, she was up and through the hatch. She crashed down onto the train's roof and rolled to the side.

The train was sliding forward on momentum alone now. At the front of the car, the Codic soldiers were gripping onto whatever they could while staring and pointing at something ahead. She was too low to see what, and she didn't have time to worry about anything else; those guards could turn around at any moment.

She rolled back to the hatch and threw down her hand.

Theo jumped. His leather gloves slipped against her sleeve. He started to slide back down, but his hand clenched around her wrist.

Solindra grimaced, but didn't complain. She let Theo climb up her arm until he could grip the edges of the hatch.

He kicked a prisoner in the face that had grabbed at his boot and pulled himself through.

Wheels squealed against the tracks beneath the car, shooting out sparks.

"Down!" one of the Codic soldiers hollered to his fellows.

Theo glanced up past them just in time to see the first telegraph pole shoot up past the locomotive's engine, spraying sand as the train pulled it out of the ground.

"Get down!" Solindra covered her face with her hands and dropped.

The train's motion ripped more poles out of the ground like a tornado in a grain field. The poles, still tethered by the wires, were helpless against the engine's power.

Theo flinched and flattened himself just in time to see the wire flash in the sunlight as it passed inches above his nose. He felt a brief, striking wind with its passage.

He rolled his head back to see the flying wire finish cutting through the neck of a prisoner just pushing his way up through the open hatch. A thin trail of blood opened up along his trachea, and then the head rolled forward.

The man's disembodied head blinked at Theo, then its eyes widened in horror and recognition before going finally still.

The train finally jerked to a halt.

Solindra squeezed out a laugh through her dry lips. She immediately slapped a hand over her mouth. She was in shock, but she couldn't stop laughing.

The Codic soldiers spun at the sounds behind them. Two of them started raising their rifles.

"Come on!" Solindra grabbed Theo's arm and swung over the edge of the boxcar.

Theo was already moving. Sparks from bullets pinged past him as he fell. Both of them crashed down onto the sandy soil below in a heap. He tried to snort out the sandy grains that flew into his nostrils.

Solindra bounced to her feet and beat a fist against the padlock on the bar across the boxcar's door. "Help me with this!"

"What?" Theo leaned back, trying to see the soldiers on the top of the car. "They were going to kill you, crypter!"

"I am *not*–"

More shots kicked up sandy dust at their feet. Solindra and Theo slammed their chests against the boxcar, squeezing out of the line of fire, at least until the soldiers moved directly overhead.

Theo growled. He glanced at the tracks. They could crawl under there and that would last until one of the soldiers climbed down. He craned his neck out toward the vast wasteland.

He shook his head. That option would only turn them into target practice.

That vicious, survivalist corner of his mind started to caress his shoulders. *Do what she wants. Let them out.* His left hand found the lock picks in the hidden pocket along his sleeve. Let the soldiers have too many targets.

Another bullet bounced off the sand next to his feet. Theo dropped his hand away from the picks. He wouldn't have time anyway.

Solindra clawed at the bar beside him. "Come on, come on!"

More gunshots retorted, but no craters opened at their feet. Theo, with his back still against the boxcar, looked up. He couldn't see anything, but the acrid smell of gunpowder drifted down from above.

A feral roar rolled down from the top of the car. "The prisoners! They're escaping like we did." He grabbed her arm. "Run!"

"Cylinder!"

Solindra and Theo whirled. The young man stared. A woman, wearing trousers, had just appeared like a ghost. Thick, long black hair curled in a crowning braid around her bronze face.

"Drina!" Solindra broke into a smile.

"Where...?" The question died on Theo's lips.

"Get down!" Drina pressed down on Solindra's shoulder. "How did you escape?"

A Codic soldier crashed down from the boxcar roof. His skull cracked open on the car as he rebounded off the metal. Above, the shouts of the escaping prisoners roared louder.

"Like that," Solindra replied. They saw the flashing shadows as the escapees leapt onto the next car of prisoners, pushing back against the few remaining soldiers. The guards fired their guns, but they were too few to stop the tide of prisoners.

Drina put a hand on Solindra's back and pointed toward the emergency dinghy. "Run!"

Theo wiped the sweat from his forehead and jumped after them. The dark-haired woman paralyzed him with a look. He froze, unable to move. It was a look of controlled, calm, hunger. He gulped and felt like a fly caught in a web, just watching the approaching spider, unable to do anything but squirm deeper into the net. His mouth dried.

Then she turned away from him and ran after Solindra. The Killing Train erupted with more people as the first escapees fished up the prisoners from the next car's top-hatch.

Theo lurched into motion. He weaved around a falling Steampower soldier. The boxcar roofs swelled with sudden overcrowding and shouts louder than thunder peals.

He charged straight toward the dinghy, gaining on Solindra.

***

Ahead in the dinghy, Jing easily picked out Solindra's fiery hair. He breathed out in relief, but kept his eyes trained on the front of the train, down the shaft of his steam rifle. The weapon's hose was plugged into the dinghy's boilerbox, and it was better suited for night shooting, since it had no loud retort or revealing flash.

It fired bundles of long, thick needles at once, each dart equipped with fins to stabilize its flight.

He squeezed the trigger.

The two Codic soldiers standing on the boxcar nearest to the engine never turned since there was no thunder from a rifle.

A spread of heavy needles slammed into their backs, driving deep into the bones and lungs.

Jing lifted the barrel up when he saw Solindra and Drina nearing. "Come on!"

Drina chased the girl like a mother hen. Behind them followed a brown-haired young man that looked familiar. He lowered the barrel and idly moved the gun in the boy's direction.

Solindra clambered over the edge of the airship. She beat her hands against its side. "Come on, let's go!" She waved at Theo and Drina.

Jing swung the rifle into Theo's face. "You can join back up with the rest of them, boy."

"He saved my life!" Solindra leaned over the dinghy's railing.

"After he put it in danger in Valhasse," Drina said quietly. "I recognize him now."

"He comes with us!" Solindra swung a leg back over the railing.

"Uh, please?" Theo slowly raised both his hands, staring cross-eyed at the steam rifle.

"No!" Jing and Drina snapped in unison.

Theo glanced over his shoulder at the locomotive, and the last block of Codic soldiers mounting a rotating gun. The metal bulk could fire nonstop as long as someone kept turning the hand crank and someone else kept feeding bullets into its guts.

The Killing Train would complete its mission right here if they had enough ammunition for that thing. The tide of people flowed away from the soldiers as they started to crank out its unending firepower.

"I can get you out of Eliponesia!" Theo grabbed the sides of the airboat. "You're trying to escape, right?"

Jing and Drina exchanged a glance.

"I know a bricoleur smuggler. She's the best."

"We can't trust him," Drina said to Jing.

"Hey," Solindra called.

The mechanic shrugged, also ignoring Solindra. "Recall the boiler. He's no friend to Codic."

The cook turned back to the bricoleur. "Are you a Steampower spy, boy?" Her scowl fell back into the approaching spider look.

He shivered, and all but saluted. "No, ma'am."

He and Solindra both flinched at the booming of the repeating gun. It spit out bullets with unending ease into the mob of fleeing prisoners.

Solindra grabbed at the steam rifle in Jing's hand, turning it away from the bricoleur's face. Theo hardly noticed. The shooting Codic soldiers stole his attention. All he could see was the fire from their gun muzzles. Endless fire.

Solindra pulled the rifle into her own hands and tugged the hose around behind her. She snapped it up to her shoulder and tried to focus on the backs of the soldiers operating the crank gun. They bobbed in her vision.

"Cyl, no!" Drina yelled.

The girl yanked on the trigger.

The soft "*phoot*" of the rifle was lost in the chaos. The expanding packet of large needles rattled against the train car. Two Codic soldiers shrieked in surprise as a couple of needles bore into their ankles. They whirled in the direction of the dinghy. More soldiers crowded around them.

Jing snatched the gun back. "Okay, it's time to go."

"What about me?" Theo grabbed at the railing of the sky-boat.

"Fine, get in!" The mechanic handed the steam rifle to Drina. "But you'll help." He bent low and started to heave out the rock ballast holding down the dinghy. Theo and Solindra quickly jumped in to help.

The Codic soldiers tugged and heaved at the crank gun, trying to move it into position to face the dirigible.

Drina's balance never wobbled as the airship started to rise, and she coiled the steam rifle's hose at her feet with practiced ease. Two Steampower soldiers charged for their ship. She kept her arm steady and gently tightened her finger around the trigger. They collapsed with a line of needles across their throats.

"Get us away from that crank gun!" She looked pointedly up at their huge target of a balloon.

Solindra chucked out the last rock and collapsed back to the center of the boat. She clutched her chest and swallowed her vomit back down at the realization of being off the ground again. "I hate sky-sailing!" She ducked back down to the deck while the ship drifted into the glare of the noonday sun.

***

With the sun setting at their backs, the remaining Codic soldiers limped down the tracks across the desert. The water tower had come into their field of vision long ago, but it only now had stopped wavering long enough to become solid. The wind teased the hose that fed the steam engines, waving it around the desolate tracks.

"Water," the smallest soldier muttered as he stumbled forward. He dropped his rifle and continued to plod down the railroad ties.

A man in black waited on the tiny platform below the water tower. He brushed a few errant sand grains off his sleeve as the soldiers hobbled up to him.

"Need water, sir," the corporal slurred.

Smith twiddled his mustache. "How many ambushed the train?"

"All of them," another soldier groaned. "They escaped. Ran away. Even the one with the metal leg, for the Hex's sake."

"Tall fellow?" Smith raised his hand. "Black hair?"

The corporal nodded. "And the lines are shot. Telegraph's down, can't even splice in." He pushed past Smith. "Excuse us."

They limped up to the spigot at the base of the tower.

Smith arced his glass cane across the spigot's switch, locking it into a closed position. "Tell me about the train."

"Nothing more to it. An airship, I guess." The corporal steeled his gaze. "Pardon us, *sir*, my men need water first."

Smith sighed. "As you wish." He lifted the cane and backed away.

The soldiers jostled each other, every one vying to be under the open spigot. The clear water splashed up against their hands and faces.

Smith pulled out his blue cipher medallion. None of the soldiers glanced back at him. He leaned against the base of the water tower with his hand pressing the sancta against one of the pipes.

He strolled away after a few moments, the glass cane clicking against the rails of the tracks as he began his trek toward the train wreckage.

The soldiers didn't notice. They didn't even pay attention to the groaning of the tower until it suddenly collapsed on them.

Chapter Six

Theo glanced over his shoulder. Drina glared at him while holding a coppery-colored metal crossbow. He looked beyond her to Jing and Solindra. The young woman was staring at his feet.

He looked down. Blackened wood crackled underfoot when he shifted his weight. The scent of seared lumber rose up from the ground like the souls of the dead.

He didn't know whose house this had been, but they didn't have a use for it anymore. Theo nudged aside another piece of scorched wood to uncover a burnt human femur.

"Hey," Drina called sharply.

He jerked his vision back to the air-dinghy. They'd landed in the middle of the rubble, and it sat with its nose rising into the air against the house's chimney. The mostly-deflated balloon shifted with the wind like an old sack.

"What are you waiting for?" Drina yelled. Beside her, Jing shaded his eyes at the sky, watching for more airships.

"Are you sure you can hit this?" He held up the white phosphorus capsule. "It's a small target."

She swung her crossbow at him instead.

"Drina!" Solindra snapped.

She lowered the weapon, but winked at Theo.

He spun around to the airship's boilerbox.

Jing whistled. "I cannot believe that those soldiers took out my matches. I mean, they couldn't hit me with a bullet, but they could hit a box of matches inside the boat."

"Why don't we just chuck the phosphorus into the boilerbox?" Solindra pointed at the dinghy's stern. "It's gotta still be warm enough to melt the gelatin."

"Um." Jing glanced at the sky.

"Oh." Drina briefly lowered her gaze. She brought up the crossbow to her shoulder. "Well, we're already here."

Theo dropped two more gelatin capsules onto the deck and listened to them roll across the solid boards. He wedged a third onto a wooden support for the balloon's ropes. He raised his hands and backed away from the dinghy. "Okay!"

Drina narrowed her eyes and slowed her breathing. "Just like shooting an earhole." She pulled the release. The string snapped forward and the bolt hummed at the airship.

The metal-tipped bolt cracked open the capsule like an egg. Fire fountained up as the phosphorus ignited on contact with the air. The spitting capsule rolled off the support onto the deck before it disintegrated into fire.

Drina elbowed Jing and said in a stage whisper, "If he hasn't been honest with us about where we're going, we're stranded."

"Codic soldiers could identify the dinghy and you know it. What? You're worried about some kid, Drina?"

"No."

Theo covered his nose from the smoke and tried not to close his eyes. He knew he would see those memories. Instead, he looked at the etchings on Drina's crossbow, glowing in the firelight.

"Where did you even find such a barbaric weapon?" he coughed.

She flashed him a grin. "What? Don't tell me you've never been outside the Steamscape before."

Theo glanced back at the fiery dinghy. "What other things were stashed in there?"

Jing patted him on his shoulder. "Do you truly want an answer to that, son?"

He threw up his hands. "Between ancient illegal weaponry and cipher medallions, I don't know what else you could have!"

"We should go." Solindra pointed at the flames where the treated canvas of the balloon was starting to smolder. "I don't think all the hydrogen has had time to—"

The airship exploded.

The crew picked themselves up from the ground.

"—explode," she finished.

They dusted themselves off.

"Let's go." Jing pointed toward the distant lights, hinting at a town. "Before anyone sees it's not just another house burning."

Theo nodded and pointed down the ruts in the road. "It'll be dark by the time we get there."

Solindra hummed to herself as she dipped her boots into the well-worn grooves. "I wonder if any survivors of the Killing Train will come this way."

Jing shrugged as he limped beside her. "Doubtful."

"You mean those people who wanted to kill you for being a crypter?" Theo sneered. "Well, are you one?"

"No." But uncertainty bobbled beneath her tongue. "At least I don't think so." She pulled the sancta from her pocket and raised it up to her eyes. "I should probably get a pouch or one of those puzzle boxes for this."

Theo put a hand up between it and his line of vision. "Might be a good idea, yeah."

"I agree." Jing turned his back to the fire and started to limp. "I know that I don't want to touch that thing again."

"When did you?" Solindra looked up at the mechanic.

"You were just an infant. And all I could see was steam. Could feel it scalding me, and there was nowhere to run away – it was never-ending, like a maze only without walls. Melting me alive as I walked." He shrugged. "Mark had a similar experience, apparently."

"Boys." Drina rolled her eyes. "Always touching things that need not be touched."

"So did I." Theo barely avoided glaring at the cipher medallion.

"Turns your fears on you, I once heard," Drina continued cheerfully.

"Why not me?" Solindra spun the sancta between her thumb and index finger.

"You're different," Jing said.

"Why?"

The mechanic stopped walking. He forced a grin. "Because it doesn't turn your fears on you, that's why."

"I'm not a kid anymore, Jing." She frowned, but started down the road again. "Do you think I could've used this to help all those people on the train?"

"I don't know," the mechanic replied.

"Can I use it to help people from now on?"

"Maybe," he sighed. "But I'm concerned with our safety first."

"Right." Theo rolled his eyes. "A crypter helping people. What would the Priory say about that?"

"You're a bricoleur," Drina said. "Many of your people *are* crypters."

"Yeah, but that's different. That's traditional. It has nothing to do with the Priory or cipher medallions. It's not some upright girl with a faux Codic accent."

"Hey!" Solindra snapped.

Drina groaned. "Are you sure we need him?"

Jing swiftly stepped in between Drina and Theo, his metal leg thumping heavily against the bone-dry ground. "As of this moment, maybe."

"Maybe not," Solindra said as she lifted her skirt and her nose. She and Theo glared at each other as they marched down the road.

***

The sun faded as they journeyed down the road. Solindra had to squint through the expanding darkness into the clump of buildings. Hardly any fires or gas lamps glowed inside the town.

"Welcome to Consequences," Theo drawled.

Deeper down the streets, a few lights began to highlight the town in an orange halo. The city itself had been shelled out. The remaining people had erected tents and other canvas structures over the foundations and half-walls of the previous buildings.

The party walked down the road into the town. Solindra smoothed her skirt. "The world is a stranger place than I imagined."

In between two half-buildings, a wooden board marred with huge, block letters screamed out against the deceits of Boras Saturni, president of Steampower. Someone had smashed a handful of whitewash across his face. A smaller poster to the side denounced the soft-spoken weekly columns of Adri Saturni, Mr. Saturni's daughter. But her face remained clear of any paint.

"Come along." Drina gripped Solindra's elbow and pushed her away from the propaganda.

Theo guided them through the streets that exploded with the reek of alcohol, sewage and the undying scent of burnt-out rubble.

Drina kept her hands inside her pockets, presumably gripping some sort of dreadful, illegal weapon. Jing had picked up a large wrench in one hand and occasionally tapped it against the other.

They passed people lounging around the canvas-walled streets, whose clothes had been turned black by coal and dirt. The street-dwellers shuffled away, eyeing them like smaller predators watching a pride of lions. The newcomers were too big, at least until the weakest member was driven from the pack – then there might be a meal to be had.

The party passed by a few belly dancers, still wearing their low-cut costumes and tassels, but they sagged against the wall like everyone else. They passed a cigarette between themselves.

Theo led them to the height of some ancient stone stairs that disappeared down into total darkness. Not even a gas lamp illuminated the base.

Drina arched an eyebrow. "We can't go down there. All that's missing is a plaque reading 'Trap Alley'."

"It's over here." Solindra pointed. She brushed away some coal dust from the sign. "Only it really says Quarry Row."

"Same thing," Jing replied.

"Did you expect to find smugglers on Main Street?" Theo asked.

"Come on." Solindra lifted her skirt and started down the stairs.

"Cyl, wait," Jing warned.

Theo jumped down after Solindra, pausing to smirk as he passed her. Jing and Drina followed. At the base of the stairs, the group waited until their eyes adjusted and then tiptoed slowly down the dark alley.

Jing's metal leg dragged across the paving stones, creating a continuous metallic slide. He pointed ahead, noting a stone archway that must have been centuries old. "That it?"

Theo nodded.

"You sure about this place?" Drina asked.

The young man forced a smile at her glare. "With the war booming like this, there might even be a line."

"I hate smugglers." Jing sighed.

Solindra cocked her arms against her hips. "Says the man who smuggled gold ingots in his false leg. Yeah, Dad told me everything about that incident."

The mechanic winced. "Probably not *everything*. Alright, I don't trust smugglers other than myself."

"Fine by me if you want to stay in the country." Theo shrugged.

"Let's just go already."

They ducked through the archway, where a fiery glow outlined a heavy curtain hanging across the side-alley.

Jing reached out and shoved the curtain out of his way. He immediately ran into a dense wall of incense.

Behind him, Solindra rubbed her forehead and groaned. With her eyes watering, she squinted through the smoky haze to see a mountain of a man standing upright in front of another curtained barrier. His thinning hair looked blue in the candlelight

Theo pushed past Solindra and marched up to the man. "It's me, Glinter."

The mountain rumbled, "They're trouble." He squinted through tiny, swollen eyes at Jing and Drina.

"Just get her, please."

Glinter shrugged. "I will see if the lady is available to receive guests in her house." He turned and vanished into the brighter glow beyond the second curtain.

Drina spun around the steam and smoke, which dimmed the light of the fat, dripping candles. "Your smuggler is a bricoleur crypter?"

"Maybe. Okay, yeah." Theo shrugged. "So this is the end of our agreement."

Jing nodded. "After we've gotten passage."

Solindra held her breath. She inched toward the shelves of candles, waving away the incense and steam with her hand. "Steamflowers!" Her fingers stretched out and hovered over the velvety blooms. The dark purple and blue flowers were open in their glory here. She caught a smattering of red and gold deep down in their centers.

"Just like Dad's." She leaned forward and inhaled, but caught nothing but the powerful incense instead of the flower's nectarine scent. The memory was enough though, and she thought of her father. It was said the ghosts in the steam nourished themselves on these flowers.

Theo wrenched her back by her shoulder. "Do you want to hallucinate?"

She glared at him and brushed off his hand.

The curtain twitched to the side and a dark-haired woman with her layered skirts and feathers in her hair appeared out of the steam. It was hard to tell the newcomer's age under all the colorful makeup and jewelry, but she moved like a sprite. Her bosom nearly spilled out over the top of her corset.

Glinter followed soundlessly in her footsteps and took up his guard post.

She smiled at Theo and opened her arms as she glided over to him. "My mysterious drifter." Then she leaned forward and kissed Theo on the mouth.

His eyes widened and he pulled away. Blushing, he straightened his shirt and stammered, "Uh. Merlina, these are—"

"Never known you to travel with anyone else," she interrupted in a voice of fairy dust and bells. "Not since your...accident."

His face was still burning. "Desperate times are even more desperate now."

Merlina raised her bright eyes to Solindra and the others. "Well then, to business." She twirled around, skirts flaring, and beckoned toward the curtain with her finger. "Come into my mists." She vanished ahead into the glow and steam.

Solindra held aside the weight of the thick curtain and walked into the glow. She blinked in the sudden flare of the gaslights. She had stepped into a circular room with two plush, opposite-facing couches in the center and a card table in between them. Merlina was just stretching out across one.

Behind her was a ramose metal tree filled with jewels. The sculpture was as tall as Solindra and branched out farther than she could stretch her arms. It twinkled with multi-colored light. Steam drifted up from holes throughout its frame, and the roots were as extensive as the branches at the top. She frowned when she saw the candles and the water boiler at its base, and then noticed the gems were just overly large, shiny stones. But they glittered like diamonds and rubies if she didn't look carefully.

The others blinked in the brighter light as they walked into the chamber behind her.

Solindra glanced back at Merlina. Her jewelry was just the same shiny stones over painted tin. The woman's hair was a mess, but it was hard to notice behind all the feathers. A few wrinkles lined her eyes that Solindra hadn't seen at first, and now she couldn't tell if this was a younger or older woman. She'd been swallowed by her pageantry. Solindra glanced back at the tree, it was the same.

Merlina followed Solindra's line of sight. "This tree connects this world to the underworld below and heaven on high."

Behind the girl, Theo groaned deep in his throat.

Solindra licked her lips. "But...but what about the ghosts in the steam? Aren't they here?"

"Yes and no," Merlina replied evenly. "Oh, did you want to talk to someone who has passed? I can ask the other ghosts if they can find him."

"Knock it off." Theo crashed down on the couch opposite of the smuggler. "We're not here for your show."

The bricoleur crypter leveled her gaze at him. "I'm for real, my boy." She rolled off the couch and swiped a candle holder off a table in one smooth motion, and then fitted a new, tall candle into it. She struck a match. The wax on the wick sizzled and spat as it caught fire and started to turn black.

Merlina smiled and returned to the couches, setting the candle between them. She stared at them over the top of the flame. "Now, what services of mine do you need? Palm reading?" She passed her gaze onto Drina and Jing. "Love advice?" She turned to Solindra. "Talk to the ghost of a loved one perhaps? Your father?"

Solindra gasped. "How did you know that? How did she know that?"

Jing grunted. "She didn't, Cylinder. She guessed and you confirmed it."

Drina sighed. "I wish we could've taken you off the mountain before now. You should have learned."

"I'm learning now." Solindra leveled her gaze at Merlina. "We want passage out of Eliponesia. Quietly."

Merlina raised her glittery eyebrows and leaned away from the party. "It will be expensive."

Jing tossed down a small leather bag. Several gold nuggets spilled out of it onto the card table.

The fortune teller held out her hand. "And I want to see it."

Theo shook his head. "No, you don't."

She ignored him and beckoned at Solindra with her fingers.

Jing nodded. The young woman retrieved the glowing sancta from her pocket. She said, "But you don't want to touch, or stare too hard at it."

As fast as a serpent, Merlina plucked the item from her fingers. She grinned as she rolled it onto the palm of her own hand.

Everyone else gasped, but the crypter only chuckled and stared deeply at the cipher medallion. "Do you know how much these things are worth? The Priory doesn't bother us bricoleurs much, you know, doesn't consider us a threat. And why should they? Not when they use these things."

Theo rolled his eyes. "The Priory is as scary as your so-called abilities."

Merlina chuckled again.

"Okay, there might be a bunch of crusty old geezers, but their power isn't real."

The fortune teller shrugged and dropped the sancta casually back into Solindra's grasp. "You're probably right. But the stories say that Steampower stole their most ancient, sacred texts about how to control the ghosts. Tried to use them as a weapon, even."

"And it's a great fireside story, Merlina." Theo exhaled and glared harder.

Her gaze passed onto the older pair. "But you wouldn't know anything about that?"

Jing remained totally motionless. Drina locked her eyes with Merlina's. "No, we would not."

"Of course not," the crypter purred. She rolled off the couch and retrieved a pen and some paper. She started to scribble. "Be on the river. Flatboat leaves at midnight. You'll have to work as part of the crew and pay them for passage too, but the River Eld—"

Solindra chimed in, "Flows straight south out of Eliponesia and into Mekani and then beyond the Steamscape. But the flatboat won't leave Mekani, if it's even allowed out of our country."

"It will be." Merlina reached out behind her for an engorged perfume bottle and started to spray the letter.

Solindra and the others slammed their hands across their noses, but the perfume still burned the backs of their throats.

Merlina rolled up the letter and tucked it inside a small tube. "This is the only way the flatboat captain will know it's real. He's memorized my scent."

Drina coughed. "We'll be smelled out by the sewer rats and thieves before we get there!"

"Now, now. I know you'll find a way to avoid them. Of all people, you know what it's like to be caught in a web."

Drina's eyes widened for just a fraction of a moment.

Solindra snatched up the tube and stood. "Thank you for your time and this letter." She turned and pushed her way through the heavy curtain. Jing and Drina followed.

Theo was behind them when Merlina called, "A moment, please, little love."

He made a face, but stopped.

She dropped into a much heavier bricoleur accent. "I fear I won't be here for you much longer."

"What? Are you leaving the country too?"

"Yes, but I waited to see you one last time. I knew you'd come." She let her fingers play in the candle flame, passing through it but not burning. "You're not going with them."

"No. Going to Redjakel to cause trouble for Steampower now."

"Don't steal the cipher medallion."

"What?" He grinned innocently and squirmed in place. "It's worth a mint."

"Now I know your momma taught you how to steal true and proper, but not this time, little love." She pulled her hand back from the candle.

"Merlina, thanks, but I will do what I need to do and—"

"They will lead you to Flame," she interrupted.

Theo froze, and then immediately uncoiled with a feigned smirk. "How could you possibly know that? I know I told you what happened, but you can't *know* that."

Her voice sounded more like a whip now. "I'm for real, my boy."

He remained motionless.

"And you need to go. Now." As he shoved aside the curtain, she turned her gaze and fingers back to the tall, slender candle.

***

The candle had burnt down to nearly a stub. Merlina's painted eyes fluttered open. She glanced up to see the curtains slapping against a strong wind. Then she cursed under her breath. She hurled her skirts to the side, jumped up from the couch and lunged for the curtained door.

She stopped and her breath caught in her throat.

The heavy curtain barring entry to the room twitched. A long glass length pushed it aside, smearing the fabric with the fresh, hot blood on its length.

"Glinter," Merlina groaned.

Steam and smoke rolled inside as Smith strolled into her sanctuary.

She deflated and retreated back to the couch. "You're here sooner than I expected."

Smith frowned. "If you suspected my arrival, why are you here?"

She wiped a tear from her eye, rubbing away some glitter and makeup. "Fate, I suppose. I was leaving on the morrow."

He shrugged, indifferent, and absently rubbed a piece of a tooth off from his sleeve.

Merlina crashed back down on the couch. "Get on with it then."

Smith smiled and took a seat on the opposite couch. He set the glass cane upright and rested both hands on top of it. Glinter's blood rolled down its length. "First, tell me about the man with the mechanical leg."

⚓

Chapter Seven

Solindra could hear the splashes better than she could see the water rushing against the side of the boat. She glanced up. The stars shone like crystals and the moons were mostly dark tonight. She squinted. There wasn't even a lamp on the prow of the flatboat.

If it could be called a prow. The boat was just a rectangle. It had no steam-powered paddlewheel, unlike all those pictures she'd seen with ladies lounging on decks of multi-storied floating hotels.

No, these were bound logs that were piled high with crates covered in canvas. There was no roof or shelter. They would sleep between the crates and could only hope to outrun the rain.

Jing shuffled up beside her, his limp causing the boat to rock. His jaw was clenched.

"Something wrong?" Solindra prompted.

"I don't like being on the water." He raised his metal leg, then lowered it. The boat rocked ever so slightly as the weight came back down. He forced a smile. "Everything will be sold in southern Eliponesia and Mekani. Even the boat."

Solindra raised her eyebrows.

"Lumber that makes up the boat. Everything goes."

"Oh." She glanced in direction of Ganther, the captain of the rectangle, and his two boys. She didn't know if they were his sons or just another pair of conscripted orphans.

She looked back down at the dark waters, but could only make out a few starlight reflections on the mutable surface. "We'll run aground when the river curves. We can hardly see where we're going."

Jing chuckled. "It's a risk, certainly. But I don't think Ganther wanted to stay in Consequences. We'll probably stop for the night after a few miles."

Ganther whistled from out of the darkness somewhere nearby. The form of a man built like a bear waved his arms. "Steam man! You come here and steer this hog for a while."

"On my way!" Jing replied. He patted Solindra on the shoulder before limping off.

After he'd left, the young woman sneaked a look over her shoulder. She set the tips of her boots into one of the edges of a crate underneath its canvas cover and peeked over the top. Eventually, she could make out the murmuring forms of the two boys and Drina off to the side. That other shape had to be Theo on the far end. Jing and Ganther were at the large rear paddle that served as the rudder.

Soon, the singing of the crickets on the nearby bank overwhelmed the splashes of water against the flatboat. The winds carried fresher-scented air from downriver.

Solindra slipped off the crate and pulled out a folded paper from her pocket. She'd wrapped the sancta in it, but replaced the item quickly. She pressed the paper against her thigh, trying to smooth out the creases.

She tilted the poster into the starlight and sighed. The girl knew that she shouldn't have gone back to steal it, but she couldn't live with herself with the thought that it might be defaced like the other one.

She really didn't know why she'd carefully cut out Steam Princess Adri Saturni's face from the propaganda poster. Solindra sighed again. How many years had she spent pretending that was her? All those years suspended on a mountain, never knowing anything about the real Codic or the real Steampower. The steam princess couldn't turn out to be any different than what she had dreamt, not like the others.

She glared ahead into the darkness. The River Eld pulled at the logs beneath her feet, but she barely even noticed the swaying of the raft anymore. This river that drained half the continent was deep, lonely, and cold.

She shivered as the craft shifted underneath. The world moved on, and she with it. Solindra wanted to cry. She wanted to clutch the poster to her chest and hold herself.

Instead, she held out the piece of poster at arm's length and slowly, achingly uncurled her fingers.

The paper fluttered off into the darkness. The singing of the crickets and the splashes of the water immediately overcame any papery sounds in the wind.

Tears started to press against her eyes, but she ignored them and turned her back on the river. She crept to the center of the boat, jaw set. Her fingers slid along the canvas tarps, guiding her more than her sight. She felt a corner.

Drina's fist came sailing around it.

Solindra gasped and bobbed back out of the way. "Drina! What—?"

The cook swung again. Solindra could hardly see her hand moving! She threw her arms up and felt the heavy thud all the way through her shoulder blades as Drina's hand came crashing.

"Remember those games we used to play when you were growing up?"

Solindra gulped. "What? Now? No!"

"You'd better!" She struck at the girl again. Solindra managed a weak block.

A shrill whistle echoed around the flatboat. Ganther jogged up between the crates, shaking his own fist. "Hey, now! Don't rock the boat!" The two young boys trailed in his wake, giggling and jostling each other.

Back at the rudder, Jing only sighed. "Oh, Drina."

Solindra dusted her skirts and straightened. She tried to glare at the older woman, but memories were starting to crowd her thoughts. *Games we used to play. With them. With Dad. Like the one done hopping on one leg while everyone tried to strike with pillows, and she had to dodge. Or the one where she had to duck and weave through the maze of ropes. Or the other one where she had to take a running person and shove him off balance...*

She glared at Drina's current smirk. She had been convinced up until this very moment that she knew this woman. The cook had never been much of a mother, but that was alright because she'd had Dad. But Drina had never attacked her before.

Solindra dusted off her skirt again and launched herself at Drina's knees. They both went down on the narrow path between the rows of crates. The younger woman growled the entire time.

Drina's laugh shattered her concentration. She patted Solindra's hair. "Well done!" She disentangled her legs from the teen. "It's not quite the same, but you know the basic motions."

"Teaching the steam princess to fight?" They looked up to see Theo crossing his arms and frowning. He scoffed.

"I'm not the steam princess!" Solindra pulled herself upright and swayed a little until the dizziness passed. "I... Wait, what's that?"

Around the entire flatboat, steam suddenly rose off the water on the deck and even across the river around them. It hissed like snakes. The sancta started to glow inside her pocket, its light escaping the fabric.

Theo gasped and pointed at her cipher medallion. "You *are* a crypter!"

Ganther inhaled like an angry swine. "Crypter! I don't take truck with no crypters." He raised his hand as if to strike, but then suddenly held his breath at a very slight thump of weight behind him. The boat shifted a little.

"Crypters don't exist," Jing said quietly from behind. "Therefore, the girl is not a crypter."

"Then what about the steam?" Ganther was breathing heavily now, his chest bobbing as much as the boat. The boys were silent on either side of him, their eyes wide.

"Fog, heated up by a nearby swamp. Maybe some of the flammable gasses had been sucked into the river." Jing smiled tightly and steered the captain toward the stern. The boys followed.

Ganther scowled. "There aren't any swamps around—"

"I'm sure there are." Jing thumped a heavy hand on the other man's shoulder, causing Ganther's knees to sag involuntarily. The captained stomped to the back of the boat with the boys.

Theo still glared at Solindra. He shook his head and turned away. "I should've just gone on to Redjakel."

"Alone? Even if you weren't, what could four of us do against Steampower?" Jing asked. "We only have one *professional* saboteur here."

"Hey! I don't appreciate the sarcasm."

"Are you so certain that was?" Drina purred. She looked up at Jing. "We could do it, you know."

The mechanic shook his head. "With the vessel?"

"What is a vessel, damn you?" Solindra demanded.

"Vessel?" Theo snorted. "You mean that old Steampower conspiracy story?" He froze and then swung his head directly at Solindra. "To create a born crypter."

"No," Drina said.

Theo kept staring.

Solindra found herself blushing.

"Who are you people?" he asked, leaning away from them.

Drina smiled flatly. "I'm just the cook."

He shook his head and stomped across the boat to its edge. After a moment, he struggled to unlace his boots and then dipped his sweaty feet into the dark Eld. The water pressed his feet down under its current. To the east—and he just now realized which way *was* east after riding the large turns of the river at night—dawn was beginning to glow. There wasn't any sun yet, and wouldn't be for a while, but the darkness was losing its grip.

Solindra sidled up beside him. "I want to hear the story."

Theo shrugged. "Not much to it. I mean, there are lots of stories, but the only thing they have in common is that Steampower wanted to make a crypter."

"Make a person? Why not just teach someone? Why *make* a crypter?"

He tossed up his gloved hands. "Like I know." He scowled ahead into the darkness. "All I know is that both sides deserve what they're getting."

"Not those people on the train."

"Not them," he growled. "But the lords of Codic and President LaBier and Boras Saturni and all of his board members! Them, *they* deserve worse. And that's what I'm going to do."

"Why?" she asked softly.

Theo coughed, surprised. The fiery wind, the screams of the dying and smell of burning meat assailed his memory. He looked down to see his gloved fists bunching. He didn't even feel anything anymore in some places. There had been too much damage to his skin.

He swallowed. "I—We, that is, bricoleurs move around all the time, especially between Codic and Redjakel and the areas in between. So both sides tried to pay us or force us to spy for them in the months before Steampower's assault." He sighed. "And *both* sides punished us. I don't know which one, but one side sent Flame."

"Of the Hex?" she asked.

He nodded.

She shivered. "But the Hex has been gone for nigh on twenty years."

"Not Flame. Both Steampower and the government used us and threw us out like trash. And what do you do with trash? Burn it to make steam."

Solindra shook her head. "I'm so sorry."

"Don't be sorry for me. I'm not sorry for me. They are the ones who will be sorry. Codic, Redjakel and Flame."

The logs that made up the flatboat groaned. Theo and Solindra rolled forward as the raft suddenly slowed.

Theo jerked his feet out of the water. "Did we hit something?"

"It's still so dark!" Solindra's hand went straight to the cipher medallion.

"Cylinder!" Drina called from the other side of the flatboat.

The boat stopped. Solindra squinted. "Is that a net? Across the river?" She couldn't be sure, and the idea was too foreign to frighten her. Her eyes explored the webbing, and she covered her nose from the oily smell.

The net exploded into flame.

Solindra felt the wind from the sudden heat push her hair back. Her jaw dropped. Even parts of the river were on fire! She sniffed; it was oil. Barrels of oil, and the net had been soaked in it too.

Someone was reclining in the fiery net, a foot propped up against the flatboat.

Theo's breath caught in his throat.

He'd seen that face before, whistling to itself. Strolling down the road toward the caravan like a man wasting a lazy afternoon. "Flame."

Flame jerked forward as if propelled by some explosion behind him. His arms spread out like the fires and the short man was smiling like a god. His chest and hips were covered with crisscrossing bandoliers holding pistols, a saber, two rapiers and other devices haphazardly stashed together. The stench of burnt flesh rolled off of him like a perfume.

The dark red-haired man jogged down the edge of the flatboat to Solindra and Theo.

Theo froze. He tried to grab the knife hidden in his boot, but his hand wouldn't respond to the screams of his mind.

Flame reached down and yanked Solindra up by her shoulder. She tried to roll out of the way, but wasn't fast enough. He clutched a rope in his other hand. It led off into the river, where a canoe with an engine bobbed in the fiery waters. All the while, the short arsonist hummed to himself. He moved as if dancing to music inside his head.

Ganther was yelling. Splashes rose up behind him as the boys jumped for safety into the Eld. Jing and Drina both brought up their small pistols from hidden pockets.

Flame's head bobbed up toward the movement. He blinked and the hum died on his lips. "What the hell are you doing here?"

"Oh no," Drina breathed. Jing blinked in surprise.

That gave Flame enough time to draw his pistol and shoot Ganther in the forehead, using the same hand that held the cord.

Solindra tried to elbow him, but only bruised herself on his armaments. He resumed humming and jerked his canoe up to the flatboat.

He pulled Solindra in between himself and Drina. "Ah, ah, ah! Now don't pop your monocle, Death, but we're off to meet the sorceress."

"What?" Drina breathed.

Solindra kicked out with her boot heel, striking at his knee, but Flame didn't seem to notice. He hopped backward, dragging her with him. The engine-powered canoe splashed and rocked wildly with their sudden weight.

Solindra screamed, "It didn't work, Drina!" She kicked at him again. "It didn't work!"

"No!" Theo yelped, breaking free from his paralysis.

Then Flame, grinning like an angry cat, tossed a canister onto one of the canvas-covered crates. It hissed and flared into life, saturating their world with fire.

Laughing, he kicked the canoe away from the flatboat and back into the flow. He tilted the nose upstream, and he and Solindra vanished into the gloomy dawn.

Chapter Eight

"Cylinder!" Drina's voice carried louder over the water than the snaps and roar of the fires.

But the young woman was gone. There wasn't even an outline of the canoe in the dawn's light.

"Cylinder!"

"Drina, help!" Jing slammed down another canvas tarp in an attempt to smother some of the flatboat's flames.

"Here!" Theo ran up with another canvas tarp, but he tripped over Ganther's body and stumbled nose-first into a crate. He closed his eyes and fought another shiver. He shouldn't be so cold with this heat, but he could barely breathe.

Flame...

He was half-convinced he was in a nightmare, and he was sure that he'd imagined that whoever it was had been Flame. That just couldn't be! It had to have been someone else.

Jing growled and smashed down the tarp again. The fires that had started with the arsonist's burning nets were spreading to the front of the flatboat. The glorified raft was already sinking in one corner where the fires had chewed through.

"Stop, just stop." Drina slipped around some smaller fires. "What can we do?"

Jing shook his head again. "Can't save the boat."

"Swim for it?" Theo eyed the fat, deceptively lazy river. How many thousands – no, millions of cubic yards of water was it draining? How could one human body survive against that?

"I sink." The mechanic lifted up his metallic prosthesis. "But this thing ain't going to hold on for long."

Drina leaned her shoulder against the rudder's handle. The flatboat started to inch toward the shore. Jing and Theo joined her, pressing their weight against the lever. The boat shifted its course.

"Not too much," the mechanic warned. "Or we'll just flip around and be backward and burning."

Theo stepped away from the crowded rudder. The craft was starting to float diagonally in the direction of the nearest point bar. He breathed through his mouth, not wanting to smell anything. But the scent crept up to his nose via the back of his throat and he whimpered against his will.

He slid closer to one of the newly uncovered crates. He hadn't dared ask Ganther the smuggler what else he'd been transporting. He tapped one of the clear glass jars suspended in frames and held up by string. He popped off a cork and the burning vapors of moonshine assailed him.

Okay, selling to barmen so that they could cut their beer and inflate their prices. The bottles clinked as the raft shifted again. Theo moved on.

The next crate held a couple barrels of oil. Also flammable.

He inched forward, closer to the fires. He wiped the tears out of his watering eyes and tried to brush away the smoke from his face.

Fire was already merrily eating at the canvas tarp of the next crate and up the edges of the wooden case. Theo yanked the canvas aside.

"Shh– Shh–" He stumbled back over Ganther's body, turned and sprinted at Jing and Drina.

"Get off the boat!" he screamed as he dived right past the pair and into the Eld. He heard his own splash, but felt only coldness as the waters closed in around him.

Drina and Jing exchanged a glance through the smoke of the fiery boat and looked back to the goods just starting to burn.

Each face of the crate was stamped DYNAMITE

Without a word, Jing reached down and picked up the nearest barrel. He stepped up to the edge and just kept walking.

The river swallowed him whole.

Drina took a running swan dive, jumping as far away from the flatboat and as close to Jing as she could manage.

He bobbed back up to the surface, still clinging to the barrel. A permanent grimace had been etched into his features. Theo paddled farther behind him.

Drina surfaced a few feet away. She risked a grin before glancing back at the boat. "Under!" Theo dove and Drina pushed herself back under. Jing tried to roll the barrel over his head.

The explosion boomed. Searing white and orange fire flared up like the sun on earth. Wooden fragments, glass and other shrapnel expanded out in front of the main fire, stabbing at the river's surface and scything through the air.

Theo, Drina and Jing rolled back to the surface. The bricoleur flailed and splashed in the water, gaping at the pieces of burning wood in the water around them.

Drina waved at him. "Help us!"

Theo, gulping for air, tried to nod. He kicked and paddled his way over toward them, unable to fight the river's flow. The water felt like the sucking sensation when he had trapped his boots in the mud, but now it was trapping his entire body, pulling him ever deeper.

Meanwhile, Jing clung to his barrel with white knuckles. His jaw was set and he stared straight ahead.

Drina leaned to her side, grabbed the barrel in one hand and started to kick, her face set in the same determined grimace. Theo, swallowing river water, joined her. Splinters cut into his fingers and palm, but he barely noticed. Eventually, they drifted downstream to the rocky bank of the river.

They stood, covered in mud and watery weeds, to see some of the still-burning pieces of the flatboat curve around the bend.

"Ganther was still on that thing," Theo murmured.

Drina shrugged. "Buried at sea is what he would've wanted. Probably. But very classical, the burning boat."

"Not in the civilized parts of the world," Jing said. "Not to mention that this isn't a sea."

The cook shaded her eyes and leaned against the barrel. "Still, fire is what Flame does."

Theo grabbed his chest and jerked forward, suddenly in shock. He tried to move his mouth, but no sounds escaped. He couldn't breathe. Flame! That had really been Flame!

Jing looked like a crate of dynamite also ready to explode. "How could he have known? No one knew."

"Not until Smith."

The mechanic whistled. "You think they're working together?"

"I don't know."

"Flame!" Theo wheezed. "That really was Flame." His eyes widened. "And I didn't kill him! I couldn't even move! Merlina even said—"

"And Cylinder is with him!" Drina gasped. "That poor child has never been away from us, and now she's with that senseless moron." She curled her hands into fists and met Jing's eyes. "But we tried to prepare her."

He shook his head. "No, we didn't. We just tried to protect her."

Nothing moved in between the three of them for a moment except the wind.

Theo pointed downriver. "I think I see some smoke that way. Might be a town, or a camp with traders."

"Or a camp with soldiers," Jing sighed.

Drina stepped behind the mechanic and pushed. "There'll be coffee either way. Come on, boys."

They stomped away from the sandy shore.

Theo licked his lips and stared down at Jing's leg, which was still leaking water. "You alright?"

Jing grunted and kept on with his steady, unending limp. "Yeah."

Theo eyed Jing's mechanical leg. "But the river, you have no steam left."

"I can fix it," the mechanic grunted.

Drina kicked at the nearest tree and then swiped her hand, bent like a claw, at its trunk. "Mark told us to protect her. Those were our orders."

The mechanic grunted again.

"Our orders. The only thing we're good at."

Theo opened his mouth, but quickly shut it.

Finally, Jing replied, "We're just going to have to figure this out on our own."

***

The smoke turned out to be from a town, housing forty to fifty people. Underneath the stronger smell of burning coal, the scent of baking bread soon teased on the breeze.

Theo licked his lips. He was already drooling. His stomach started to yowl and tremble on its own and he couldn't help himself. They stepped out into the dirt street. A waterwheel turned alongside a building on the river, and several small steampipes left the tiny boiler house to spread their fingers throughout the town.

The only two visible people turned their faces away from them and ducked inside the nearest structure. Theo slowed his pace and leaned back to the other two. "This ain't such a good idea."

"Too late now." Drina pointed ahead to what was both the dry goods store and the local eating hole. The scent of honeyed wheat baking amplified in the wind. Theo nodded dumbly, his stomach already protesting.

The boards creaked against their boots on the wooden sidewalk as they stepped up to the store. They pushed through the doors to find what appeared to be most of the town inside. Pale faces with sunken eyes swung toward them.

The men were smoking their pipes almost feverishly. Women, in respectful if dirty high-collared dresses, rested shoulder to shoulder, leaning on each other. No one spoke.

The only person not staring at them was a man in the back, obscured by the crowd, and playing the keyboard. The notes were twangy and slightly out of tune, but nevertheless, the player was pulling out a graceful melody.

Overhead hung a dead ceiling fan, usually powered by a pair of chains that disappeared into the establishment's ceiling. "No steam," Jing murmured.

"No children," Theo whispered.

This is a trap, the dark voice said. The bricoleur's fingers tingled.

The piano hit a discord and the player grunted.

The man in black twisted around on the player's swivel stool. Smith flipped the bowler hat back on his head, but didn't smile.

That survivalist instinct voiced itself again as it massaged the back of Theo's neck. *Run away. This government's man won't bother you. Leave them to their fate.*

"I heard the explosion." Smith pulled the glass cane away from the wall and leaned his weight on it, still sitting in the chair. "Sound carries so far on the water. As far as a rumor, they say." He stood up. "Where's my vessel?"

Theo froze, just as helpless now as he had been with Flame.

Drina suddenly sniffed. She brushed her face, still damp with river water, and streaked the mud across her cheek. She shook her head. "She didn't make it."

Smith tapped his cane on the floor. "You've learnt to act, Ms. de Avila. Well done, but I doubt you've ever shed a tear at a death."

She sniffled again, but couldn't hide the flash of surprise and then contempt from her face.

Smith frowned. "Please." He reached into his pocket and tossed out a yellowing photograph. It drifted across the air and landed in front of Jing's metal foot. Theo stared. He subconsciously backed away from them.

Smith continued, "Yes, I know who you were, Ms. de Avila. Or should I call you by your true name, Ms. Death Spinner?"

Still glaring at him, she squatted and picked up the photograph. Her own face stared back at her from over twenty years ago. Jing glanced over her shoulder and grimaced.

They were all there. Mark Canon/Silvermark holding his silver-plated rifle. Stetson James/Parrot nonchalantly drinking a brandy while still managing his trademark smirk. There was herself, glaring at the cameraman with a taut garrote cord in her hands. Jing/Ghost was behind her, and he looked the same as ever, metal leg included. Next to him was Sava Zhidkov/Steam Slayer leaning on his homemade, shoulder-mounted cannon. And lastly, Flame, just Flame, holding what appeared to be a magical fireball but was actually a mirror lost in the camera's flash.

The Hex.

Theo snatched the picture from Drina. He found his thoughts stuttering. The photograph was even labeled and dated with a Codic military archive stamp.

The Hex.

Smith smirked. "It was your leg, Mr. Li, which pointed me in your direction."

Theo stepped back away from them. He raised an accusing finger. "Y-You! Y-You knew Flame!"

Smith swatted Theo's hand aside with the length of the glass cane. "Killers, the lot of them, and so on and so forth." He narrowed his gaze at Drina and then Jing. "Where have you hidden my vessel?"

Jing shook his head.

"I'll give you a medal for not just walking into town with her, but if you don't tell me where the young lady is, I shall have to boil this town's children alive." He retrieved his own cipher medallion from his vest pocket, just as casually as one would retrieve a pocket watch. "Not that I would ever suspect you to care about them, but if you don't, well, mob rule is so messy."

He shifted back far enough so that the trio could view the huddled crowd behind him.

"They know that only I can safely rescue them. If those poor kids die, and you did nothing to save them...Tsk, tsk."

"You're lying."

Everyone spun to find this new confident speaker. Theo nearly slapped his hand over his mouth as he realized it was him. The vicious corner of his mind eased out his next words like a snake gliding through the grass. "You've got Ghost here. The Hex are Eliponesia's patron saints." He nodded at Jing. "He can do anything with the mechanics and steam. That's why he's called Ghost."

Smith raised an eyebrow, probably stretched it to the limit of his patience. He leaned forward. "Young master, I know more than the stories. I know their histories. And I very much doubt that even Ghost can speak to the steam ghosts better than me."

Theo also leaned in and whispered, "But what does the mob believe, sir?"

Smith stood up straight, a scowl replacing any smirk he might have worn. "Who are you, boy?"

Theo shrugged sharply. "Just a bricoleur."

"Is that so? I am Deputy Liaison to President LaBier."

"So it is Codic that wants her," Drina said.

"Just dead, I assure you." Smith offered a stiff smile. "Although I am not surprised that this vessel survived with protection from you. Your sudden dissolution was a disaster for both the government and Steampower. But as you can see, we've learned to live without you."

"But not with each other, apparently," Jing remarked.

"You never found the Hex though, Mr. Smith," Drina growled.

Smith doffed his bowler hat. "*I* was never hunting you. Nor am I frightened by your legend, but Codic might still have use for your skills." He glared. "But alas, you cannot be trusted."

"I will never work for Steampower or Codic again." Drina drew up her chin. "Unlike you."

Smith chuckled. "Dear, I only draw my wages from Codic. I work for the Priory."

⚓

Chapter Nine

This room smelled like perfume and wine. Solindra hadn't seen anything since that night on the river. Flame had stuffed a bag over her head, and she had no idea how long it had been. It felt like days. Or weeks. Or hours. She couldn't tell.

But she knew she had gone from a long ride on the water to marching through some paved streets, and now she was in this sweet-scented room. She gulped and pressed her shoulders against the back of the chair. No escape that way; it was taller than she was.

And dangerously comfortable. Her head nodded forward and she fought against a yawn.

Someone yanked off the hood. She blinked in the soft, warm sunlight of the room. The ceiling was high, and gold paint and foil lined the gothic arches overhead.

Flame eclipsed her vision. "You got weird eyes, girlie." Immediately, he turned away to a sylph sitting behind a huge, mahogany desk. "Your delivery. Special."

He stood directly in Solindra's view of the other woman.

"Unburnt this time," a mellifluous voice said evenly.

Flame snorted. His motion caused his pistols and swords to grind against each other. "It was only his toes. And fingers." He paused. "And nose. He was fine."

"He only lived two hours, Mr. Flame."

The Hex member shrugged. "My fee."

A heavy leather pouch clinked as the woman rolled it across the desk. She sighed, and even that sounded like the most expensive thing Solindra had ever heard. She felt like she was wasting this woman's time, and she should pay for it.

"And…?" he prompted. "Your information is the best in the world. Maybe the rumors about you are true. How else could you have known about this one?" He jerked his thumb at Solindra.

The voice replied gracefully, "The board considers you to be more perilous than what you can deliver to our war effort. Your life is to be liquidated, Mr. Flame."

He chuckled. "Oh, I'll just burn down their homes, steam chariots and families before they'll ever ignite me." He hummed to himself a little. "But they'll whine, and then they'll treat me like *I'm* standing in *their* way again. Pah!" He started cleaning out his ear with a finger, humming to himself.

"Yes, they say that you're a fine asset as long as you're in the enemy's camp, but sometimes you venture home."

Flame shrugged. "I am what I am."

"Please go now, sir."

"But don't you want to know who was guarding this little strawberry? You'd be surprised."

The tone of voice didn't change. "Mr. Flame, you are dismissed."

He sneered. "There's only one woman I'll take that tone from."

"And I strongly suspect that you saw her recently."

Flame clicked his heels and hummed to himself before turning away. He slammed the door behind him.

"Please forgive him."

Solindra had already forgotten him. She stared. She knew the slender face of Steam Princess Adri Saturni. The young woman hadn't been able to forget the picture of the face she'd so recently tossed overboard.

The small woman loomed so large in her vision. Adri really was svelte, but wore a beautiful forest green dress with a padded bust and rear bustle to make it look like she carried some attractive weight. Her blond-white hair was bound up in golden chains, winding smoothly into an array of curls against her dark face.

Adri folded her slender fingers together on the desktop. "I had to tell him that you were a spy. To protect you, you understand. I'm not sure how much he knows about vessels."

"More than me," Solindra replied sharply. Then her jaw dropped and she shriveled up inside. How dare she raise her voice at this woman she had dreamed of all these years! But her tongue continued on without her, "I'm not even sure what a vessel is."

"A very useful person in the war effort," Adri answered evenly.

"Why is there even a war?" She was already flying and light-headed, so why not ask? She gulped. "Why did Steampower attack Codic? Everyone says that Boras Saturni just wanted it all. That Steampower wasn't enough anymore. I rode the Killing Train. I saw the burnt-out cities. What is it that Steampower wants? Because I can't think of anything it doesn't already have."

"Love."

Solindra froze. She blinked, suddenly off-balance even while seated.

Adri graced the room with a smile. Her eyes sparkled. "It's such a sad tale, what my father did for my mother and this horrible catastrophe that followed."

"This can't be about love." Solindra's voice sounded hollow even to herself. "I rode the Killing Train…"

"Love stories made famous usually do not end well." Adri straightened her shoulders against her high-backed chair. "However, it is a tale for later, little bird. I think for now you need to know what you are."

Solindra's throat dried. "How did you know about me?"

Adri pursed her lips. "Smith is too confident in his own cyphers."

"You had him followed?"

"No. Why bother to follow the man when one can follow his words? He dutifully reports back to his masters like clockwork." She pushed the chair back and rose as fluidly as water. "More over lunch, perhaps? I imagine your stomach is turning by now."

It was true. Solindra clutched her gut and felt her stomach rumbling underneath her skin. She barely glanced up as the steam princess moved to stand beside her.

Adri reached across the desk and lifted up a dainty glass bell with a long telegraph wire attached inside the clapper. It chimed like a songbird. Within a minute, servants wheeling trolleys of food with steaming meat, vegetables and breads padded silently into the office.

"I'm in Redjakel, aren't I?" Solindra swallowed, trying not to salivate at the sight. "That's where Steampower's heart is."

"Steam Central." Adri nodded and her smile spread while the servants laid out the feast on the buffet. Everything was on gold or silver trays. Wine sparkled in a crystal pitcher at the end of the line of steaming, sweet smelling food.

Just as quickly and silently, the servants streamed out again. Adri kept staring at Solindra's otherworldly eyes. She unfolded her fingers toward the buffet. "Please, my dear."

In a daze, Solindra managed to unlock her legs and shuffle to the table. Adri did not follow. Could all of this food be just for her? She couldn't eat this much in two years!

Still in that almost dream-like state, Solindra loaded a silver plate with food. She stared at the array of forks, not knowing which to choose, and licked her lips.

Adri appeared at her left, holding two crystal wine glasses. She held one out in Solindra's direction and then turned and swept back across the room to the desk. She set both glasses on what looked to be diamond coasters.

The steam princess sipped her wine as Solindra returned to her seat. The girl tried to balance the plate on her knees. She didn't dare set it on the desk.

"You will act as my personal maid – no one else need know anything more – and in return, I will teach you how to use a sancta."

Solindra swallowed a mouthful of bread that was as light as a cloud. "But what about my fam—my friends?"

"Oh. Oh dear. I'm afraid they were lost on the river."

"They survived. I know them." But she hesitated.

"And Smith had set a trap for you in the next town. It was too much for any soldier, I'm so sorry." The smile replaced any concern. "But you have shelter here and shall want for nothing, not even during this dreadful war."

Solindra dropped her eyes to the silver plate overflowing with food. "But..."

Adri brought Solindra's crystal chalice in front of the young woman's face. "Have a sip, bird. You're safe within these walls."

Solindra eyed the gilded framings of the office again. She accepted the wine into her fingertips and its sudden weight surprised her. Its scent wafted above the glass, sweet and tangy.

Adri folded her hands into her lap while sitting up straight at the edge of her chair. Her smile beamed. "Now eat up, and then there is a hot bath being drawn for you in the next room. After that, we can discuss everything."

There was nothing left for Solindra to argue.

***

An hour later, Solindra drifted on the edge of sleep in the tub with just her nose poking above the water. It was so warm. She was certain heated pipes ran though the walls of the tub to keep the water from cooling. And she was glad of it.

It was silent except for the little notes of a silver music box in the shape of a tornado. The metal funnel spun, singing out cheerful melodies.

She could forget the screams of the Killing Train here. The water carried her weight, leaving her floating in this perfumed world. She could even forget there was a war in the moment, or that she had ever left Pitchstone.

The scent of spiced chicken meandered its way into her nose. Her gray eyes bounced open, and she lifted her head.

More food and wine were waiting for her. She hadn't even heard anyone setting them up! Had she fallen asleep?

She glanced at the table beside the tub. A towel that could probably wrap around her twice laid next a new floor-length navy dress. Her old outfit had vanished.

Solindra splashed up a tidal wave in a crashing effort to lunge out of the tub. Her old clothes were missing! Dripping wet, she pawed at the pile of towels, perfumes and dress.

She clutched the towel to her chest and leaned back against the tub, staring blankly ahead. Her mouth instantly dried.

It was missing.

Surely Adri wouldn't have gone through that act just to steal the thing. There were easier ways!

But...but the sancta had belonged to her father. She'd stolen it from his grave.

And now it was missing.

She scrambled to get inside the new dress, and then raced barefoot to the washroom's door. She slammed it open.

A plump woman on the other side of the door automatically ducked into a curtsey. She nailed her gaze to the floor. "The lady of the house is waiting for you. This way."

Solindra reached out to shake the servant, but then pulled her hands back. She nodded. She didn't dare trust her own voice. Instead, she followed the plump woman through the huge maze of vaulted corridors. Everything gave the illusion of openness and space – from the high ceilings to the huge windows, all gilt and gold. There was also food everywhere, just sitting in bowls along the hallways: apples, grapes, oranges and more. Solindra had eaten a proper orange only once before in her life.

The servant wound her way mutely through the palatial estate. Solindra couldn't believe they were inside the city – not with the gardens and courtyards. This was a country manor inside the city. Nothing was stained by grit or smoke at all, and no steampipes were visible. She tried to fix her drying hair and hide her bare feet beneath the skirt.

Birds sang through half open walls to courtyards. Solindra followed the servant around another enclosed corridor that ended with two massive doors.

The woman pushed on through into a larger, domed room. Solindra swung her head around. The space was much taller than it was wide, with a tall stained-glass dome on top and a pit below.

She stared down into the red ember glow of the coals below. Steam was rising up from the water being sprinkled on them by some sort of small fountain.

In the center of the room was a training circle, suspended by thick cables. The floor was bronze lattice-work with hundreds of interconnecting poles hanging down beneath it.

Adri Saturni glided barefoot across the suspended metal frame like an angel, or a ghost. She had also changed outfits, and now wore a shorter skirt that was seamlessly woven into her lace leggings. She turned to face the newcomers. The overhead light of the above dome caught the sparkle of the chains in her hair.

"Ah, my vessel." She beckoned with one hand, and unfolded her fingers to reveal Solindra's cipher medallion in the other.

Solindra's undressed foot hovered over the edge of the circle. She set it down. The metal felt cool enough, despite the steam below. She jogged out a few steps toward the proffered sancta. She stopped. Her feet were burning at the middle of the circle.

Adri didn't move, still standing barefoot in the center of the ring.

The younger woman gritted her teeth and marched forward, sure that burnt skin was peeling from her soles as she walked.

The steam princess nodded. She waved behind her with a free hand. The servant closed the double doors and vanished. Then Adri curled Solindra's fingers around the red medallion. "Here is your sancta, or cipher medallion. Either is acceptable. And this..."

A male servant with a face carved from granite marched out onto the ring, carrying a rifle. The wooden stock had been polished, but bore scars of use and battle. Everything metal had been plated with what appeared to be silver. It had a pump and cocked like a shotgun, so it was faster than the normal lever-action rifles.

"And this," Adri hefted the rifle, "belonged to someone I think you knew well." She passed it along to Solindra.

The girl imagined it would be heavier, but it wasn't. It had just enough weight to be real. "Who?" she formed on her lips but didn't dare whisper.

"A man who may or may not have been a traitor. However, his actions brought you to me alone, so I will consider him favorably." She reached out and touched Solindra's fiery hair.

The vessel flinched, but held her ground. She closed her eyes and squeezed the rifle against her chest. Something seemed familiar about it, like a scent she recognized from long ago.

"I knew Silvermark hadn't killed you like he'd claimed before vanishing."

"Silvermark?" Solindra frowned in thought. "The Hex."

Adri pointed at the rifle. Solindra followed her line and saw an inscription engraved just to the side of the trigger. *Veritas temporalis est.*

She didn't know the language of the ancient empire, the one civilization that those in Steamscape had finally surpassed only a few decades ago. But she knew her father's favorite saying. *Truth is temporary.*

"Mark Canon's rifle."

Solindra hugged it a little tighter.

"Oh. It looks as if you never really knew the man, not if you can't recognize his own gun." Adri reached out and pried the rifle from Solindra. As if in a dream, Solindra had no power to hold onto the gun. Her arms wouldn't work. They were too heavy and too slow to stop the sylph. Adri turned around and handed it back to the granite-faced servant.

"Maybe when you've earned it, little bird."

Solindra stared as the man walked away. Something inside her slipped free. "No!" She leapt forward, never taking her eyes off the rifle.

Adri grabbed her arm and spun her around. She narrowed her eyes and leaned into Solindra's face. All sweetness had evaporated like the steam around them. "Silvermark stole a valuable asset from us. You. If you survived into adulthood, my father had wanted to build you up to destroy the Priory. The Hex betrayed both us and Codic and stole you away. Ripped apart years of research and planning, expensive years. And just to steal a baby from its mother? Your mother."

Solindra gasped. "My mother?"

"Yes, but the poor woman died of a broken heart after you were stolen. All because the Hex decided that a mother wasn't good enough to raise her own child."

"No," Solindra wheezed. "No! Stop it! My father was a good man!" She staggered away, slamming her hands over her ears.

"Father?" Adri sneered. She stalked closer. "You had no father. Silvermark was just afraid that you would replace the Hex. You would have been a dragon."

Solindra gasped for breath, her chest heavier with each inhalation. She shook her head dumbly. The room was spinning, and the steam rising up from the embers below clouded her vision. She remembered sitting on her father's knees every morning while he read the telegraph dispatches. She remembered his chuckles when she'd try to steal the threads of paper. That had been real!

"But he died."

"Good." Adri turned her back and did something Solindra couldn't see. The training circle started to tremble beneath them and then it split down the middle.

Half of the circle rose, carrying Adri up like a soaring angel. Solindra's half sank a few feet closer to the fire below.

She didn't notice. She stormed up to the line of slick poles, grabbing them and shaking them. "I dare you to say that again. I dare you!"

Adri stood on the lip, smiling serenely down at the young woman. "First, you come up here. If you can."

Solindra heaved up at the bars, still clinging to her cipher medallion in one hand. No good. The metal was too slick with condensed droplets. The bars, having been much closer to the fire, hissed at her touch.

She withdrew her hand, noticing the blisters rising. Her bare feet were starting to feel the heat again.

"Use the steam, child!"

"What?" She didn't know how to do that. Not unless she could fly. Then again, she had not known what she'd been doing on the Killing Train either, and that... Well, that certainly hadn't worked out in her favor. But she remembered the feeling.

She brought up the cipher medallion and tried to ignore the blisters forming on her feet. She'd let that sensation surge within her and then just let it out somehow, like a primal yell.

Below her, the steam started to gather and swirl.

Solindra glared up at Adri and then turned her entire attention to the red sancta. It seemed to expand in her vision. She thought she saw her father's face in its depths.

The steam became a tornado under her feet, scattering the embers at its base and spraying them across the stone floor and walls of the cylindrical hall.

It pushed up from underneath her feet, whipping up her hair and her clothes. The steam should have been scalding, but it could not hurt her unless she allowed it. She didn't fear it in the moment, hardly even felt its tingling warmth.

She rose up, all the while staring at the cipher medallion. When she was even with Adri, she simply walked off the steam tornado and onto the raised platform.

Solindra had meant to keep on walking and use those steam winds in the grand slap she was going to deliver to Adri's beautiful, flawless face.

The steam princess brought up her own hand. Something purple glowed inside of it. Solindra's tornado vanished and the young woman was left reeling for balance, her back and heels leaning out over the edge of the platform.

Adri grabbed her in one hand. She held out her own purple cipher medallion in the other. She smiled and pulled Solindra forward onto secure footing. Then she replaced her medallion back inside her dress. A friendly smile lit her face and she clapped. "Well done, Solindra, well done. Better than I'd dared dream." She walked across the circle and flipped a dial on the lever panel. The circle rattled as it began to reset to its planar level.

The steam princess smiled wider. "I apologize that I had to act in such a manner."

"Act?" Solindra stumbled, off balance.

"But I knew the only way you can make the steam react is through anger at the moment. Forgive me, my little bird. I can show you how to do that without such an emotive stimulus, but it won't be easy." Adri strolled off the training circle.

Solindra followed. She didn't know what else to do. At this point, she felt frozen and hollow, like an old tree trunk in a blizzard. "How did you use the cipher medallion? Everyone— *almost* everyone who has touched it has terrible hallucinations. But you're not a crypter, are you?"

Adri just smiled. "Perhaps. Depends on how one defines a crypter. I did the rites for myself, and I have the research, stolen straight from the Priory. I can teach you to use your sancta. In return, you will help me to end these nonsense atrocities of this war."

"Me?" Solindra hesitated stepping out of the ring.

"It may not look like it, but we—Steampower, excuse me—is going to lose this war." Adri's face softened. "An untrained eye can't see it now. Codic has more soldiers, but we have better, far more capable war machines than they. However, such technology is beset by many...mysterious accidents."

Solindra licked her lips, trying to keep pace. "Ghosts in the steam."

"The Priory's work, no doubt. It's been suspected they've been dipping their fingers into Codic's government for a while now." She offered another brilliant smile. "But you can control the ghosts in the steam too, and far more powerfully than those stodgy old men. You never fed on your mother's breast, only on steam. Who knows? You can probably even talk with your lost father again through the ghosts, and demand to know why he stole an infant."

Chapter Ten

Smith tapped the glass cane against the floor of the dry goods store quickly. His lips were pressed into a thin line. "Where is my vessel?"

"A Priory Reaper," Drina growled. She, Jing and Theo remained motionless. The only sound in the room was the creaking of the door in the wind and the hushed breathing of the assembled townspeople. Nothing moved except for Smith's tapping cane.

The man in black exhaled. "It will take me less than two seconds to destroy the heretical thing, and I've already wasted too much time on this venture. I didn't know *you* were involved." He doffed his bowler hat to Drina and Jing. "So, well played, but the game is over. Where is she?"

"Blown up," Jing said. "Smuggler was carrying dynamite, and wouldn't you know, he smoked too close to the damned crates. You heard the explosion, you said so."

"Your work was finished by an idiot before you could do it." Drina stuck up her chin.

Smith frowned. He glanced over his shoulder to the townsfolk. "Go find me a red-headed young woman, probably hiding by the river. Do so, and your children will be able to thank you in person."

Most of the people stiffened at the remark. Two or three of them glanced down at the floor, refusing to look at Drina or Jing, and hustled out the door. The majority of the local population remained motionless, rooted with fear.

Theo swallowed. He could feel the tension in the room as if he could feel a tightrope beneath his feet. "And take some government stranger's word against the Hex?"

Smith lifted up his own cipher medallion. "Some stranger who has already demonstrated that he is more powerful than an old campfire story."

"The Hex is real." Theo straightened his shoulders. "They don't have to sneak in during the night and steal your children away."

"Yeah!" A young man around Theo's age pushed his way through the crowd. "They'll save us. My old man said that he saw—"

Smith swatted him across the mouth with the cane. That finally shook the people into motion. Several moved to catch the falling teenager while the others packed closer in to Smith and Theo.

The Reaper raised both his cane and free hand. "Folks, listen to me. All I want is this traitor girl whom these people are harboring. I want nothing of your town or your children."

"You're a crypter!" Theo shouted.

The following silence stunned him. No outraged shouts erupted. Instead, he heard the sharp intakes of breath from Jing and Drina behind him.

"And?" Smith said into the echoing silence.

Theo nearly swallowed his tongue. "And...and everyone knows what crypters do! Twist the ghosts in the steam to your bidding! And, oh yes, that they steal children away in the night. *Am I close, sir?*"

"Walking on fire, boy," Smith growled.

Theo could feel sweat stinging his forehead. The added weight felt like it could tip him over in a gust of wind. Surely Smith and everyone else could see it too. But he set his jaw and continued, "Talking to the ghosts goes against nature!"

"It *is* part of nature!" Smith slammed his cane down. "As much as dying is."

Theo took a step back, slightly faster than he'd meant to, but it put him closer to Jing and Drina. "But the Hex has always protected us from unnatural enemies!" Through the air and in the floorboards, he felt the tension in the room tightening. The tigers would leap all at once.

Smith ducked his head. "Well played, my young foe. I had scant information on you, Mr. Theodore Meilleur. I won't be out-talked again." He removed an almost flat cylinder three times the size of an egg timer from his jacket. Water sloshed inside the glass tubes. "And you've made their decision for them."

He flipped it around to show that his blue sancta had been fastened into the device. He pressed his thumb down on the plunger on the top. "Can you live with yourself?" The water distorted the rising glow of the sancta. Bubbles started to form as the water began to heat. Smith pocketed the device.

Suddenly, an impenetrable cloud of black smoke choked the room. Its acrid taste seared the inside of Theo's mouth and nostrils. He struggled to open his eyes.

Smith was gone. People were shouting and shoving; someone knocked Theo aside. The bricoleur had grown up knowing to watch for the doors and behind counters and tables for the person in the center of the smoke, but Smith had been surrounded by people on all sides. If it had just been a distraction, it had been a good one. If it had been something more…

Theo tried to spit the acrid taste out of his mouth. He shivered. Crypters – the Priory could keep the lot of them. His world stuttered to a stop.

How the hell had Smith known his name?

Someone shouted something very near to his ear.

"What?"

"I said, the boiler tower!" Drina slapped him upside the head with enough force to send him staggering forward.

"What?" Theo managed.

Drina smacked him again. "Logic, stupid."

"The boiler!" a woman screamed. "They were here the entire time?"

Drina, Jing and Theo rode the tide of the surging crowd down the street to the boiler. It was the squat, square tower with one side overhanging the Eld that they'd seen on their way in. A massive wooden waterwheel turned ponderously, but the sluice had been closed, allowing no new water into or out of the tower itself. The wheel brought the water up, splashed it against the concrete of the tower and spilled it right back into the river below.

Several people hurled open the double wooden doors at its base to reveal the metal framework, supporting the bulb of the boiler itself.

"No fire," Drina said as calmly as if she were looking at a broken wagon wheel. She stuck a hand through the door, ignoring the mob. "But there is heat."

Theo squinted, trying to see the boiler in the darkness of the tower. "How can we get in there?"

Jing shook his head. "Those things are built to stand up against fire and time. We can't drill in there before the water boils." He waved his hand toward what felt like an invisible fire.

A descending silence surrounded them. Everyone had turned to them as the heat continued to rise all around them. Theo immediately began to scan for hidden cables. Smith had to be controlling this through some trickery.

He shoved the mechanic's back. "You're Ghost, right? Do something."

Jing forced his muscles to remain taut and not shake his head. "This is a crypter's work."

"What?" Theo blinked.

"It's not like I can outsmart the ghosts with mechanics! Besides, the ghosts aren't real, it's all just dissolved aether."

"But you *are* Ghost."

"Kid, that was just a pool-hall name to make us seem larger than life. That's all."

Theo's mouth hung agape. "Folks pray to you!"

Jing pulled the bricoleur aside. "Well, I've never heard any prayers, except maybe very personal ones along the lines of 'please don't kill me' and those never ended well, not when we were in the service."

"But you're not in the service now!"

"I hadn't noticed, kid." He reached out and put a hand on the metal of the tower. He could feel the vibrations of the panicking children and the heat cascading down the line. "Never did a favor like this before in my life."

"You raised an orphan," Theo snapped.

"Because Silvermark said to."

Drina gritted her teeth. "If we're not doing anything else now, we should at least be getting ready to steal a boat."

Jing still stared up into the tower. There was no fire to quench, no drill fast enough to get through that bowl. He imagined young Cylinder in there. He remembered raising her and imagined finding her in that tank.

What would he do? Crypters used steam, and steam meant water.

"Death, I need my tools."

"Death?" Theo echoed.

"Right-o," Drina called. "They'll be whatever we can nab."

The mechanic nodded, kneeling down and opening up the compartments in his leg housing. He snapped his head up to the crowd. "There's a hatch on top, isn't there?"

One man twisted his hat between his hands. "Yes, sir."

"Well, get some men up there and start digging those children out!"

"There won't be enough time," Theo murmured as several townsfolk, men and women, ran to the far side of the tower, presumably to a ladder.

Drina returned, carrying several spanners and a large wrench. "What've we got, Ghost?"

Jing snatched the wrench from her arms and marched as quickly as his metal leg would carry him to the waterwheel. "Simple enough!" He heaved himself up and out onto a thin, wooden walkway. "Standard river pump. Wheel turns, collects water and pumps it up into the boiler." He wedged the wrench in between the sluice and the turning wheel. "Displacement, no suction. The water just has to move up into the boiler because of the weight of water behind it after it passes through a one-way valve."

"Break that valve, should all spill out." A flash of a smile crossed Drina's face.

"Right." He heard the scrabbling from the top of the boiler and shouts from the hatch. He yanked the sluice partway down and jammed the butt of the wrench into the valve, shattering the cast metal. He slammed the wrench home again and the cheap valve flew apart, sending pieces flying up past his face.

Nothing happened. No water trickled.

A young girl screamed from inside the tower, her voice muted and tinny to their vantage.

He brushed aside the flakes of metal and poked his fingers inside. They ran right into the freezing wall. Jing bent down and brought one eye level with the pipe.

The water was frozen inside the pipe. "What the hell?"

Above, the girl screamed again.

He looked down at Drina and shook his head. "He's using the aether to pull the heat up to the bowl. It's freezing down here at the bottom because he's pulling all the heat upward."

"Freezing?" Drina echoed.

"But the ghosts are only alive in the steam – in the heat," Theo protested.

"Perhaps not to a crypter." Jing frowned.

"So what do we do?" The bricoleur glanced over his shoulder at the crowd. Too many were still just standing and watching. "I think we're out of time."

"The hell I am." Jing hefted the wrench and slammed his metal leg down off the walkway, back onto the ground. "No machine has ever beaten me before. And no crypter occultism either."

He limped around the walls of the tower to the open doors. "Right," he grunted and walked underneath the bulb of the boiler. "Drina, Theo, help up top." He didn't turn around. Instead, he started to climb with his wrench in hand.

**

Drina shoved her way through the mob at the base of the tower. She didn't even bother with the overcrowded ladder, and instead dug her fingers directly in between the stones of the tower and started to climb. Her movements were slim, efficient and infinitely practiced.

Theo raised his eyebrows in surprise and then started to climb as well, wedging in his boots and thrusting up with his legs. Beside him, a screaming young boy fell, splattering Theo's cheek with warm water. The bricoleur turned his head to see him caught by several other people below.

Theo caught up with Drina at the edge of the open hatch. Steam was already starting to curl off the water's surface. At least ten remaining pale and horror-scarred faces were waiting inside. Once he'd processed their faces, his ears allowed him to hear their screams. A couple of the smallest ones were just floating in the water, being too short to stand.

He reached across the open hatch, next to a bearded man from the town, and yanked his hand back from the waves of heat from inside the boiler tower.

"Move back!" The Death Spinner elbowed her way past the man. She threw down a thin, gossamer cord with a weight at the end. "Grab on!"

Many small hands seized at it, scrambling with all their fury.

"We're out of time!" Theo screamed.

***

Jing jammed the wrench into the arm-thick pipe that fed the tower. He could see the frost on it below where it curved into the sluice outside. Up here, it was sweltering. He lodged both feet into the spidery framework of metal holding up the boiler itself.

Muscles bulging, he started to heave the wrench to the side. He counted his breaths and kept on pulling.

With a jerk, the pipe shuddered in its place. The metal squealed and turned almost a quarter of an inch. Bolts popped along the wall.

Jing kept applying the pressure and turning the wrench to the side. The pipe continued its slow twist, like an old ballerina.

Beneath the wrench, the metal started to glow a dark orange, as if the ghosts were attacking the new bend in the pipe. Jing didn't stop to wonder why. His entire world was consumed by the tug of the pipe.

The tube was now twisted halfway around itself. The heating made it even more pliable and easier to twist than he'd hoped. On the other hand, it made it harder to break.

Droplets sizzled as they flew from the pipe, landing on his forearms and face. He didn't even feel them; his entire world was bending this pipe.

His chest, back, neck and even his leg contracted together with his arms. His entire body felt like one single muscle. He heaved on the wrench.

The pipe snapped. Steaming water gushed free.

Jing leaned back out of its path as far as he could. Blisters and red burns were already growing on his hands and forearms. He eased his way down the network of supports and beams and back to the floor, pausing briefly to wipe the sweat and water from his face with his arm.

His muscles twinged and sagged. He hadn't moved like that in years. He glanced back up to the pipe, twisted purely enough with a neat snap in it, like a child's toy. Chalk that up to another legacy of the Hex. He couldn't help but smirk; they were back in the saddle.

He pushed his way back outside. The people were crowding around soaking, sobbing children. He fought against a smile at the reunions.

Drina was leaning on the edge of the tower, all but ignored in the rescue of the children. Theo was behind her, pale but standing up straight.

She shook her head slightly as he approached. "Some of the littlest ones had drowned long before. The rest... many of them will be scarred."

"But they're alive."

She swung around to fall into step with him. Theo dumbly started to follow, just swallowing. They stepped through the townsfolk, who were too focused on checking and crying over their children.

"And now we vanish." Jing swung away, ducking around the corner of a building.

"Are you with us?" Drina turned to follow, but looked back at Theo. "Or this is goodbye? None of us owe each other anyway."

Theo glanced back over at the townsmen. But the Hex had just gone, disappeared like the steam, even though he knew they were just around the corner of the building. Of course he knew that.

He curled his fists. "You owe me, Flame." He kicked up dirt as he ran after them.

"Well, well, he decided to come," Drina drawled. She tossed out a couple coins into Jing's waiting palm.

"Thank you," the mechanic quipped.

Theo fell into step alongside them. "I am not going to be cowed by you, Hex or not." He stuck up his chin, trying to hide his trembling as the weight of knowledge finally caught up with him. "So now what?"

"Get back to our last orders: Solindra." Jing didn't glance down at him.

"Orders?" Theo scowled. "Whose orders?"

"Silvermark's, before he died."

"And that's it?" Theo sneered.

"Of course," Drina scoffed. "I know I've killed some loudmouths outside of orders before."

"Death," Jing warned. "We're here for Solindra."

"Right," she said. "But we don't even know which side Flame works for now."

"But he took her alive," the mechanic mused. "So she's got to be out there somewhere, and probably not by the same people who are bossing Smith around."

"In Redjakel then?" Drina guessed.

The mechanic shrugged. "Possibly."

Drina sighed. "It's the best lead we've got."

Chapter Eleven

"Without the fire, Solindra."

"Yes, Miss Adri." The vessel scowled at the full bowl of water in front of her. Her eyes flickered to the servant woman carting away the steaming bowl. This new ceramic bowl that had been left glistened blue through the clear water, but the liquid was tepid. Solindra tightened her brow in concentration.

"It's pointless, Miss Adri." She pushed the bowl away with her free hand and fingered her cipher medallion in the other. "I know the ghosts are there in fog and water, but they're only alive in the steam. It can't be done on a bowl of cold water."

Adri shook her head and the golden chains in her hair tinkled together like tiny bells. "The aether is merely the medium through which energy can be transferred. That's all we do, transfer of energy." She held out her own purple sancta above the bowl. "You don't need fire. People have quite a lot of water in their bodies too. It's something to remember if you're ever in danger."

Solindra was only half listening. She watched as tiny bubbles began to form and then rise underneath Adri's sancta. Soon, the bowl was bubbling along happily, and fresh steam curled off the water's boiling surface.

The steam princess pulled her cipher medallion away from the table. The boiling immediately faded. "You do it, little bird."

The young woman frowned again and held up her sancta. After a moment of nothing, she dropped her hands. She suddenly pointed to the window. "Do you think we can do this lesson outside?"

She sighed while staring at the world beyond the glass. In this high room, she could see enough of the city. Redjakel's Light District had not been touched by the war. Boiler towers and electrum-coated skyscrapers reached up toward the clouds. Steam-ships drifted regally above them.

Down below, steam-coaches and horse carriages danced around golden fountains in the avenues. Women in the most brightly colored dresses strolled down the streets with their bustles and parasols, showing not a care in the world.

Adri slipped up behind the vessel. "Remember, none of this would be possible if not for the aether in the steam. Our technology would fail."

Solindra pressed her hands and nose against the glass. "I've always wanted to see the cities like this! This is nothing like Valhasse. This has plazas with fountains and restaurants and—"

"You can't, Solindra."

The girl's face seemed to melt.

"You can't be found out. You're too precious. You know how the common folk distrust crypters, especially after the assassination of President Falklind."

Solindra sagged. "That's just a story. It was never proven."

"You know your factual history. Good." Adri stepped up to the window and also put her hand on the glass. "But the truth is often pliable. People chose to believe the story, so it's more true to them than whatever actually happened. And so every last crypter was hunted."

"I know, but…"

"People hated us long before that. It was just an excuse for what they already believed. And yet, the Priory are the ones holding up Codic. I surmise they're fine with the general fear of crypters as it keeps their competition down."

"This is a whole war against crypters, isn't it? Is that the truth? Steampower is attacking crypters." Solindra pulled her hands away from the window and watched her breath fade from its polish. "This whole war is just so your father could go after the Priory?"

Adri tapped her fingernails on the glass, and even they chimed. "Blinded by love. Not a hatred of crypters. The fool."

"All of those people… they don't *know*?"

"Of course not, and why should they?"

Solindra reeled away from the steam princess. Her hands were suddenly shaking. "Because they don't know why they're dying."

"The truth wouldn't stop them from dying." Adri touched her chained hair. "What matters to me is that the longer this war drags on, the worse it will go for the Saturni legacy."

"Saturni legacy," Solindra repeated. "What happened?"

"My mother's cousin was a minor member of the Priory, and my father was cordial with them then. But that wasn't enough for Helen Saturni, and somehow she stole a copy of their sacred codex. She smuggled it back to Steampower with the help of Parrot. She, however, could not escape the Priory's underworld."

"And Steampower went to war to get her back." The younger woman's eyes misted.

"Eventually, yes. Now my father will rip out the Priory, branch and root. He's tried covertly over the years. The only thing that held him back for over twenty years was the threat of her death. Alas, somehow, my father had received word that she passed a couple weeks before his initial assault…"

Solindra wiped her gray eyes. "That's so sad."

Adri's face remained blank. "I have never wanted to destroy the Priory. They know more than we think they do. I did the crypter rites my mother had smuggled despite the perils, and I know in my heart that there is more to be had."

"But what about me? Where do I belong?"

Adri lighted the room with another smile. "You, my dear, were a product of the research into the Priory's manuscripts. We used them to build you, a true crypter."

"What?"

"Vessels are created when a pregnant woman does the Priory's rites. It had to be done when the child was viable outside the womb, for the mothers rarely survived the process. Neither did the infants we cut out from their guts."

Solindra stepped away from the steam princess. "No. No. That's too horrible."

"But you lived. That is why you are so very important for a Steampower victory. You do want to help me, yes?" She smiled as radiantly as the sun. "Or at least aid all those people on the Killing Trains that you spoke of? All of that is Codic's doing, not ours, and I need your help to stop it."

Solindra still retreated a few steps away from her. "You're a crypter. Why can't you?"

"My dear, I am not a vessel. I am not as powerful as you can be. Also, people know me, and they can't know that I am one with the steam." Adri followed and reached out. She started to intertwine her fingers in Solindra's flaming hair. "But I do want to know the ghosts' secrets. I want to know your secrets."

The vessel inched further away.

Adri advanced. "The Priory just wants you dead. But you're safe enough from the hunt here."

"But why are they hunting me?"

"The Priory fears you'll be stronger. You never had to study. You never had to sell your soul. They consider you to be not even human."

"I don't understand."

"Neither do they. They think this is all just mysticism, even if they know more than we do now. Our current tools of scientific observation are not yet sophisticated enough to show us the ultimate answer. But it does offer a current empirical reality, a world we can measure and attempt to understand. The Priory doesn't apply such scientific standards to their abilities."

Distantly, a large bell began to ring. Its sweet notes fluttered like a flying bird.

"Four o'clock," Adri said. "Let's go meet the man who started this war."

***

Serving a pitcher of wine was not what Solindra had imagined when she dreamed of meeting Steampower's leaders. Of course she was playing the role of Adri's maid, but she'd never expected to actually be one! Adri, meanwhile, sat with her ankles crossed in a chair with her back to the window, facing away from the long, carved table.

A huge telephone chimed on the corner table, and a well-dressed lackey scrambled to answer it. He held the corded receiver to his ear and then hung his nose over the speaking tube. Next to it sat a typewriter wired into a small electrical box attached to a telegraph.

Solindra tripped over her own heavy skirt while gazing around the room. The wine nearly spilled onto the stupid servant costume. This corset and bustle were ridiculous. The magazines she'd coveted had never mentioned anything about style being uncomfortable.

Men in heavy jackets lined the conference table in the center of the long room. They smoked and sipped their brandies and placed them beside the wine glasses on the table.

She bobbled and staggered for balance to keep in the alcohol in the pitcher when the far doors to the room opened with a crack akin to thunder.

The last true steam baron in Eliponesia, Boras Saturni, entered the room, coattails flying. He pulled off his top hat and half cape and tossed them to the servant trailing him. He ran his fingers over his dark beard.

He slid into his seat at the head of the long table, and then looked up in surprise. "Adri?"

She smiled and smoothed her skirt. "I just wanted to help, Papa."

"Fine, fine." Saturni spread out his fingers on the table. "Gentlemen, let's call this board meeting to order." Behind him, his assistant rang a glass bell. The men at the table set down their glasses and turned to face the steam baron.

Saturni relaxed back into his seat.

"Now, as you gentleman know, we are not new to this war industry. We've built the machines for nigh on eighty years. You know that I was just another compressed steam salesman when I was a boy, so I know how long a long day's work can be. And, gentleman, we have a long day's work here if we want to end this venture."

One of the men in suits put a hand on the table. "I have news that Eliponesia's overseas colonies are crumbling. Codic won't get support from them for much longer." He leaned back with a smile on his face. A round of "hear, hear" and harrumphs circulated the table.

Saturni frowned. "And we won't get raw supplies from them, either. Alright, send them some money to prop up the friendly forces that way. Can't stop production."

His servant took notes. "Yes, Mr. Saturni."

"People are not very happy with us," Saturni continued. "We need something to boost their spirits. Those folks outside of Redjakel, I mean."

"We're safe enough here, haha," another man put forth.

"Do they need anything?" someone asked. "Are they low on supplies?"

"They're low on morale," Saturni replied sternly. "They're running in fear and hoarding, which is bad for us in so many ways. We need a resolute war face out there."

"How about some survival kits?" a man with a cigar suggested. "Tent, canteen, matches, that sort of thing. Put in some informational fliers about how Steampower is helping them."

"Get them involved." Adri's voice was like warm honey flowing in the room. She smiled. "We need to get everyone involved in the war effort in some fashion, even if it's just embroidering Steampower napkins for the boys in the blimps. People are bound to support the effort if they have to sacrifice for it. Obviously, one cannot be overt in stating such an intention, but get some rallies going, get the word out about how they will help themselves by helping us."

Silence pervaded the room.

After a moment, Saturni clipped off the end of his cigar and lit it. "You do that, Adri. Get your girls sewing. We'll continue without you here now. Thank you."

The steam princess stood up straight. "Why, Papa, I thought I'd spoken another language. I suppose I really don't look like my mother."

Saturni's cigar dipped. He grunted. "It wasn't a bad idea, darling."

"But it might be an expensive one," a chair remarked. "Although we might get some free labor because it's patriotism. I don't need to remind anyone that until we win this shindig, we're losing money, and everything boils down to money."

"No," Adri snapped. "Everything boils down to physics and the five elements and every atom that makes them up. Money is just a febrile shared dream of civilization."

Saturni grinned stiffly at the board through a puff of smoke. "Now, now. Pardon us, gentlemen, the doctor has said that she has developed neurasthenia. It's so new, the University of Medicines only invented it last year."

Adri scowled.

Solindra tried to hide a gasp. She'd read about that in a magazine a traveler had left behind a few months ago. It meant that someone of the intellectual class had succumbed to urban stresses.

The steam princess lifted her chin and stalked away from the table.

Solindra knew she should drop her eyes, stare at the floor and quietly follow Adri out of the room. Instead, she glared directly at Saturni. Her hand slipped into her pocket with the sancta. She could do it. If she could touch him, she could boil him alive, from the inside out. Then this war might be over.

Adri tapped her shoulder. She shook her head.

As they turned to leave, Solindra heard Saturni saying, "Codic has got some information it shouldn't have, and it has been seriously damaging to the war machine and it's not entry-level bullshit. Surely one of you sirs has been offered a deal by them. I will say now that listening to them will not be profitable to your health."

Time slowed down. Solindra inhaled for as long as it takes a glacier to move. Shadows seemed to lengthen out from the corners, and a new shadow was rising behind her. Through the window, she heard and felt what seemed to be every thump of the individual blades.

A copper-colored helicopter platform was rising up to the board room behind the window. The things were hard to steer, and dangerous with their two rotating blades driven by a steam engine underneath the platform. There were smaller blades on each side facing outward to help guide the platform, but the controls were just a mess of levers and dials.

Those levers were left unchecked. The masked man on the platform was aiming his rifle. Saturni's eyes were just now starting to widen.

Adri grabbed Solindra by the neck and threw them both to the floor. Solindra immediately started to roll over, her hand pawing at her sancta. She stared up through the window at the dual spinning blades. There was steam driving that engine. If she could just get the cipher medallion close enough...

Adri placed a hand on her shoulder, and Solindra felt her chest constrict. Cold fire danced along her skin. Before all feeling numbed, she felt the prickling of the hammer shape of Adri's sancta through her corset.

"No," the steam princess whispered. She pulled back her hand and the freezing weight from Solindra's shoulder stopped pulsing.

The rifleman fired at Saturni's chest.

But not before Saturni's assistant began firing with his own pistol. In the same instant, they exchanged a volley of gunfire.

Saturni recoiled in his seat and stared at the red smear across the leather from where the bullet had clipped his ear. The blood trickled into the hole in the back of the chair.

The assistant stepped forward and landed another shot in the chest of the assassin. The stunned rifleman staggered back and collapsed off the helicopter platform, plunging out of sight. The machine tipped up and soared into the sky now that it had lost the counterweight.

Solindra finally remembered to breathe. She pushed herself up to her knees and hands and stared at the floor. It seemed solid enough.

"Get those girls out of here!" was the only thing she heard. She thought it was Saturni's voice, but she was far from certain.

"Come along." Adri pulled Solindra up by the shoulders and brushed off her dress as they slipped outside the room.

Solindra was still shaking as they walked through the vaulted halls of Steampower's headquarters. Adri just walked with a slight frown on her face, as if she had drunk sour milk.

Suddenly, a tall, handsome man around Jing's age, wearing the black uniform of a courier, winked at Solindra when he stepped into her path. She flinched and grabbed at her sancta, but Adri stepped directly in front of her.

Judging by his calmness, she figured that he couldn't possibly know what had just happened. She was still trying to slow her breathing.

He handed a thick envelope to Adri. "To you personally, my lady." With another wink, he was gone.

Neither Solindra nor Adri watched him leave. The vessel tried to read around the other woman's arm, but she couldn't get a view.

The steam princess immediately rolled the letter up. Then she smiled. "I think it's time to fly away from this gilded cage."

$$\mathbf{1}$$

Chapter Twelve

"We don't even know where Flame is." Theo groaned and kicked another rock down the road. He inhaled more dust as he breathed. It was so thick that it created a low-hanging haze on the horizon, and the humidity made it stick to his skin. A town was visible in the distance, or at least the mirage of a town against the desert scrublands. They'd left the trees a few days behind by the river.

"Be glad of that," Drina replied. "It's not him that we're worried about."

"Cylinder's got to be fine. He took her alive" Jing looked straight ahead as he limped down the road. "I hate to imagine what might've happened if she'd been with us when we encountered Smith."

"You know he's circling us like an eagle again," the assassin said. "He has to be."

"Doesn't matter. We still find Cyl."

"We could just shoot him," Theo offered.

"Better be sure of that shot, boy." Jing didn't look down at him either. "More than just aim. The man's a born crypter."

"Not a *born* crypter," Drina whispered. The wind picked up around them, stealing their breath for conversation and bringing even more dust into their eyes and ears.

As they drew closer, the shadows of the town's buildings became more solid. They didn't look burnt out either.

Jing clumped down his metal foot. "This all brings us back to Flame, who is our only lead."

"No." Theo bunched his fists. "Because the next time we see him, he's going to have his candle snuffed out."

"You'd better be sure of that shot too, son," Jing said.

Drina lifted an eyebrow. "And you might want to, maybe, I don't know, *be armed* first?"

Theo growled, but couldn't stop the flush from lighting up his face.

"Or, knowing Flame, maybe calling him names will make him explode. Or you might discover your final heat tolerance. And he's got Cyl." She scowled. "I can't even guess that vituperative jackass's motive. Could be money. Could be Flame being Flame."

Jing nodded. "Remember when he used to try to grab the rising sun at sunrise like a kid chasing a rainbow? The ultimate fireball, he called it."

"And we don't know where he is."

Theo felt his entire body lock up. "Yes, we do." He gulped, finding himself unable to even bring his arm up to point.

Flame waved at them from the road in front of the town. Smoke and fire were starting to rise up from behind him, towering high over the buildings. He spread out his arms and smiled like a miracle-performing saint as he walked out of the growing furnace behind him.

Then he grinned like a toddler, his sabers and pistols all rattling together as he started to jog toward them. "Mm, nothing like the scent of chaos. I'm sorry I stole your spy and set your boat on fire. Let's go get some coffee!"

Theo still couldn't move. This was the second time he'd met the murderer, and he couldn't move!

"Spy? What spy? Oh." Jing lumbered in between the bricoleur and Flame.

"So you went into contract work too?" He held his empty palms up to both Drina and Jing. "Guarding a Codic spy though, that's a bit beneath us, don't you think?"

Drina just forced a smile.

Flame checked over his shoulder to see the entire town. "Too bad it was already abandoned before I got here." He smacked himself in the forehead. "Coffee, right! Um, the next town then? My bad."

Theo was vibrating as if in a very personal earthquake, unable to make his muscles respond to his mental commands.

Flame leaned over toward Theo like a melodramatic actor. He shaded his eyes. "What's he for?"

"Training him up," Jing answered.

"What?" Flame barked a laugh. "You trying to put players back on the team? The Hex is over, man."

Theo ripped off his gloves and raised his scarred hands. He tore at his shirt to show the mess that was his chest. "You did this to me!"

There was no reaction. No furrowed brow of thought, no perplexity or recognition. Flame eventually shrugged. "Eh, you survived. I don't see what you're complaining about." He patted Theo's head and grinned. "What do you fellas think about this war, huh?" He rubbed his hands. "Best fun I've had in years! No more sneaking around at night!"

"You did this to me!" Theo screamed again.

"What?" Flame blinked. "Sounds like *someone's* a little obsessed if you ask me." He whistled and pointed at his head, circling his finger. "Hey, I figured you'd be moving away from the river–"

"You did this!" Theo shoved Jing aside with all the strength of rage. He marched forward. "You burned me. You murdered my whole caravan. You killed my family!"

Flame leaned away from the spittle. He inserted his pinky finger into his ear and wiggled it. "So? I murdered my whole family too. And you know what? It got me a job." He licked his extracted earwax.

Theo sputtered between rage and confusion. He stood motionlessly, trembling out of both emotions.

"Can I kill him?" Flame looked at the mechanic. "You can find another apprentice."

"No," Jing said.

"Fine." Flame shrugged. He rubbed his palms together again. "Where's ol' Silvermark? I want to know what happened to him after he went crazy and stole some dyin' bitch's baby."

"Dead," Jing said.

Flame spun around like a dancer and dipped his face next to Drina's. He winked. "Finally did it, huh?"

The Death Spinner shook her head. "He died of influenza."

The pyromaniac laughed. "I don't believe it. Not unless you figured out how to poison somebody with the flu."

"You killed everyone I knew!" Theo screamed.

Flame's eyes flickered back over the young man. "Are we still talking about this?"

"Y-You! You devil!"

Drina pulled down Jing's arm and whispered, "He's gotten crazier through the years."

Jing shrugged. "Or maybe we've gone sane." He cleared his throat and picked Theo up in one hand by the back of his neck. "Down, boy."

"What?" Theo kicked at the air uselessly.

The Hex members ignored him while Jing set the bricoleur back down, but kept a squeeze on his shoulder. Drina pointed at Flame. "Why are you here?"

Flame batted his eyes. "The folks over in Redjakel want me dead, so I thought I'd switch sides for a while. By the way, do you know that their idea of fire control is to shut their river-gates and flood the city? No joke! Town on fire and all gates closed to make a flood. This is fun at its finest!"

An empty, wide-eyed silence saturated the air around them. Only the sounds of the winds fanning the flames could be heard.

"Did you do that?" Drina finally asked.

"No." Flame still grinned. "It's too big, so then I remembered I saw my old friends and thought that they would want some fun too."

"Only us? What about the others?" Jing murmured.

"Eh. Playboy Parrot's supposedly working somewhere inside Codic, and Slayer is sailing with some foreign trading company on the other side of the world – provided he ain't dead yet." Flame shrugged again. "But I think the three, no, four of us could do it. I've got this balloon hidden on the library's rooftop, so we'll have a superb view. I'll even bring some half-pennies we can throw at people."

Theo broke free and charged. Jing caught him up in two arms, but the enraged young man carried him a few feet down the road. "Did you throw half-pennies at my mother too? Did you throw half-pennies at my brothers?"

The bricoleur wrenched against Jing, but the mechanic's grip was steel.

"I like him." Flame smiled. "He's got an inner fire." He tilted his head to the side. "Look at it burnin' in his pretty eyes. So pretty."

Theo dug his heels into the ground, suddenly reeling away from the insanity. Jing let go.

Flame ducked forward in the moment of movement and danced back before.

"What…how did you—?" Theo could see his few remaining phosphorus capsules in between Flame's fingers. "Hey!" He grabbed at his pockets.

Flame suddenly twisted apart one of the capsules and threw the sparking, fiery powder into the air. "You're trying to replace me! He's supposed to be the new Flame, ain't he? You're building a new Hex!"

Both of the other Hex members started to laugh, all the while never diverting their eyes from him.

"Please!" Drina chuckled. "Not unless Silvermark ordered it. Oh, and he can't."

"And I don't *want* to go back to playing for both Steampower and Codic, especially now." Jing managed a grin.

"Both sides?" Theo rasped. But his mouth was already drying out. "All of you used to play both sides? Like what they forced us to do?"

Flame waved a hand in front of Theo's face. "Poor bastard is just stuck in the past." He whipped his fiery grin back to the other two. "So, Redjakel then?"

Drina crossed her arms. "We want our spy back first. Then we'll talk about Redjakel and Theo's anger troubles. But our spy first."

Theo inhaled to scream again, but his throat trapped his words. That vicious voice in the shadows of his mind massaged his shoulders and breathed in his ear in Merlina's sultry voice, *attack him now. He's there and not expecting it. You owe the girl nothing.*

Theo planted his feet and looked beyond Flame into the burning town behind him. "Solindra first." He closed his eyes and tried not to hear the raging thunder inside his own head. His survivalist voice seethed against his denial. He felt the heat flare out across his skin.

Drina stepped between Theo and Flame. She poked the short pyromaniac in the chest. "*And* if you don't stick to the plan this time, I'll tell Theo here your real name."

Flame stamped his feet and marched around in a circle. "Fine! But maybe I'll just throw you out of the balloon too! And that is *never* my name. I'm Flame, alright?" He stopped so suddenly that it looked as if he'd walked into a wall. He pulled back his hair and flashed a smile. "Coffee?" He leaned toward Theo and said in a stage whisper, "Whatever else she says, just remember that she can stick needles in between your vertebrae so that you're paralyzed and you'd never even feel it."

"Flame!" The assassin snapped her fingers. "Cylinder first. Then Theo gets to work out his scars on you. Blood debt, you know the rules."

He sagged. "Aww... But those rules aren't civilized. We do live in the Steamscape, you know." Flame looked at Drina with puppy eyes. "I get to fight back, right?"

"Not against a blood debt."

"Let him." Theo tugged his gloves back on his hands. "It won't matter."

Flame cupped his cheeks in his palms. "Such fiery eyes."

Jing half-smiled. "Then how many unpaid blood debts do you owe, Drina?"

She cocked a grin. "None. No one's alive to claim them."

Theo made himself look into Flame's all-too-cheerful face. "We need to get Solindra back. And soon too, so that my ghosts can pay you back. So where the hell is she?"

Flame's face twisted as if he was going to sneeze. "I don't know about where she is *now*. Adri's not so cuddly like me." He threw open his arms for a hug, causing his pistols, rapiers and homemade incendiary devices to jangle together on his bandoliers.

"Adri?" Jing repeated. "Steam Princess Adri? What could she possibly want with Cyl?"

Drina rolled her eyes. "What could any powerful person want with a true crypter?"

Chapter Thirteen

The wind pushed Solindra's hair up and over her shoulders, spreading it out like an electric halo. Solindra, Adri and her other servants stepped through the opening glass doors and onto the roof of Steam Central. Solindra gasped, first at the sting of the wind, but then at the metropolitan vista. They looked down at the skyscrapers, the markets, the rooftop gardens and the entire world below.

Adri gestured to the machines on the roof: a wire-frame helicopter powered by a boilerbox, and two other rounder flying machines, each with repeating guns on their arms. Menacing monster teeth had been painted onto their bases. The helicopter pilot and two huge men walked across the roof to each of the machines.

Solindra stared. She'd never seen anything like those two armored helicopters. Titangles, she recognized them from the magazines and she'd heard Jing talking about. Flying battle machines. They were mostly spherical with a large dome in front so the pilot had excellent lines of sight. But they looked heavy. Chains of bullets had been casually draped over a side of one.

One of the titangle pilots stowed the bullets before climbing into the cockpit. At the same time, the helicopter pilot flipped on the switchpack in order to ignite the fuel that would heat the boilerbox. It must have run on something far more efficient than wood or coal because the fire immediately flared into life and the scent of gunpowder and coal filled the air around them.

Adri smiled. "I make certain that I am often seen flying in this fashion."

She nodded to the two silent servants behind them. The women curtseyed, and one of them pulled on a blond-white wig. Together, they walked out to the waiting helicopter.

"Oh," Solindra said. "A decoy. Especially since your father was almost killed."

"Yes, a pity that." Adri turned away just as the two escort titangles and helicopter lifted off and flew between the electrum-coated skyscrapers.

The younger woman hovered behind, watching the display as if it were a parade. Soon, the helicopter rose like a ballerina, perfectly spaced in between the two flying titangles. They sauntered into the air, graceful as hummingbirds.

Solindra let slip a smile and sighed.

"Come, little bird," Adri called.

She dropped her gaze and stooped to pick up two large haversacks and put one on each shoulder. Then Adri handed Solindra a long, thin but heavy case. She winked. "In due time."

The steam princess let the roof doors blow shut behind them. She checked her belt pouch for her sancta and a small four-shot pistol. The purse was a narrow, leather pouch with a slot for a woman's fan and pistol, now the height of fashion in the city.

Adri stepped up to an interior gated door and waited. Solindra, wheezing a little under the weight of both haversacks and the long case, bent her knees to fit through the cage door. The steam princess then floated out onto the elevator platform.

The cage bobbled when Solindra walked further onto it with her luggage and she stopped, holding her breath. She squeezed open one eye and stared down into the black, seemingly bottomless shaft below.

Adri chuckled. "It's perfectly harmless, unless you've been eating too many chocolates." She let her hand glide over the control levers. "Now please close the door and let's be on our way."

Solindra grunted and rammed the cage door home. Adri pulled down a lever and the elevator began to sink.

After a while, there was light from below. Solindra squinted through the slots in the cage's bottom, trying to see the destination of their controlled plummet.

Adri moved more levers and the elevator slowed its descent. It finally stopped, hanging a foot above the landing.

Solindra stared. Below was a moving chain as wide as her arm.

"This part is a bit of a drop, or so I've been informed." Adri slammed a lever with a red handle home. The overhead cable detached and the entire cage bounced down onto the moving chain. Instantly, the chain caught and began conveying them along.

Solindra pressed her nose through the bars. "What is this place?"

Adri raised her chin and did not look around at their surroundings. She sighed elegantly. "Maintenance and escape tunnels, I believe. A few unofficial labs." The cage shuddered as it rattled along its new track. "This chain also powers the water pumps up into headquarters' boilers. There are deep wells here."

Solindra looked down through the cage's bottom. Beneath the moving chain she could see the water, the oil in it shining almost like aether bands.

They rode in the semi-darkness for a timeless moment. Solindra couldn't tell how long had passed in the gloom. She covered her eyes. Ahead, a green lantern was glowing.

Footsteps from ahead broke the stillness. The steam princess reached back and grabbed Solindra's shoulder. She shook her head.

"I read something about a project down here..."

"Something feels wrong." Solindra grabbed the bars of the cage as it rumbled forward.

The sound of shattering glass and snapping metal echoed ahead in the darkness and someone cursed explosively. Then even more footsteps sprinted away in the other direction.

Adri pushed Solindra against the cage bars and gripped her cipher medallion. Shimmering like a liquid, a wall a steam out of the oily water below encased their chests and leads in a large cloud.

"Don't move." Adri pressed the sancta close to her chest.

"I don't see anything," Solindra hissed.

"That's what I fear."

Unbridled screaming rose from several throats. It rapidly faded to choking sounds, and then the only sound was the cage moving inevitably forward on its chain toward the origin of the unseen terror.

The machines continued to grind and clank in the everlasting gloom.

Solindra turned to Adri, eyes wide. "What...?"

Adri shook her head. She pointed.

The cage passed by several dead men. It was too dark to see their bodies clearly. Solindra leaned closer. One of them was slumped over some sort of metal canister, but she couldn't make it out. She tried to reach out, to see better, but Adri's steam bubble made it too foggy to make out any details.

Adri whispered, "Don't move. Don't talk." The cage kept moving forward on the mechanical pull of the chain.

Eventually, the steam princess brought down her hands and the steam bubble faded. "Go ahead and open the door. I don't think either of us wish to stay here."

Solindra breathed in the damp air. "What was that?"

"A waste of breath. Silence."

"Yes, ma'am." Solindra dug her shoulder in and wrenched the cage door sideways. She stood there, toes hanging over the edge, hands on the haversacks as she watched the lantern growing larger. It highlighted a small metal platform and a darker hole behind it, suggesting a tunnel.

They jumped. Adri's shoes barely whispered as they glided down onto the walkway.

"Oof!" Solindra swore under her breath, and her knees seemed to crack like a whip as she stumbled her landing. The two haversacks bounced forward, throwing her entire body off balance, not to mention the long case on her back.

The empty cage clattered on down its track without them, its rattles louder with less weight pressing down onto the platform.

"Come now." The steam princess marched into the darkness beyond.

Solindra waddled behind, trying to balance herself and run at the same time. She tripped over another still-warm corpse. The boy could have been no older than ten. His face had contorted and he stared at something horrible that was beyond her vision.

"He ran far." Adri slipped up beside her as silently as a hunting cat. She stepped around the corpse as if it were an inconvenient puddle and onto the roughly hewn stairs beyond the body.

The vessel followed and banged her toes on the second stair. It was too dark!

She stuck out her hands until they bumped into a slick, uneven wall. She tried another stair.

Adri moved like a ghost through the poor light, her footfalls barely making a whisper. She smoothed out her skirt. "Poison gas. Chlorine, mustard, bromine or something else. Even I don't know much about this. Some sort of mechanical defense against people trying to break into Steam Central." She frowned. "At least, that's what I heard. Papa has begun to keep the information to himself since he suspects there is a spy on the board."

Solindra shivered. How would a machine know friend from foe?

"Come, let us leave this place."

After a few minutes of cussing and stumbling, Solindra gasped at the sudden sunlight. Adri held open the door for just a moment and then strolled on ahead like she had been walking on the clouds.

She pulled on a dark wig of her own and smiled as she saw the red carpet and silver ropes guiding the crowd to the golden-colored blimp. People here dressed in ornate clothes matching the expensive appearance of the private air-dock. Adri and Solindra breezed through the gentlemen assigned to keep the riff-raff out.

The blimp took up most of the sky as they stared up at it.

Adri pulled on her white gloves. "We must fly, my dear."

Solindra shook her head. Her feet felt heavy, as if they were growing roots. Her stomach heaved at the thought of sky-sailing. "N-No."

Adri smiled sadly. "Smith is a determined man, I'm afraid, so we can no longer linger here. Now I'm the only one left who wants to protect you from the beasts."

"Like the Priory?" Solindra asked.

Adri nodded. "Yes, bird." She opened her hands. "I know not for certain, Solindra, but I fear that you are not safe here, either. Perhaps Papa's would-be assassin was only so daring because of rumors that a vessel had been found. Yes, there are stories, and we are not safe in the city."

Solindra stuck out her chin. "Drina and Jing are still out there. I don't believe for a moment that Smith was able to stop them."

"Because Smith is after you, not them." Adri smiled sadly. "Even if they live, you are not safe. Especially here, despite an army of soldiers between you and he."

From the corner of her eye, she could see the wire-frame helicopter and its two titangle guards approaching the air-dock.

Adri placed a gloved hand on her shoulder. "But I will protect you." She didn't even look up as their entourage sailed overhead.

***

Theo whistled at the wire-frame helicopter and its surrounding titangles. "I ain't seen that before." He leaned over the side of Flame's descending airboat and its rotting hull.

"So close," Drina murmured gazing at the distant skyscrapers, "but armored walls. Didn't they say Adri likes that sort of thing?"

Jing kept his gaze level with the Redjakel's crowded streets. "It's just as well. We can't get near her with Smith still in the wild."

"Now, now." Drina laid a hand on the mechanic's arm. "Smith is a bastard, but he is as civilized as the next man."

Unfortunately, that next man was Flame. He was leaning on a line and whistling to himself. "Er, what?" He grinned and clipped Theo's shoulder with an open hand. "Redjakel! You'll never find dirtier whores than here!"

Theo felt the heat across his flushing face. "In front of a lady!" Despite his hatred for the man, all he could think about was a woman's presence.

That woman cracked her own smile. "No, he's right, but he's not talking about the poor girls on the street." She pointed to the line of skyscrapers.

The largest building Theo had ever seen came into focus. It was golden, or at least its sleek stones and metal looked golden. It wasn't adorned with reliefs and art like most everything else in the Steamscape. Sheer, sleek, slick...devoid of art so that it became art itself. Other buildings had giant clockwork displays and showed off their elevators, but not this tower that overshadowed all of them.

Drina sighed and cupped her chin in her hands, resting her elbows on the railing. "Steam Central. Outside hasn't changed much."

"Do you think our Cylinder is in there?" Jing wondered aloud.

"We're going down," Flame called. "Ghost, lend me your leg here. I need the weight."

The mechanic nodded and slowly limped over to Flame. His weight creaked over the rotting boards of the hull. "I can't believe you paid money for this wreck."

Flame kept up his grin. "Old beaut, little creaky, but I wouldn't trade her for the world – seen me through so much."

Theo looked down at the city below through a hole in the hull.

Their landing was smooth. They docked down in a central hub for trains, carriages and airboats. Dozens of elegant dirigibles and hundreds of smaller airboats crowded the docks.

Sheer busyness on a scale that Theo would have never imagined infused the world around him. He felt a laugh gurgling up from his belly. How could he have thought he could cause trouble here? This was nothing like Consequences or Valhasse.

Their hull scraped against the dock's ship-catch, causing some splintering sounds from below.

Theo took one large step toward the railing and *crunch*! His leg slipped through the rotting wood and stuck out through the hull.

Flame grabbed his stomach and laughed, slapping the railing. "She knows what I like! She knows what I like!" He leaned forward and kissed his control console.

Jing collared Theo and lifted him out of the hole with one hand.

"I hate him! I hate him! I hate you!" the young man roared.

Flame just laughed harder.

"Hey! You can't dock here!" a grounder yelled up at them. A man with his hair parted and plastered down the middle of his scalp ran toward their ship. He waved a clipboard. "That is not a Steampower built ship! You know the rules!"

The prow fell off the boat into a pile of firewood. The man stared at it and then started waving his arms. "Get it out of here or we will!"

"Oh no," Jing muttered.

"No problem. No problem." Flame smiled and held his hands out wide.

"It's old! It's ugly! Get it away from the others or you'll have fines up to your neck, friend!"

Theo had to admit the grounder had a fair point. The new, sleek and polished hulls of the Steampower vessels with their gilt and gold webbing around their balloons did make Flame's ship out to be a dead duck floating amongst swans.

"I can fix this." Flame held up his hands as he approached the grounder. He reached into his bandoliers. The grounder stopped breathing, his eyes widening, suddenly realizing that he wasn't paid enough for this.

Flame withdrew a cigar from a bandolier and waved it at the man. "You look like you could relax. You want this one? Here." He tossed it to the grounder. "I'll take this other one."

His other hand pulled out a stick of dynamite. He struck a match with the calloused thumb of his other hand and lit the stick.

Jing snatched Theo's shoulder and hauled. The grounder was also running, holding his clipboard over his head. Theo turned to catch up with Drina. The mechanic followed as quickly as his metal leg would allow. Drina was muttering. "He's gotten crazier, I swear."

Flame stood there, eyes closed. Meanwhile, the dynamite fuse spit fire and shortened, still held in his hand like a tulip.

Finally, with a shrug, he launched the explosive high up over the tall deck of the nearest Steampower-built ship.

It exploded in the air. The hydrogen in the air-ship's balloon caught aflame and carried the heat and fire into an even greater explosion.

Theo stumbled, his senses numbed by the heat, pressure and noise. The blast of the explosion pushed him down. When he dared to look over his shoulder, he saw that Flame was still standing nearby, arms wide, like a man bathing in sunlight. The young man watched Flame's eyes glowing in the fire's reflection, even as the burning canvas and wood fell around him.

Theo realized there were more reasons than just revenge to kill this man.

The balloon of a second ship exploded a fiery death and its burning debris punched through the rigid balloons of the ships next to it. The next dirigible went up when the flames climbed up its support ropes, and it exploded, spreading even more fire to other ships.

The bricoleur didn't look back this time and instead tried to keep up with the stampede. He tripped over a squirrely businessman and blundered through the crowd of screaming, fleeing people.

He managed to keep his head above the flow, enough to see the fire patrol and soldiers running toward them.

He also spotted Jing, towering over the crowd a few feet away. Once they squeezed through the last of the ships, Theo felt the pressure on his shoulders ease. The flow was spreading out. He rubbed his ears, unsure of his hearing in the moment.

He pushed and shoved until he made it over to the mechanic, and he saw Drina there with him. "Where's—?"

Flame, grinning through a cigar, sidled around one of the ship's hulls.

"They have 'no smoking' signs," Jing commented.

Drina chased some embers out of her long hair. "Aren't the Steampower higher-ups trying to kill you? Maybe you shouldn't cause all of their soldiers to run at you."

Flame held up his hands. "In my defense, I didn't want to pay the fine."

"You destroyed your ship," Drina said.

"Piece of junk anyway. Who cares?"

"I think you just did more damage than any of the battles so far."

"And I'm ahead in the game!" Flame danced in place.

Nearby, alarm bells cracked and air-raid sirens howled above the din of the burning airships. Flame clapped his hands and pointed. "The river! I told you they blocked off the river to help with fire control!" He leaned over with the force of his laughter.

They turned to see massive gears on floodgates turning.

Drina pushed Theo's arm. "Time to fly. Just like all the other emotionally scarred urbanites." She nodded her head toward the soldiers, still trying to advance through the crowds in a semblance of a ragged formation.

They ran, joining the sea of people escaping the docks.

Theo wiped the sweat from his forehead. He leaned against the wall and wheezed. The concrete almost felt icy. The cool air of the alley soothed his lungs after their run from the dockyard. Jing, Drina and Flame all watched him. None of them were breathing hard.

"Come along, youngster." Jing pointed with his thumb. "Let's get something to eat. You look like you need something for your strength while we plot our course in the city."

Theo coughed. "But what about Solindra?"

"Smith first." Drina scoffed at him. "We discussed this."

"But what about setting the city on fire?" Flame whined. "I'm sure this guy who is after you is as flammable as everyone else."

"He's a crypter, Flame. Priory man."

Flame's upper lip curled. "Snarlin' water cheats. They don't play fair."

The party walked further down the alley as a squad of Steampower soldiers ran past its mouth.

Theo stretched his shoulders and slowed his breathing. "I need to send Merlina a telegram."

"Are you stupid?" Drina rolled her eyes.

"She's the closest thing to family I got left."

"Right, so why do you want to chance Smith tracing a telegram to her?"

"Oh."

After a few more minutes, they came into a space between windowed buildings. Theo bit his tongue. This place had looked so clean and so pristine from the air, but its alleys stank just like the ones in Valhasse.

They rounded another corner. A man in what had once been a nice suit, now ripped and greasy, tiptoed toward them. "'Scuse me, and I ain't never begged before in me life, but me girls have taken a turn." He coughed explosively into his glove. The spasm came from deep in his throat, rich with phlegm. "And me wife was killed when…"

Drina held out a couple of coins without a word.

The man closed his torn open-gloved fingers around them. "Thank you, madam." He shuffled along.

Flame leaned over. "Those were coated in poison, right?"

"No." The assassin stared straight ahead and kept walking.

Flame stared as if he'd seen the sky falling down around him. He hummed to himself, cracked his knuckles and jogged to catch up. "So you definitely see why this place needs to be cleansed?"

Jing quirked an eyebrow.

"It will flush out your spy and her hunter."

Drina sighed. "Smith isn't going to fall for us sticking a wig on you, Flame."

"Aw, but I liked wearing your dresses for sneaking into places."

Theo stopped and stared. "What?"

"Hey man, I might be strange, but I am not crazy." Immediately, he resumed humming to himself.

"Smith is a terrier, so we need to throw out something for him to fetch." Jing tapped the wall of the building, just a couple of beats in telegraph code. "Theo, you need to send Merlina a telegram. You also need to send one to your dead parents. And everyone you have ever known. Talk about daisies growing or some mystical bricoleur story. Talk like it's a code."

Theo swallowed. "And Smith will come in for the kill."

Chapter Fourteen

Theo jogged a little after he stepped outside the telegraph office. The receipts in his hand rustled with the motion, their bright red Steampower stamps blazing in the sunlight. He jigged around the corner to where the three Hex members were loitering.

He held up the papers. "Alright, since each telegraph office has a code key, Smith will know where these originated." He rubbed a thumb over one of the stamps. "But I really don't like the idea of waiting to find Solindra…"

The shadows of Jing and Drina obfuscated the sunlight as they leaned over him. "You know we raised that girl," the mechanic warned.

"I *meant* we should put more effort into finding her." Theo gulped, his eyes flashing back between Ghost and the Death Spinner. "Um. Because that's our goal."

"No," Drina corrected. "Your goal is to kill Flame here."

"Yeah!" Flame nodded encouragingly.

She pointed between herself and the mechanic. "*Our* goal is to protect Cylinder."

Flame clapped his hands. "The sooner we get her, the sooner the boy and me get to fight. Fun."

Theo crunched up the receipts and held them between him and the Hex like a shield. "This was expensive. Um. I know how to make money gambling."

Jing rolled his eyes. "Right, like we're going to trust a bricoleur with our money."

Flame chirped, "I can make money gambling, too! It's called the Clockwork Boom." He jerked a glass grenade from one of his bandoliers, and yanked out the pin. The gears above the black powder and shrapnel mix began to spin.

"If you run before I throw, I win."

Theo felt coldness roll over his entire body. He wanted to skedaddle, but his legs had grown roots. Flame wiggled the weapon in his hands, and Theo heard the metallic screws and lead shot tinkle against the inside of the thick glass.

The gears rolled through the timing mechanism to their end, and then raised a metal file to strike the flint. Fire hissed into life at the top of the casing and the fuse carried the fire deeper into the grenade.

Flame shrugged and tossed it into the open window of the nearest building.

It exploded. The building rattled. Smoke shot out of the window, and the shrapnel scored the stone of the building directly across from the window.

He dusted his hands. "I guess you won that round. Good times."

A woman screamed inside the building, but it was a scream of surprise at least, and not of horror or pain.

Flame shrugged again and started walking.

Jing sighed. "One of these days you are going to blow yourself up, laughing."

"I know."

Nearby, constables' whistles flared up, screeching across the early morning air. The party kept walking nonchalantly into a wide avenue.

Flame spread his hands. "You know, I can get you inside Steam Central."

Jing's nostrils flared. "I thought they'd ordered your death."

"I still know the building and the new defenses. But it's just this Smith feller, ain't it? He's got you scared, and Drina, that's not something I think I've considered about you."

She lifted her chin. "It's not me I'm scared for."

Flame teased out another clockwork grenade and smiled. "We need to do something while we wait for Smith to come kill you."

"Game fields." Theo turned his whole body without bending at the knee and started to totter away. "Gambling is so much safer than you people."

***

Redjakel's fields were far more civilized than the gladiatorial arenas of the lands outside the Steamscape. Here the players were volunteers, not slaves, and that marked the difference. Also, the games were not designed to actively kill the players.

Theo snorted under his breath as he wound through the crowd. The air around him felt oddly cool despite the cheering of the nearby people. He glanced around the stadium and the fans.

He whipped his gaze back. He thought he'd seen Merlina across the way, on the other side of the stadium. He shielded his eyes and stretched.

Nothing. Just another girl with feathers in her hair.

He shook himself free and looked at the players. Lion polo. What a game. He leaned his shoulder against one of the shaded awning's wooden pillars and watched.

The players, including a few women this time, he noted, flew a few feet over the ground on hover-plates, controlled with foot pedals. Cougars and lions attacked from below. Each player carried a polo stick and tried to score the ball into the goals.

He listened to the roar of the large cats above the crowd. Then he glanced over to the scorecard. Some poor kid was only a plank away from being a meal himself while hanging a giant 3 over the 2. It looked like the Steampower mechanics team was beating their compressed steam salesmen counterparts.

A player, wearing a full suit, took a moment to club a lion on its skull before turning his attention back to the game. The lion howled and swiped with its paw, missing the moving man's coattails by half a foot. It elicited cheers from the crowd.

"If you're really with us—"

Theo jumped and spun around.

"—then you need to stay with us," Drina finished. Jing and Flame strolled up from behind her.

The bricoleur shrugged. "I am. The girl didn't do nothing but try to help me once."

Then he let his eyes wander back onto the polo course and the little jets of flames keeping the hover-plates and their riders from the lions.

A lion swatted a player off of his hover-plate and onto the field below. The man went down swinging with his polo stick. The lion roared in victory and the crowd cheered as if he'd scored the game point as the man was mutilated by the pride.

"Civilized indeed," Theo muttered. "It's not right, those people–"

"I worry more about the cats," Drina interrupted. "The people can be eaten for all I care."

Jing shook his head. "Never saw the point of these games. Animals are just being animals, and I mean *all* the animals."

"Showmanship."

"Pardon?"

"Showmanship," Theo said. "It's all about the show, not the safety of the players or the comfort of the animals. It's all about the illusion of the show. So that gentle sir probably won't even care if he's missing an arm, not if he can walk away with his head high. At least as long as the crowd's watching."

"I think he's dead." Flame pointed.

Drina looked at the field and shook her head. "That's why we preferred war. Just targets, and not nearly as much ridiculous pageantry."

Theo continued, "But pageantry, or at least the imagination of it, is why everyone fears and loves the Hex."

"Smarter than you put forth, kid." The assassin shrugged. "It's a fair point, I suppose."

Theo stared across the stadium and into the stands on the far side of the arena. Merlina winked and waved at him. He blinked.

She was gone. The bricoleur rubbed his forehead with his gloved hand. "I think I need something to eat. I'm starting to see things."

***

Jing pushed aside some young chimney sweeps, barefoot and in tattered jackets so soot encrusted that their original colors had been lost. They sneered at him but ducked out of the door of the cheap deli.

Drina paid for some bread and soup. Flame lurked outside while Theo kept an eye on the sweeps through the window, wondering what would happen if they tried to pick Flame's pockets.

But the kids just passed the arsonist by.

The Death Spinner flashed a grateful grin at the baker before turning away with the bags of their food. Her smile faded when she turned. The entire room darkened as Steampower soldiers eclipsed the doorway.

Jing and Theo stiffened, but didn't move. The corporal in the lead walked past them and to the counter. He slapped down a pile of paperwork and stared at the baker. "The company is going into baking now. You'll have to close up shop."

The baker was fast becoming as pale as his bread. "But..." He licked his lips. "But I'll be out of business."

"So bake for the company." The corporal shoved the paper closer to the baker. "And hurry up, I've got twelve more shops on my roster alone. And—Hey!" The soldier leaned over the counter and swiped his hand through the coins. "You knew the deadline to switch currencies!"

The baker held up his hands as if at gunpoint. "It's what the c-customers have!"

"Pah!" He scattered the coins with his hand.

Drina held up the bags of food and smiled at the soldiers in the door. "Excuse me, please, gentlemen." They grumbled, but stepped aside. Jing tapped Theo on the shoulder and nodded at the door.

Outside, Theo locked his knees. "We can't just go! The poor man needs help!"

The assassin shook her head. "Our mission is Cyl."

Jing took one of the bags of food. "And what are we going to do? We can beat up a few soldiers. Fine. Then they'll come back with their friends."

115

"But, but…"

Drina shrugged. "Learn to pick the fights you can win, kid. And oh, not to take on Steampower and Codic by yourself. That wasn't working out so well for you, if I recall."

Theo stamped his fist into his palm. "Hey! I didn't have anything to lose."

"Didn't you?"

The bricoleur stared hard at Flame's neck. The pyromaniac just hummed to himself and took a bowl of hot soup from Jing. The mechanic held out a sandwich for Theo.

He knocked it to the ground. "I'm not hungry anymore."

Drina rolled her eyes. "Your stomach doesn't know it can live on disgust."

Theo backed up a step. "Is this really what the Hex was about? Just picking the fights you can win? We loved you because you won against the odds! We feared you because you could show up unseen anywhere! How is that possible if you only pick the fights you can win?"

"Because those attacks were planned out and practiced." Drina bit into her own slice of bread. "This is really good. That poor baker."

Theo smashed his hands against his ears. "I don't believe this. I don't want to believe this."

As one, the members of the Hex just shrugged. Soup drizzled down through the patches where Flame hadn't shaved, or more likely, the parts that hadn't burnt off over the last week or so.

Theo looked away. Movement caught his eye. Across the busy avenue and in the black shadow between two skyscrapers, Merlina bounced a curtsey and waved at him. A cart passed in front of her and she was gone.

"You okay, kid?" Jing prompted.

Theo mutely shook his head. "I think… I'm worried you know. What if Smith does trace that telegram to Merlina? I know she said she was leaving, but…"

Jing replied, "There's nothing we can do."

"Like with the baker?" Theo snarled, more viscerally than he'd meant.

Drina shrugged. "If you insist, we'll slip him some extra coins to get by." She held up a bag she had stolen from a soldier's belt. "Fair enough?"

He shook his hands and breathed deep. "Um. I'll be right back." He turned and started to jog through the steady traffic of buggies and people across the avenue.

Drina pulled a long, thin cord out from her pocket. "I think I'm going to put a leash on that young gentleman."

Flame brightened up and opened his mouth. A hand disappeared into a bandolier.

"No," she cut him off.

"But—"

"No." She continued to loop the cord into a makeshift lasso.

"Okay, how about I strap him up with counterweights and my own special dynamite, so that if he moves, he'll explode?"

Drina frowned and caught Flame's gaze. "When is that ever a good idea?"

"Good idea it ain't. It's just fun."

Jing said, "Flame, you're not even funded by Steampower or Codic anymore. Where are you even getting your equipment?"

Flame whistled and looked at the sky. "Well... I got friends."

"You terrorize people into giving it to you, and then I bet you blow up half of them anyway."

The arsonist held up his hands. "They gotta respect the Hex, you know."

"You never did that when you were part of the Hex. Silvermark would have never allowed it."

"He was too strict," Flame whined. "I'm glad I'm off his leash." He glared at Drina while she knotted up a thin lasso. "But I see you've taken up the yoke."

***

Theo pushed the last person out of the way. The caped man snarled something after him, but the bricoleur didn't bother to listen.

Merlina wasn't here.

Of course she wouldn't be, he told himself. But at the same time, he'd seen her. He knew it.

The bricoleur trudged into the alley between the buildings. It remained dark, and he blinked his eyes until they adjusted. It remained darker than it should have been.

He licked his lips and let his fingers drag along the building as he walked forward. It was something solid at least. "Merlina? Was that–? Are you–?" But he couldn't finish. The questions were just too stupid. How she talked to the ghosts with a straight face in front of all those marks every day he would never know.

He stopped, but listened to his footsteps still echoing against the walls for a moment. The cement underneath his feet rumbled. He hopped back.

The concrete swelled up in front of him like a bursting bubble. Pieces broke apart as the ground punched up from below with the sound of snapping bones.

Theo stared as a huge metal pole exploded up from the ground. Torn wiring stuck out of it like a frightened cat's tail. It sparked a couple of times and died.

A tiny aether band curled around it, drifting up past Theo's nose. He stared cross-eyed at it.

The ground began to fall in on itself.

He jumped. A gray curtain of gas erupted like a geyser out of the hole, sending him careening for balance. He spun on his heel and tried to sprint.

The collapsing alley was faster and it snatched him into the earthen maw. He grabbed at the pieces of flying cement, but nothing was anchored enough for him to grab onto. More chunks bounced off his skull and into darkness.

And then… he wasn't falling. Nothing had caught him, but all of his weight seemed to have left his body. He gasped, or at least he tried to. There was nothing to inhale.

He screamed. There was no sound. His throat ached and he felt the air passing from his lungs and through his mouth, but not a whisper escaped him. His blood felt like it was boiling and all he knew was coldness. So cold that it didn't even feel cold anymore.

He held up a hand in front of his face and wondered where the light was coming from. Lights. Hundreds tiny little lights swirled in this void.

A blob of luminous color passed between his hand and his nose. It shifted through the colors of a prism, drifting through this place like oil in water.

It passed. Dozens more floated around him, drawn toward his body. Then he noticed how his fingers were changing from bright red to a pale blue at the tips in these strange lights.

He tried to scream again, but he felt like he was choking. His lungs were aching. He inhaled desperately, but there was no air.

Something grabbed his foot and yanked him up.

Now he had nothing left to scream with. Something pulled him through what looked like a cloudy updraft and then suddenly he was back in the alley.

He hacked and heaved, but he was breathing again. His head throbbed like it had been hit with an axe and his vision was blurred. He curled up into a ball.

Drina coiled her makeshift lasso. "Leash was a good idea. What is that?"

Theo dared to open an eye, chest still heaving.

"It couldn't be…" Jing trailed off.

"Aether." Flame stuck out his hand into the slowly rising gray fountain, tittering as the weightless cloud drifted between his fingers like silk. Twists of rainbows curled in and out of the band. The stream rose high up between the buildings to join its brother bands in the sky and above.

Theo gulped. The fifth element was only visible when it was in contact with the other four material elements. That was why the sky always had aether bands high up in it where the air met the edge of the sky.

Theo held his heaving chest and stuck his fingers under his arms. What was such a concentration doing buried under an alley? Someone had committed a corruption of nature.

***

The buggy bounced as its wheels rolled over the gravel road. Solindra bit her lip much harder than she'd intended when the carriage hit another pothole. She stared through the narrow windshield while her hands fumbled with the control levers. The vessel still didn't even know what half of those gauges meant, but she'd figured out speed and engine pressure.

She'd never driven before, not even a buggy with a horse, but she'd grown up under Jing's tutorship and would be damned if this could beat her.

And that blimp ride! She'd thought sky-sailing in such luxury would quell her stomach, but that indulgence hadn't been in Adri's plans. They'd spent the entire trip in some dark corner by the door with the cold air pressing through the seams. When the blimp had docked at a waystation in the mountains, they'd slinked off.

Solindra had thought this would be like home, but it was Steampower-built, owned and operated. It ran like clockwork: efficient and mechanical. The blimp's staff had even come off the airship to run the waystation. No one had been there before them, and no one after.

Almost no one. Adri and Solindra had waited until the blimp was climbing higher than the foggy mountains before stealing the steam buggy from the waystation's carriage house.

Solindra grinned. She'd never stolen anything before! Of course, the question of why Adri had stolen something that she had free access to had been nagging her for the entire trip, but she did her best to ignore the question.

Now her attention was on this slender, rocky road. But it was smoothing out and widening as they drove down into the valley.

"Codic!" She gasped and pointed. "I see it!" She jerked on the levers and gears, slowing the buggy to a halt.

"Hm?" Adri raised her head, absently pulling off her dark wig. The reclining couch had been bolted to the floor of the metal buggy.

Solindra pointed through the front windscreen. "Almost there." The looming mountains were the outer walls of Codic's fortress. The ancient city was squat and hunched compared to Redjakel's soaring skyscrapers. Some of the buildings looked carved out from the native rock, rising high up into the backs of the mountains.

Adri patted Solindra's shoulder. "Good work. Now perhaps we can end this war together."

Chapter Fifteen

Theo's mouth was still dry. He, Flame, Jing and Drina had backed into the cusp of a crowd staring at the rising pillar of aether. The column had consumed the entire alley. Cords and swirls of rainbow twisted around inside. No one had seen aether this close. It was always above the clouds, above the sky.

The Death Spinner tapped the bricoleur on the shoulder. "Watch for whoever seems to react differently from the rest of the crowd."

"What? Why?" Theo hissed.

"Look for who doesn't seem surprised, who seems angry instead."

Theo took several short, sharp breaths and sliced his gaze away from the aether cloud. He scanned the crowd, looking for marks as if he were a child again. But his gaze was driven back to the aether. He'd never been so close. No one had ever been so close. All the fools who had tried with their hot air balloons never bragged about it, and they came down half-frozen or not at all.

Drina bumped him with her elbow. "Do act suitably awed. They might also be watching us."

Jing loomed over them, but he kept his face toward the rising aether. "Steampower troops, seven o'clock."

Theo sneaked a glance. They were staring as slack-jawed as the rest of the crowd. Then again, he guessed, the average grunt wouldn't be guarding such a secret.

He didn't even know how the aether could be contained. He didn't dare think about who could have possibly done it. His mind closed that door before he could get a foot through it.

Flame kept striking matches with his calloused thumb and tossing them into the aether.

The broken pole with frayed wires laid at their feet. Jing tapped it with his boot, but didn't move his eyes away from the cloud. "Containment barrier. Somehow, they contained it."

"But it's lighter than air. Obviously." Drina nodded up to the heavenly aether bands.

"They put a roof on it, Death. That's easy enough. I just don't know how they got it down here in concentration. Where did they harvest it from, and how?"

Theo shivered and rubbed his still cold fingertips. No one could fly that high; everyone knew that.

Jing continued, "It's dissolved in everything."

"They sieved out the ghosts?" Theo asked incredulously.

"No, not in such a large field. I don't know. But I damn well want to find out."

Flame chuckled. "Everyone who has messed with pure aether has died. Oh, I know the stories that you mechanics swap."

"'Scuse me. 'Scuse me." A blond boy, possibly about ten, was shoving his way through the crowd. He didn't even glance at the impossible cloud, as if seeing such miracles were commonplace. "Hey! Anyone named Theodore Meilleur here? Mr. Meilleur?" The child put his hands on his hips. "Look, I was told he was here." He waved a yellow paper over his head. "Telegram for Theodore Meilleur."

Jing tapped Theo on the shoulder and pointed.

Theo barely glanced away from the aether. "That's me, son. What are you—?"

"Telegram." The youth shoved the paper into his hand and walked away.

"Uh, okay." The bricoleur flipped the page over.

Drina plucked it from his hand before he could read it. "Paper can be poisoned, but the boy was holding it just fine. Oh my."

"Death?" the mechanic prompted.

She passed him the note.

Flame whistled. "What is it?"

Theo took a half-hearted swipe at the missive. "It's for *me*."

"Smith," she said.

Jing passed the telegram back to Theo. He turned it around. Stamped by the typewriter, the telegram stated, "Do not waste my time. C.S., Esq."

Theo swallowed. "It's proof he is after us, at least."

"I can always set him on fire," Flame pointed out.

"That's not always the answer, you know," Jing replied, still watching the rising aether. The colorful cloud was finally starting to shrink as the underground storage slowly depleted. He nudged the broken pole with all the wiring with his foot. "I fear we may have bigger troubles now. If there's more of this, no one in this city is safe. Not us. Not Cylinder."

Drina snapped her fingers. "Flame, we may need you to do what you do worst."

The pyromaniac grinned and the fires sprung alight in his eyes.

The assassin said, "We make a run for Cyl at Steam Central. We'll just have to deal with Smith along the way. Our best ally is speed, as well as breaking from the pattern that we've already built with him."

Jing nodded. "Sounds like Silvermark. I agree."

Flame raised his hand, which happened to have a clockwork grenade in it. "Can I also set fire to Steam Central?"

Drina batted his hand out of sight. "Sure, why not?"

"Okay, I agree then," he replied.

Then they turned to Theo. He gulped and rubbed his still cherry-red fingertips. "I– I don't know about this anymore." He looked past the group to the hole, still silently spewing up the gray and colorful aether to the omnipresent bands in the sky.

***

Solindra dropped her gaze from the bands of aether high up against the heavens. They looked closer up here in the mountains. Much more like home.

That was the only thing similar. Solindra had dreamt of Codic, but she'd never imagined it correctly. Her magazines only had showcase pictures, apparently. She'd read about the Tears of the Sun Waterfall, but never imagined how high it fell over the city at the mountain's base.

Codic's buildings weren't as sleek nor as tall as Redjakel's, but there were more of them. The capital still had pieces of its medieval wall surrounding the city. It also smelled wrong, and not like the mountains should smell at all. There was no pine or even a chill on the wind. Codic's few factories were busy pumping out heat and smoke.

Solindra looked back up to the aether bands. They were at least something familiar. She felt for the weight of the sancta in her pocket while Adri led her down another avenue, but she kept her eyes in the sky. She needed aether to make it work, and their world needed to run on the ghosts in the steam. But water ate aether like a fire eats wood.

She nearly ran into a child. The young girl turned her face toward her, never rustling her massive jade hoop dress, and just glared.

Solindra thought she'd nearly trampled a doll. They made dolls that moved like people on internal clockwork, but this was a real person. The girl's face was painted white with extravagant rouge across her cheeks.

The vessel gulped and jogged around the girl after Adri. She had nearly lost the steam princess in a knot of people.

This was where she'd always wanted to be? She scrunched up her nose. It seemed too foreign. They passed by the fabrics emporiums, the dress stores, and even a chocolate shop. She remembered the day she'd torn out a picture of a chocolate fountain and pinned it up in her room for months.

But, as the smell of chocolate overwhelmed her, all she could think about was the Killing Train, or those downtrodden workers in Valhasse. Codic and Redjakel dozed in comfort and the war they had precipitated wasn't even bothering them!

Solindra grimaced and marched after Adri. They were on a mission to stop this chaos. She accepted that. While they walked, several government soldiers tossed the steam princess a curious glance. They whistled and waved while Adri ignored them.

The vessel wheezed under the weight of the two haversacks and her father's rifle on her back. She had been right about what was in the carrying case; she had peeked while Adri had dozed inside the carriage. Adri had not given her any ammunition for it though.

She was surprised to find that she liked the weight of the case. Of course, it was her father's rifle, but that was the second thought in her mind. She liked the gun itself.

"Miss Adri?"

The steam princess glanced over from underneath her dark wig.

"What are we doing here?"

Adri smiled. "We're attempting to end this fracas. You know that."

"With what? Is there a peace treaty in one of these bags?"

The older woman shook her head. "Not so much. But as you witnessed, Papa doesn't listen to me. I don't have power to sign a peace treaty. I do, however, have information as well as... other things."

They leaned into the slope of the rising hill.

After a moment, Solindra asked, "Like what?"

Adri paused. She glanced around the street and over her shoulder. She leaned close to Solindra. "Well, you might as well know. I have it on authority that my mother may, *may*, still be alive, and that's what Papa wants."

The vessel's eyes widened. Adri grabbed her hands. "Please. This is a secret. I don't actually *know* if she is. And I dared not say this where someone in Redjakel may have heard. I didn't know you well enough in Steam Central. Please forgive me for keeping this secret until now."

Solindra nodded.

Adri released her grip and risked a smile. "Thank you."

"Are we here to break her out? Using our cipher medallions?" Solindra felt her heart hammering in her chest at the thought.

Adri frowned. "Do not be ridiculous. I am here to negotiate in a meeting."

"Oh." Solindra felt her blush rising up from her neck like an invading army. "But then why not tell your father? If he went to war over her–"

"Because I lack proof." An edge glinted somewhere in the steam princess's voice. "You are my servant, remember that."

"I thought I was just playing your servant."

"It doesn't make a difference here." Adri snapped her fan open with a sound like a gunshot.

"Well if we're not using our crypter abilities, then why just the two of us? Surely some soldiers–"

"Solindra, respect!" Adri smoothed out the front of her dress. "Steampower crypters, here? I don't think that would go over well."

Solindra nearly tripped over her own boots. She stammered and felt embarrassingly pink in the face. "But—but, you could…"

Adri spun around like a twirling leaf and smiled. "Never fear. I have a plan, little bird." She held out her hand. "Your sancta, please."

"What?" Solindra turned her shoulder between herself and Adri. "No."

"I can't trust that you won't attempt to use it here, especially since you are questioning me. I will not let your childish follies jeopardize my mission."

The vessel stuffed her cipher medallion deeper into her pocket just as the street exploded.

Chapter Sixteen

"Solindra!"

Nothing.

"Solindra!" Adri pawed at the smoke stinging her eyes. Her dark wig lay askew on her crown. Bits of rubble smoked on the avenue all around her.

The vessel threw back part of a door. It crumpled in on itself at her touch. She rolled onto her side and started coughing.

The steam princess bent over and shoved the broken door out of her way. She reached down and forced a grin. Then she held out her hand.

Solindra stared and took Adri's hand. "And here I thought you'd never lifted anything heavier than a champagne flute."

This time, her smile sparkled. "Well, you are part of my plan, after all."

"Yeah." Solindra's brief levity faded as she turned to face the aftermath. The fronts of the nearest buildings were blackened and sagging. Bodies lay along the street, most moving and bloody, but some completely still. Small fires burned up and down the boulevard.

"Oh no. Oh no." The vessel whipped around in a circle. "Where are the soldiers? Where are they? Oh no…"

The perfect doll-like child lay spread-eagled on the street. Her makeup was streaked and smudged, and her beautiful dress torn and bloody.

Solindra swallowed a laugh. She punched herself in the gut and doubled forward. She didn't know why she was laughing! She pointed. "Look, she's human. She finally looks human."

She surveyed the damage again. Somewhere down the street she saw blurry blobs of people running in their direction. "We didn't...Steampower didn't do this, did we?"

Adri slid her wig back into place. It looked ragged and parts of the hair were singed. "Glad to know you've chosen a side." She shook her head. "I want to end this, Solindra. Please believe me."

"Where are *our* soldiers?"

"This was not done by soldiers, little bird." Adri lifted up the hem of her skirt, now stained and torn. "Saboteurs and spies. Just enough to show them that we can strike at their heart, you know? This is just a message. There's nothing here worth guarding or attacking."

"But they're people." Just like on the Killing Train. Steampower was as awful as Codic.

Solindra hesitated over the perished doll-child. "Where is your mother, little girl? Why is there no one here to cry for you?"

"What was that?" Adri stepped off some of the broken boards and picked at her dress. "Oh damn. I needed to make a good impression too. Our lives depend on that impression. But it does appear that Steampower missed the fact that I am here. At least that part of my plan is working."

Solindra didn't hear any of it. She had her ear turned to the chocolate shop. The front wall was going up in flames and an upright horse trough had blocked the door. Someone was screaming inside.

Through the fire-framed window she saw a very heavy man on the floor. A petite woman in a purple dress and ruffled collar was trying to shake him awake. She tugged on his arms, but he was too heavy for her.

Solindra dropped the haversacks and rifle. She ran toward the flames. "Help! Help! There are people trapped in there."

No one was able to answer her call.

The horse trough was blazing, its flames riding right up against the door, spreading its claws into the structure itself. The remaining water was bubbling and the steam was hissing.

Steam.

"Solindra, no!" Adri shouted from behind. "I said no!"

The younger woman fumbled for her sancta. She held it out at the horse trough. "Come on, blast you! Come on!"

The steam began to rise faster and swirled like a dust devil. She formed the vapor into a ball, squeezing it together tighter and tighter until almost no more water remained in the trough.

The ball was already leaking like drops of sweat – the water too dense to stay together so tightly. Solindra swept the cipher medallion across the store's façade. Water splashed all over the flames, dampening the majority of them immediately. The embers hissed against the water.

Solindra rushed forward and stamped out what was left of the fires. She dug her shoulder into the horse trough and heaved it over. Panting, she pushed open the store's door.

The woman in the purple dress stared at her. "You're a crypter. Crypter!"

The vessel stumbled back a step. "What?"

"Crypter!" But Solindra could see she was just terrified, almost as rabid as those on the Killing Train.

She ran over to the fallen man. "But is he okay?"

The woman fell over his body, protecting him. "Crypter!"

"I said *no.*" Adri pulled on Solindra's shoulder from behind. She snatched the red sancta from the teenager's hand and pocketed it. "Get our bags and let's depart!"

"But I was helping..." Solindra let herself be dragged back out into the street. Now the vessel could see the oncoming soldiers clearly and her hands itched for her father's gun. She picked up their haversacks and the rifle's case.

Adri pulled her back inside the chocolate shop, snorting at the woman in the purple dress as she glided toward the back door. Solindra stumbled along in her wake.

The steam princess slammed the back door closed after them and started to march down the alley. "If this presentation doesn't go right, we'll both be doomed like my mother."

Solindra gasped for air. "I thought we were here to rescue her."

"Maybe. If it suits us."

"Suits us?" The vessel froze. "If it suits us," she repeated incredulously.

Adri snapped her fingers. "Yes." She whirled around and leaned into Solindra's face. "This is war, child. What did you expect?"

"Not to be willfully sacrificing somebody else. Sacrificing your own self, that I can understand, but—"

Adri cut her off with just a glare.

Solindra felt her feet melting in the alley below her. She stuck out her trembling chin. "Or like the Hex."

"The Hex? We made the Hex into heroes and villains at the same time because it brought us victories. Because they brought both fear and hope in one easy envelope. They were never as real as they seemed to be."

"But…"

"No buts. This is why we are here. We are to negotiate with men of true power."

Solindra gulped. "Who in the Codic government knows about you? Or me?"

"No one but me knows about you presently." The steam princess shook her head. "Child, it's the Priory with whom we'll meet."

As they strode through the far end of the alley, a man dressed exactly like Smith stepped out of the shadows behind them. He gestured with his hand to an old-fashioned carriage, just now pulling into the alley's mouth. Horses' hooves neatly clipped against the pavement. Adri stepped forward. "See, the Reapers can be as courteous as they are unrelenting."

***

"Anyone looking?"

Theo leaned his head around the corner of the intersection. He flashed an up sign with his hand.

Flame bounced on the thick metal of the trap door. It locked away a maintenance shaft that connected to Redjakel's underworld.

"Start of a long road to Steam Central though. Probably guarded, possibly trapped." The arsonist nudged some of his metallic powder back into a perfect circle and then hopped over the line. He rubbed his hands together and grinned. "Do you know how many rusty items are around? Thermite is so easy to make!" Then he frowned. "But a pain in my heel to light. Do you know how hot of a fire is needed?"

"Where do you get the aluminum to make thermite?" Drina asked, ignoring his inquiry. "Stuff's not cheap anymore."

"Theft," Flame replied.

"What's taking so long?" Theo called.

Flame sneered. "This is art, my boy. Now where the hell is my blasted lighter?" He pulled a switchpack out, his version of a lighter, but it was really the standard ignition trigger for most machines. This one was affixed with magnesium at the top, something that could burn hot enough to bring thermite to life.

"You know, I think I'll build a couple of these things with thermite *in* them already. Just flip the switch and go." He grinned.

Fire flared between his fingers and he struck it to the magnesium. In obedience to its master, the thermite exploded in fury inside its fiery fountain. Metal melted.

A perfect circle opened wide into the trapdoor as the center collapsed down into the shaft.

"We can't hide this," Drina murmured.

Flame shrugged. "So? They'll blame it on Codic. We're fine."

Jing also shrugged at Drina. "Deed's done, Death."

She flipped her hair and grinned. "I thought that's what I'm supposed to say to you."

They hopped down the hole in the trapdoor and into Redjakel's muggy, smelly underworld. Drina paused to slide a plywood plank over their new entryway.

Flame yanked out an electric torch from one of his bandoliers. He flicked it on and the light bulb inside hummed to life.

Theo trailed his fingers along the slick lead pipes. Steam was escaping somewhere, but it was long condensed and chilly down here. There were dozens—no, hundreds of pipes all linked together. He squinted ahead. "Hey. I think I've got something." He reached forward and pulled back a large cloth, soggy in the underground dampness. Paper would've disintegrated already.

"It's a map." He turned it around. "Ha! Steam Central is that way."

Jing snatched the cloth map from his hands just as he took his first step. "Flame." He held out his hand and the pyromaniac tossed him the electric torch. Then the mechanic flipped the map upside down and shone the light through from underneath. "Actually, Steampower is the other way. See?"

"What?"

"Old soldier trick, boy. Don't worry, you're just too young to know. It's meant to be read upside down. You can tell by how the Steampower logo is at a ninety-degree angle."

"What?" Theo crossed his arms and frowned.

"Anyone following us?" Drina called.

They listened. There was no clink of glass on the street above. No shuffling footsteps.

"No," Jing said, "but if we don't know what we're going to do, then I highly doubt Smith does either. He probably isn't far behind."

"Wonder if we'll find another aether containment field around here." Flame's heavy boots echoed like thunder in the metal cavern.

"Likely not," Jing murmured. "They seemed to know exactly where in this maze to hide one though."

The others fell into step alongside him, with Jing shining the light through the map to illuminate the pipe-filled, dripping world.

"Close enough to the old days, eh?" Flame chuckled.

"Just about," Drina replied.

Flame suddenly snarled, "But rescuing the girl, *that* girl, is what made the Hex fall apart. I wish I knew the first time she and me met. Don't get me wrong, I've had my fun since, but you just can't get into as much trouble by yourself, know what I'm sayin'?"

Drina shrugged. A small, double-edged knife had appeared in her hand.

"So what's bricoleur boy still doing here?" The pyromaniac jerked his thumb. "Does he really think he can kill me?" He batted his eyes. "Or is it love?"

"It's you," Theo spat. "I'm only here to be the retribution for your crimes."

And that vicious voice caressed Theo's shoulder like a lover. So why are you waiting? What's your excuse this time? Is it the girl? No. You're still afraid you'd freeze up again, little child, so afraid of getting burned again—"

Theo grabbed his ears. "Shut up!"

The Hex members stared at him, eyebrows rising.

"I think he may have spent a little too much time at high altitude." Flame rolled his eyes skyward suggestively. Then he toddled on down the hall, humming to himself.

Theo's ears were so warm he thought could singe his hands through his gloves if he touched them. He lowered his arms and trod mutely in the Hex's footsteps.

Jing and Flame murmured over the map. Drina kept checking around corners, throwing knives at the ready. She seemed to be more and more frustrated that she didn't find anyone as the hours marched on.

Flame clapped his hands. "Here it is! The door to Steam Central. It's probably rigged." He immediately dug his shoulder into the large gear wheel to open the portal.

"You just said it was rigged," Drina said.

"Only probably." Flame heaved and the wheel came loose, spinning around several times on its own.

Jing yanked Flame back by his shoulder. Several darts shot out across the entryway from compressed steam coils along its vertical sides.

"You were right," the mechanic said.

Jing held up his metal foot and kicked the door in. Nothing else happened.

Drina picked up one of the darts and sniffed it. "Flyweed Toad. That'll stop your heart."

Two Steampower soldiers peered into the doorframe.

"Hello." Flame smiled and held up a clockwork grenade.

"Put your hands—"

Drina had thrown two knives at their throats before Flame could strike the grenade's fuse. "That will be too loud."

"Too late." With a shrug, Flame tossed it down the metal cave. Whistling, he leaned against the wall.

"Run!" Jing bellowed.

They dived through the open door. Theo heaved it shut and leaned against the thick metal.

The door coughed at the grenade's eruption, but it muted the thunder and barred the shrapnel.

Through the portal, Theo could hear the escaping steam hissing like a bag of serpents. "You broke something."

"It's what I do." Flame grinned.

"Why didn't you mention guards?" Drina waved another knife in the arsonist's face.

"It's new. They are in a war, you know."

"They don't seem to notice," Jing mused. "Hardly any city defenses. Sneaking in here was too easy, even for us. Here, let's get these bodies into the pipes."

After they had dragged out the corpses and retrieved the Death Spinner's knives, they stepped inside Steam Central proper.

Theo's jaw dropped upon seeing the domed ceilings. He spun around, becoming dizzy as if high up in a balloon, gaping at the opulence around him.

Ahead, a stained-glass picture of Steam Princess Adri as a praying angel glowed in the sunlight.

"Ah!" Flame snapped his fingers at the stained glass. "It's this way." Humming to himself and clicking his heels, he trotted down another palatial corridor.

Theo watched Flame's back. He knew he would just stand there and stare at Steampower's glory otherwise. But the gilt still reflected in his eyes. This was like the illusions they'd sold as kids, tinfoil mirrors and glass gems, only this wasn't an illusion. This was real.

Drina and Jing silently kept pace behind him.

"Adri's place ain't none too far now," Flame commented.

Ahead of them, a dumpy servant rounded the corner. She gasped at the sight of Flame and his cohorts and dropped the empty bucket she'd been toting. Then she frowned. "Oh. It's you."

Flame grinned and waggled his fingers.

She bent down to pick up the bucket. "You know there's a kill order on you now. We have to be quiet, but we hear things, you know."

"Which is why I didn't tell them I was coming."

"Where's Ms. Saturni?" Jing asked from the back of the group.

The servant threw up her free hand. "She and the new girl left days ago."

"Where did they go?" Drina demanded without missing a beat.

"Like I would know."

The assassin slid closer. "When are they returning?"

The servant rolled her eyes and pushed past the party without another word. Her footsteps echoed down the hall.

Jing rubbed his chin. "So Cylinder isn't here."

"Good." Flame rubbed his hands together. "Forget the girl and let's get to work." His eyes glimmered with inner fires.

Drina held up an index finger. "Cylinder first."

Flame sagged. "But, Drina..."

Theo tugged Jing to the side. "We're not really going to burn Steam Central, are we?"

The large man sighed. "Someone probably will. I think the average person would be better off if we could aim Flame at Redjakel's board."

Flame nodded encouragingly. Jing said, "He's actually useful if you send him off in the right direction."

Theo scowled.

Jing raised his eyebrows. "Let me riddle you this. Why did you explode that boiler tower in Valhasse if you're so opposed to violence?"

"Because...because I wanted to help."

"No." The mechanic shook his head. "You wanted revenge. You wanted to hurt the people who hurt you. But you know that's not the general worker. You could've been that poor bastard on the assembly line if things had been different."

"No, but—"

"Or those guards in the hall not ten minutes ago."

"It was us or them," Theo protested. "I understand that."

Jing's voice darkened, "They work for the enemy, but does that make them the enemy?"

"I think so. But I am—"

"From what I see, the only difference here is a scared kid who doesn't mind playing in the ponds, but the ocean is just too big for him."

In that moment, Theo's face matched Flame's in burning intensity. That vicious voice shouted at him to go ahead and burn down Steam Central. They deserve it. You might even be doing those poor factory workers a damn favor again.

He swallowed the metallic tingle on his tongue and straightened his shoulders. "I am not scared, Ghost."

"I hope not."

Flame whistled. "Adri's office is this way. It's a dollhouse, but life-sized." He trotted down the maze of identical hallways, leading the others. They passed no other guards, not this far inside where the gentlemen of the company preferred quiet. At a huge, polished door with carved angels on it, he stopped and waved his hand. "Ghost, if you would be so kind."

Jing knelt down and swung open the hatch on his mechanized limb. From inside the door panel, he eased out a set of slender lock picks.

"Always prepared, huh?" Theo rolled his eyes.

Jing didn't glance away from the doorknob. "You'd be surprised at how many locks suspicious people leave between them and us." He chuckled and slipped the hook and the rake into the keyhole. "But this deep into Steam Central, this isn't much of one."

After a moment, the handle turned. Drina pushed open the door so wide that it bounced off the wall. Nothing stirred inside. "Now look for anything. Like a telegram or—"

"Don't bother, Ms. Death Spinner. Adri's smarter than that."

Smith lounged at the steam princess's desk in the sunlight. He held his glass cane in both hands and frowned. "You could have used the front door if you'd dressed well enough." He pointed the cane at Flame and his bandoliers. "But not when they've a bounty on your head, I suppose."

Flame shrugged. He leaned toward Drina. "This is Smith, right?"

She nodded, eyeing the Reaper's jugular.

Smith sighed loudly. "You and Adri have cost me much time. I should get word to the Gentlemen about this vexing process, but I do hate to make incomplete reports. So, Mr. Meilleur or Mr. Flame, as you have no attachment to this vessel abomination, may I pay you in gold? None of this current debacle need be mentioned."

Flame shrugged.

Theo stiffened. "I am a man of honor, sir."

"Please." Smith kicked the chair back and rose. "You're a scoundrel and I admire you for that honesty. All honorable men are, they just lie to themselves about it." He slammed the glass cane against the floor. "This is a damn fine offer. Do we have an accord?"

Theo swallowed and stepped away from Drina. He turned his back to Smith to face the Hex instead. "Yeah. Yeah, I think we can work something out."

Chapter Seventeen

"Theo!" Drina snarled.

Smith swung his cane between the bricoleur and the assassin. "Mr. Meilleur has made a decision. Please respect it, Ms. Death."

Theo gulped and stepped back another foot. He hated himself, but that vicious voice was in control. He felt like a prisoner inside his own body, as if that dark corner of his mind had finally reached out and seized him.

He couldn't move. It was like the first time he'd met Flame.

"I will kill you, boy!" Drina raised a throwing knife and let fly. Smith's cane batted it away, but not before Theo flinched.

She grinned. "I'll even let you see it coming, and you'll be helpless."

Beside her, Jing was shaking his head. "Why?"

Theo swallowed again. "Because you're working with him!" He stabbed a finger at Flame, who gasped like an accused innocent. "Because you made me work with that murderer. I'm just doing what I'm doing to survive. You'd do the same. You've done the same. But no, your boss decided to kidnap an infant, and suddenly you're not the Hex anymore? You—"

Smith swung the tip of the cane up into Theo's face. "I think that's enough, Mr. Meilleur." In an instant, his own sancta flashed in his palm, and then a cloud of steam as thick as the morning fog materialized throughout the office.

Drina jumped forward, knives leading. She ran forward until her knee crashed into Adri's desk. She hopped back, cursing. The steam lifted and they were gone. Only the breeze through the open window moved across the room.

"What now?" She tossed a look back at Jing.

He clenched his jaw. "Stick to our plan. Find anything that could lead us to Adri and Solindra."

Flame stomped his boots. "What about me? What about what *I* want to do, huh?"

They ignored him. Jing tapped his knuckles on the desk. "Adri wouldn't stay away from safety for long."

"That's right." Drina nodded to herself. "We need a trap. Need a web."

"Right. I just hope Adri's habit of hedging her bets means keeping Cylinder out of trouble, too."

***

Solindra stumbled over her own boots because she was too busy staring. The chilling spray from the waterfall brushed up behind her. She'd forgotten all about the horse-drawn carriage trek up the mountain in an ancient stagecoach. The ride had been followed by a blindfolded walk. Once they had gotten close enough, the Reapers had removed their blindfolds and walked them on the narrow stone passage around the curtain of water. She looked down past the Tears to the city so far below.

The slick route had led along a rock wall with brass handrails on both sides. The path and brass had both been worn smooth through use.

She gazed into the light of the gas lamps at the temple's façade. It was an archway higher than the cave entrance itself, made in the likeness of ancient heroes, gods and demons. It was brass, aluminum, gold and platinum. The metals gleamed in the lamplight. Decorative gears whirred along. Steam hissed out from the mouths of gods.

"Leave your items here." The dark Reaper whom they had met in the alley pointed to a natural alcove in the cave.

The two haversacks slid from Solindra's shoulders with ease, but her hand hesitated to push off the strap holding the rifle's case. She held her breath.

The nearest Reaper took a step toward her.

She forced her hand to glide over the leather. She was an adult now, a young lady. She could do this. Gently, she eased the rifle's case onto the floor.

The Reaper nodded. Adri stepped up beside him, and Solindra mutely fell into place behind the steam princess. She shivered as they walked under the arch. It felt like a living thing to her and she couldn't fathom why. It was just clockwork and steam.

Gas and electric lamps lit the rounded hall that led into the heart of the mountain. After a few minutes, Solindra squinted. Blue and white flashes of light were dancing on and off, creating bizarre

137

shadows. She stopped and grabbed the wall after a faint pop of thunder.

A large metal grate blocked the cave ahead.

Their Reaper guide stopped. "The Gentlemen are waiting. Entry is always a little dangerous, but you should be fine. Just don't hesitate." He propped open the grate with a gloved hand.

Solindra jogged down after Adri, and the Reaper slammed the door behind them. The bolt struck home, but there was no lock. The man then turned his back to them and stood guard.

Adri and Solindra pushed into the large cavern, still trapped underneath the metal. Electricity arced through the air of the cavern all around them. A massive metal cage rose up through the natural dome of the inside of the mountain. Lightning reflected against the metal and slashed in the space between the rock and the cage. Somewhere, Solindra could swear she heard a huge engine running over the popping thunder.

"Electrical cage," Adri whispered. "Safe inside, at least from a bolt of lightning. I just don't understand why they did it. It's not a practical defense. Not unless they can harness the aether in lightning," she added sarcastically.

As their eyes adjusted, they saw a huge circular table, hollow in the center, with seated figures every few feet. Gas lamps glowed inside the empty ring, but it wasn't completely empty. Steamflowers, currently closed, created an ivy-like garden tangle in the center.

The high-backed chairs made it impossible to actually see any faces in the pooled shadows. Several butlers fluttered between the seated figures. Heads turned expectantly to the women.

Adri smiled warmly. "Thank you for receiving me, gentle sirs." She started to circle behind the chairs. Solindra stepped silently after her.

The steam princess let her fingers drift across the top of one of the leather chairs as she passed. "I know that you, sirs, are Codic's true government, whatever other blather LaBier claims. I don't see him at this table, do I? No, I came to the soul of power."

A figure yawned in one of the high-backed chairs. Solindra squinted, but couldn't make anything out against the unsteady shadows. He said, "Yes, yes, you've been useful in allowing us maps and access to Redjakel, and now you've come for your price."

"You know that I read your stolen scrolls. Many people have." She scored her fingernails across the leather top of one of the chairs this time.

Hands and jaws clenched around the room. The stiffening silence seemed to darken the electrical arcing lights.

"And now I'd like to join you at your table." She smoothed out her skirt and took her place in an empty chair. "I have always been truthful with you gentlemen, which is a valuable trade during wartime, is it not? Yes, your scriptures were stolen, read, experimented with and forced into production. This you know."

"It does not dwell to speak of such things," said another voice, deep and red.

"You no longer have your secrets. The Priory's grandeur can only be regained if you defeat Steampower."

More silence.

Solindra swallowed and wiped her forehead. So she was Steampower's traitor.

The vessel glared at the back of the steam princess's chair, and thought, you have two sanctas right in your pocket and we'll both be killed if they find you have them. I thought you weighed the risks first.

And if she *had* considered the dangers of bringing those here, what had made her decide that having the sanctas was the less dangerous choice?

Solindra tried to shrink herself on the spot, tried to blend into the darkness and almost backed into the cage.

"We know this," a new, crisp voice clipped. "Holy writ debased on *infants*."

"I believe there is only one vessel left?" Adri raised her voice like a question. In that instant, Solindra felt her cheeks drop several degrees in temperature. Her breath froze in her throat.

"If *your* information was correct, then yes," a voice snarled.

"That thing must be destroyed." Another thumped his fist on the table.

"Hear, hear," echoed around the table.

Solindra gulped and stared down at her trembling hands. She was nearly crouched behind the chair.

"But we know better than to trust Saturni women!" an elderly voice croaked.

"Your mother is still a prisoner here!" a much younger, diamond-edged voice snapped.

"I know," Adri said into the rapidly cooling silence. "Her bones have probably fused with the walls of her cell by now. Who do you think sent word of her death to Boras? I had to do something to break the stalemate."

She smiled into the dead silence, broken only by the pops of thunder. "I have helped you far more than you know. You, the Priory, now have an opening to strike back at Steampower and regain your honor. I can help you with this."

"What do you require?" an old voice asked softly.

"I want Steampower itself. But don't worry, I'll still fly the flag of Eliponesia."

"Is that all?"

Adri paused, almost a hesitation. "I wish to join the Priory." She stood up and leaned forward on the table. "I can give you exactly what you want, your honor: your scripture back and an end to this war."

Silence reigned.

The diamond-edged voice finally spoke. "No. Plans are already underway in Redjakel based around information you have already provided to us. We cannot allow you to join this sacred fraternity, princess, but thank you for your help this far."

"I have the vessel," Adri crooned.

A gasp escaped from Solindra's lips. She could only hope that no one heard as she stared at the floor. Adri had lied to her!

A butler gave her a long glance as he passed by with a tray full of wine glasses. Of course Adri would betray her if she had already sold out her father. She felt like an idiot for not realizing it before.

"So will we," that smooth, gem-infused voice stated. "We've intercepted a number of its supporters' telegrams in a very crude code in Redjakel. We know where it is and we don't need your help. One of our most distinguished Reapers is on the task."

Solindra straightened up. Jing and Drina were in Redjakel!

The voice continued, "But we thank you for your service, Ms. Adri Saturni. Do please excuse us for the remainder of this meeting. We're sure you understand."

Adri snapped up out of the chair. She lifted her upper lip like a wolf baring its fangs. "You should ignore your other enemies from now on."

With that, she marched through the glow of the lightning's dance to the tunnel. Solindra trotted along behind her, trying to mask her heaving chest.

Adri slammed open the metal grate and stormed past the guarding Reaper, who calmly closed the door and resumed his post. Solindra heard him slide the bolt home behind them.

"Laughing at me! Laughing at me!" Adri's knuckles were white in her curled fists.

"They're letting us leave." Solindra twisted her neck around to see if anyone was following.

"Decorum!" Adri snarled. "Leave the old bastards to sniff their flowers. They think they're being polite when they have *no idea* how *stupid* they are! Oh, I will make them regret this." The steam princess slowed her stride and a wicked grin slid up her face. "Well, you were lucky."

Solindra looked at Adri's face and felt like vomiting.

"You and me, little bird. I will have new, better plans."

"But…" Solindra licked her lips. She couldn't force out the words screaming in her mind. Betrayal! Ego!

She stopped and tried to unswallow her tongue. "You would've sold me to them like a slave!"

Adri raised an eyebrow. "I'd be more careful with my words in this place if I were you."

Solindra followed the steam princess in silence the rest of the way out of the tunnel. They passed through the mechanical arch. Four Priory Reapers stood between them and the path alongside the waterfall. Its roar was almost deafening.

"Adri, I don't think they are letting us go."

"Ah, true gentlemen. Having their butlers do their work for them." Her fingers dipped into her pocket and she slipped Solindra the red cipher medallion behind their backs.

The tallest Reaper drew a dagger from his belt. "This will be over soon."

"I have different plans," Adri snarled. "And I am so glad you didn't ruin my surprise." She whipped out her sancta into both hands and leveled it at his chest.

Two handless limbs of water reached out from the waterfall and yanked him straight back. He disappeared into the curtain of water. The dagger clattered to the stone floor. The others stared dumbly at the sancta for a moment in absolute surprise.

"Solindra, move!"

A blast of steam, hotter than any furnace Solindra had ever been around, screamed right between herself and Adri. She rolled toward their haversacks. She felt the heat radiating along her skin and the air felt too hot to breathe.

She crouched behind the bags and saw that one of the Reapers was turning toward her. The other two were pressing Adri closer to the cave's far wall. She was holding up her purple cipher medallion as a shield. The two Reapers with their own devices were stealing water from the falls and blasting her with scalding steam while they marched forward.

Solindra jerked her attention back to the nearest Reaper. He brought his sancta on level. It was like looking down the barrel of a gun. His expression was empty, bland, even.

She did the only thing she could think of. She clenched her sancta and swung her arm around wide, stealing a swath of the boiling steam from the other Reaper's attack and wrapping it around her attacker's neck.

She jerked the cipher medallion down and it read her intention. The steam dropped down into his mouth and then his lungs.

His face twisted into a silent scream, but his throat no longer worked. Red and black burns circled his entire neck. His eyes bulged and his body convulsed as it burned.

Solindra looked at the device trembling in her hands. She felt like she should have burned her hand by now.

The body finally collapsed at her feet, horrified and blistered.

She yanked up the rifle, clutching it to her chest, unable to believe how lucky her panicked attack had been.

Only a few feet away, the two Reapers with their backs still to Solindra held their sanctas out at Adri. Steam slid along their arms in blasting, scalding streams.

Solindra dropped the rifle case's strap over her head and crouched. She glanced between the exit path and Adri. She glanced at both again, unable to move.

Adri feinted toward the archway and then dived right between the two Reapers, somersaulting under their swings. She rolled right back to her feet and lunged for the path around the side of the water. She swung around, one hand on the railing to the exit path and beckoned rapidly at the vessel. The Reapers stood in front of the shadow of the mechanical arch with Solindra caught between them and Adri.

Adri threw out a hand. "This way! I will show you the power that these old fools have squandered by not combining it with our technology."

The vessel started toward Adri. The Reapers were closing in from behind. But then she stopped, staring. She inched backward and shook her head. She glanced behind at the Reapers, raising their own cipher medallions and shook her head again.

Solindra adjusted her father's rifle on her back and then pressed her sancta into her chest. She turned and leapt into the waterfall.

Chapter Eighteen

"I am aware that you don't know where the vessel is." Smith sat with his back to the wall inside the private lounge he had purchased for the evening. "Otherwise you wouldn't have gone to Adri's office." He returned to writing out his letter to his employers in a smooth, flowing cursive.

"You were looking for clues to Solindra's whereabouts too." Theo glared hard at the bottle of spiced cider and the self-boiling pot of coffee beside it. The tiny boilerbox below the pouring jar hummed along nicely.

"Yes, and it appears that Adri is well armed in the civilized art of secret-keeping. I didn't expect to find much, but even a careful man, or lady, gets careless at some point. The trick is to intercept that point." He turned the letter over and kept writing. "For example, you did catch me off guard in the town with that nasty business with the children."

Theo's fingers seized tight against the handle of his coffee cup.

"Never fear, Mr. Meilleur. As a professional, I admire such temerity at times. I am not a vindictive man."

"Lucky for me."

"After this war, what are your career aspirations?" Smith didn't stop writing to look up.

Theo coughed. "What?"

"A significant percentage of my comrades have fallen to Boras Saturni's machinations. You were raised a bricoleur, so you're familiar with the fundamentals of the aether ghosts."

Theo crossed his arms. "My only goal is to kill Flame. I am a vindictive man."

"Your goal is personal. It can wait. We have professional business first."

"Yeah. That's what the Hex said too."

A knock echoed from the center of the door. Smith raised his eyes at Theo in no uncertain manner. The young man oozed out from his seat and trudged over to the door. He cracked it open. "What?"

A boy's young hand held up a sealed envelope. "Special telegram for Mr. Martin Coxwell. Station boys said he'd left a message that he'd be here."

"Do accept the missive," Smith said.

Theo snatched the note and slammed the door. The boy kicked it from the other side. "May your next boilerbox explode in your face!"

Smith held out his hand. "I do loathe resorting to pseudonyms, but the Hex makes it a necessity." He slit open the envelope and removed the telegram.

"Well, where do we go next?" Theo suddenly flinched deep inside his heart. Solindra had tried to save him; she had smiled at him. Why was he even doing this?

And then the image of Flame burned through Solindra's sly grin. Because Flame was more important, that's why.

"Our hunt has been postponed and we're to destroy Redjakel. Tell me, have you ever heard of an aether bomb?"

***

Solindra retched again and clawed her way farther up between the boulders. She gasped for air but couldn't stop the convulsing of her stomach. The vessel lay clenched and helpless, fighting for breath, and unable to do anything but collapse against the black rocks.

The dark water nipped at the heels of her boots. The wet weight of her clothing acted like an anchor. Silvermark's rifle on her back pinned her down.

"Hello?" a voice quavered.

Solindra's head snapped up, or at least attempted to. Above her, someone stood on the rocks. She squinted, but couldn't see through the water and exhaustion clouding her eyes. "Dad?"

She hacked again and focused all of her remaining strength on the figure. A boy, no older than seven, looked at her with pure terror etched across his face. He dropped the pail he'd been clutching and skedaddled.

The bucket bounced down, almost hitting her head, but it ricocheted off a boulder instead and rolled to the side of the young woman.

Solindra surrendered. She could do nothing but focus on breathing. Her muscles weren't even shivering anymore, despite how freezing the water had been. She just didn't have the strength.

So how in the hell had she had the strength to jump off a waterfall? She remembered swimming with the current in the river – and that was the only thing that had saved her from drowning. But not much of the fall itself.

There had been a ball of comfortable steam, floating down the waterfall slower than the water around it, cushioning her and protecting her from the rocks. The cipher medallion had glowed like the sun.

The vessel retched again, unable to fight the spasms. She was cold, wet, lost and alone.

Darkness closed in around her.

***

"My shrill steam whistles!"

Solindra jerked her eyes open, but still wasn't entirely certain if she was dreaming or not. It was still dark.

"Oh, you poor girl. What happened?"

She squinted through the moonlight. There was the boy who had dropped the bucket, Now he was trembling behind an elderly woman. The plump, grandmotherly soul was trying to reach down between the boulders toward Solindra.

"Wha...?" managed to fall out of the vessel's mouth. She swallowed and tried again. "W..." With a mental sigh, she gave up.

The woman managed to grip one of Solindra's hands with farm-grown strength. "As cold as a ghost you are, child. Davey, get down here and help an old lady out."

Half-conscious, Solindra had no power to stop them pulling her away from the river. She lifted her foot and tried to put weight on it only to collapse down into a pile. Once again, darkness closed in on her.

***

When she opened her eyes this time, it was almost black. No stars, no wind, no light glowed overhead. After a moment, she started to see. Enough moonlight spilled in through the rounded mouth of the cave to squelch any panic, if she'd had the strength to panic.

Solindra felt around her front pocket. The sancta was safe. When and how she'd put it back in her pocket was a mystery to her. She rubbed her face against a scratchy cloth, presumably a blanket.

But she was breathing, she noticed, and no longer straining to do it. She heard others breathing all around her, perhaps dozens of people. She squinted in the dim blue moonlight. Many children, some as small as toddlers and others closer to her age, lay curled together on the floor.

Solindra twisted around in her seat. Torchlight beckoned from deeper in the cave. She grunted and pushed herself up onto her knees and then her feet. She reached out a hand to steady herself on the stone.

Taking shuffling steps, she slid toward the light.

The old woman sat in a rocking chair, knitting. Solindra blinked – she had half expected the woman to have been a dream all along. She knew she'd seen her father at the riverside, too, and that was wrong.

Also wrong was the sight of a woman making scarves in the middle of a cave by torchlight.

Solindra leaned against the wall and fought off a wave of dizziness. Crates and burlaps bags took up most of the available space around.

The woman stopped rocking. "Still got some crackers here if you'd like some. Stale, but what isn't these days?"

The teenager blinked again, just to make sure that she wasn't dreaming. The old woman's hair looked slightly blue in the light and very thin, but her hazel eyes sparkled.

"I'm Elclei, dear." She started rocking again, and the chair's creaking bounced off the walls.

"Elk-lay?"

"From the lands beyond the steam, young miss."

The vessel patted her chest with a shaking hand. "Solindra."

"You'd better have a seat."

She obeyed, grateful for the relief. "You don't look like a barbarian."

"And you don't look like a piece of driftwood, Miss Solindra."

The young woman blushed. "Where am I? Surely I'm not out of the Steamscape."

Elclei shook her head. "No, you're near Ronna, west of Codic."

Solindra frowned. She couldn't place herself on the map.

"No sign of your boat either."

"It…" She swallowed. "It, um, dissolved."

"Mmm." Elclei didn't react. Instead, her fingers spun about her knitting needles. The torch flickered again.

"Why are these children here, Miss Elclei?"

"Safer than town, miss. Killing Trains are driving closer every day. Now I know they're supposed to be on our side and taking away the Steampower loyalists. I honestly think it's a way to get rid of those that aren't useful to them. If they catch any young men sans uniform or any citizen without a government-stamped card these days, or they just don't like you, well, you're off to the desert. Cards cost near fifty silver dollars now."

"But it wasn't this way in Codic! I was there…" The squeal of the Killing Train's whistle echoed in her head.

A draft whistled by the torch again, and this time, some of the pitch-wrapped cloth fell off. Little fireballs collapsed down onto the stone floor next to the crates of supplies.

"Blast." Elclei squinted and held up the scarf to her eyes. "Can't see in this."

Solindra eyed the little flames burning themselves out. She pointed at a glass lamp with an electrical filament on it. "Why not use that?"

"No electricity out here, miss. Although we might have some ammunition for that gun of yours."

Solindra forced a grin, trying to shove away the memories of the Killing Train. "I think I can help." She crawled forward and spent the next few minutes dipping into crates and perusing through the burlap sacks.

When she was done, she had laid out two delightfully ornate brass candlesticks, a glass jar, some sticky pitch from the torch supplies, a large iron nail wiggled loose from a crate and the electrical lamp. Using the nail, she pried open the bottom of the lamp to reveal a coil of copper wiring.

She chuckled. "Pay dirt." Then she wrinkled her nose and kept looking around. "Are there any cooking supplies like some lemons or grapefruit? I need the juice."

Elclei smiled sadly. "No, can't say that there are."

"Vinegar?"

The old woman shook her head. She tossed her gaze into the deepest part of the cave where most of the glass had been piled. "There's some ancient wine that was smuggled out. It's probably vinegar by now. They said it'd be worth a fortune, being from the time of Eliponesia's barbarian days, but they couldn't find a buyer. Still, I say, vinegar's vinegar."

"Perfect!" Solindra scrambled for the glassware. "Hmm."

"Blue bottle on the left. Dusty as a demon."

The vessel pulled up the bottle. "This one?"

Elclei nodded. "But I don't see what you could possibly use it for."

Solindra kneeled back down in front of the supplies and grinned. "I had a guardian who taught me a lot about machinery."

Ghost. The thought arrived like a train crashing into the terminus. Adri had said they were the Hex. Jing was Ghost!

She tried to close out the idea and set to wrapping the copper wiring from the lamp around the brass candlesticks. Next she coated the insides of the candlesticks and the wiring with the pitch and placed them inside the jar. They poked above awkwardly. "Don't touch those."

She double checked the wiring's connection to the filament on the lamp. Then she filled the jar with the centuries old wine. She held the bottle as far away as she could. "That stings my eyes."

Elclei chuckled. "Vinegar's vinegar." She set her knitting down into her lap to watch.

Solindra dropped the nail into the ring created by the copper wires and pitch. The filament began to glow with warm, soft yellow light. It wasn't much at all, fading away into darkness only a few feet beyond the lamp.

Solindra wrinkled her nose. "I tried. Sorry it's not more."

"My word!" The old lady grinned and then sighed. "Only wealthy people have electrical lamps. That's what makes them better than us."

"It's hardly even glowing. If I could get some sodium-mercury batteries up here, then maybe…"

Elclei turned her stitching into the meager light. "It's enough, dear. Did you hear that Steampower outlawed wool? You have to buy it from them now. I think these socks are now illegal."

The old woman set back to work. "Now, if you're none too tired, you can start boiling water for laundry."

"In here?" Solindra shook her head. "The torch is already too much smoke, let alone to build a fire."

"No worse than in the cities. And no fires outside at night neither."

The girl smiled. "Fair enough, I suppose."

Elclei nodded deeper into the cave. "There's firewood and a pot. Davey brought back the rest of the water."

Solindra pried the torch down from its crude sconce and tiptoed into a new, bulb-shaped opening. She gathered up the firewood and lit it. When the fire was hot enough and embers glowed down deep among the flames, she set the pot atop it. She continued to build up the fire around its base.

She sat back against the wall and sighed. Her head drooped forward and she realized exactly how exhausted she was. In fact, she hoped Elclei would forgive her if she fell asleep. She wondered how hard the lands outside of Steamscape were since the old woman hadn't seen it fit to give her a reprieve after her ordeal. She was awake, so she could work.

She jerked her eyes back open. The steam was flying off the pot now, crowding out the smoke around it.

Steamflowers unfolded their blooms along the walls of the cave. Solindra smiled and inhaled the fragrance, and curled her fingers around the petals.

She raised her hands, leaving the sancta in her pocket, and tried to form the shape of the flower within in the steam itself without the cipher medallion.

The steam continued to rise, but no flower formed.

Solindra's head rolled forward again. She guessed she needed that damned device after all, just like every other crypter. With the heady scent of the flowers still in her nose, she rested her back against the wall again.

She jerked her head upright at the sound of footsteps. "Elclei! I didn't hear you..." She gasped and froze at the figure whose skirts swirled in the steam.

The vessel licked her lips and squinted. "Merlina? How did you find me?"

Merlina pressed a quieting finger to her lips and beckoned.

工

Chapter Nineteen

Solindra rubbed the sleep from her eyes. "Merlina? What are you doing here?" She tried to fight against a yawn.

"Talking to you," the fortune teller said with a barb in her voice. But she smiled and winked.

"Yes, but..." She squinted. Merlina wasn't in focus, not with all the steam and smoke waving around her body.

"But nothing. Come along, girl, it's time."

"For what?" Solindra pushed herself up off the floor. She limped after the bricoleur crypter, her muscles still weighed down with exhaustion.

Merlina danced instead of walking, like those belly dancers outside of her little den of crime. She held up her arms and rattled her hips. She spun in a circle, never stopping the shaking of her waist as she moved through the steam. Ahead of Solindra, she vanished into the darkness of the cave.

The vessel stopped. She rubbed her eyes again. No one was there. No echoes, no voice. Just the gathering steam blowing past her skirt and into the darkness beyond.

"Hello?" she quavered. Her foot hovered in the air, stopped halfway through its next step.

Merlina's hand shot out of the blackness. Her bangles clanged together like tiny bells.

Solindra took the hand, held her breath, closed her eyes and jumped into the void.

It felt like passing through a strong downdraft.

The scent of honeysuckle tickled her nose. She opened her eyes to the light of a garden. Green vines wrapped around marble pillars holding up the roof. Those vines smothered a central, spiral staircase that disappeared into the ceiling and the floor, leaving no way up or down. She stared at the aether's reflections on the water and the shadowy bands high in the bright sky. The moons looked so much closer from up here.

Merlina flounced down on a long sofa.

Solindra rubbed her temples. "This is just too weird." She inched toward the edge and stared down. A massive light, made by mirrors and electrical lights, swiveled overhead. Down below, a garrison of soldiers swarmed in front of the famed barracks. Ahead of them was nothing but the sparkling ocean, illuminated by the beam and the bands.

"The Lighthouse of Vilosa!" Solindra gasped. She stumbled away from the lip. "But…But this was destroyed in earthquakes centuries ago!"

Merlina dipped some grapes into her mouth. "That's what you were taught, yes."

"What does that even mean?"

"It exists. Beyond the steam. In the imagination of the ghosts, as you say."

Solindra frowned. "The ghosts don't have imagination. They're just dissolved aether."

"Perhaps just a memory of it then. A pattern etched into time itself. Why don't you ask them that?" She laughed.

"Ask them?" Solindra repeated doubtfully.

"Isn't that why the Priory is after you, my dear?" Merlina reached overhead and plucked some fresh grapes from a vine.

"No. It's not because of the ghosts." She bunched her fists. "I know I can't trust anything Adri said."

Merlina smirked and swallowed a grape. "I don't think she lied to you, as such. I think she just omitted what she didn't want you to hear."

"She wants me dead now, too. She, Steampower and the Priory. By the way, she was nothing like what I had imagined her to be." Solindra wheeled for balance, eyeing the nearby edge with wary eyes. She sat down right where she was, on the floor. "They all want me dead. I don't know where my family is. I don't know what to do next."

Merlina smiled sadly. "*Veritas temporalis est.*"

Solindra scowled. "What does it mean?"

"What it says. Truth is temporary."

Steam swirled up from nowhere, weaving in and out of the flowers and the grasses. Thickly, like fog, but with a welcoming warmth. It smoothed her skin and whispered in her ears.

Solindra buried her face in her hands. "I don't know what to do. I don't even know what I want anymore. I got to see Codic and Redjakel. I dined with Adri, I can make the ghosts obey me, but none of it was what I wanted."

"It's not about what you want, dear. It's about what you need to do."

"Oh? And what's that?"

A male voice drifted through the steam, "I need you to do what I never did."

Solindra froze. She mechanically swiveled her head toward the sound. Her hands froze halfway from her face at the silhouette. She gulped. "Dad?"

Winds pushed the steam aside to show Mark Canon. He smiled beneath his beard. He held his arms open.

"Dad!" The vessel pushed herself to her feet and dashed over to him. He wrapped his arms around her.

"You've grown so much!" His grin started to recede. "I will walk you home. There's too much to say and not much time."

***

With the lights of the garden vanishing behind them, Canon and Solindra walked into the dark of the cave. The fire surrounding the laundry bucket had faded to glowing embers, but steam still wisped above the pot.

Solindra sniffed and swung back into the same spot where she'd fallen asleep. "Dad, I'm not sure about any of this. The only thing I'm sure of is that you can't leave me again!"

"I'm always right here, little Cylinder." He stepped back, becoming nothing more than a shadow in the embers' light. "Right beyond the steam."

"Dad. Dad!"

Canon had vanished.

"Solindra. Solindra."

The vessel jerked her eyes open. Elclei was shaking her shoulder. When she noticed Solindra's face, she smirked and stepped back. "Tsk tsk." But her smile warmed. "Fire had burnt down." She waved her hand at the cheery flames. "I had to rebuild it."

"Dad!" Solindra rolled to her feet, steadying herself against the rock wall.

Elclei raised her white eyebrows. "There's no one else here, child."

The young woman lunged forward, but the distant wall of the cave was smooth and solid, and lined with the potent steamflowers. But Merlina and her father had appeared out of that passage that was right there.

Solindra ran her hands over the stone. "No, this is wrong. He was here. He was right through here..." She leaned her back against the wall and sank back down to the floor. Tears bubbled up from somewhere deep inside.

Elclei gathered up her skirt and circled the fire. "I think it was just a nightmare, dearie, especially after what you've been through."

She shook her head. "No. This place is the nightmare. Everything's wrong on this side of the steam."

The old woman shrugged sympathetically. "Just as you say, girl. Now I think you should get more rest, because it looks like your trip down the river's still got its grip on you. After all, you passed out here well enough in the least comfortable place I can imagine."

"But my dad was here..."

The old woman held out her hand for the girl to stand. "Maybe, maybe." She wheezed a little bit under Solindra's weight. "In the lands beyond Steamscape, when I was but your age, steam was nothing special. We believed the aether bands were the chariot trails of the sun god. When I was forced to work for Steampower as a child – before I was brought here – we figured the steam was enslaved like a person to turn its metal teeth. How silly I feel about it now."

Solindra felt out the passage with her free hand. It was still too dark to see. "I guess civilization has worn off onto you then."

"Yes, but what I'm trying to impart is that my whole world changed. What I thought was real was only real for the time I thought it was. Everything changed when I was brought here, and now that I'm old, I'm afraid soon that everything will change for me again."

Solindra shook her head. "I don't understand."

"Codic fashion. I bet you've always believed in those clothes."

The vessel was glad for the darkness to hide her blush. "Yes, but it's silly now after what I've been through."

"Exactly." Elclei chuckled. "But have you noticed that the wealthy have their clothes on their portraits painted over every ten years or so?"

Solindra laughed and wiped away a tear. "I'd heard that, but that's just to keep their clothes with the current trends. I read in the fashion journals that some of them would perish of embarrassment if people saw them in outdated styles."

"Don't you think life is a little like clothing then, Miss Solindra?"

The girl shrugged. "I don't know."

"Everything I've ever known has always changed. And it will again." Elclei paused as they came into the part of the cave where the children had been curled up in their bedrolls. Some of the older ones were already up and watching the entrance. A blond-haired boy turned and waved at them.

He cupped his mouth. "Me and Davey and the others are just about ready. Is there anything else, Miss Elclei?"

The old woman wrinkled her nose. "Flour, my lad." She nudged Solindra, who was wiping her tears on her sleeve. "Would you care to join them? May do you more good than sitting around here and think yourself stupid all day."

Solindra sniffed and nodded. "Yeah, just let me grab a couple of things." She pushed herself back toward the room with the supplies. In the sparse glow of the lamplight, she dug her hands into a bag of ammunition and checked the caliber on the bullets' stamps.

Gold! No, this was better than gold; these were bullets.

The vessel spent the next few moments checking over the rifle. Adri had prepared it for use before she'd given it to her. At last, she loaded it and then strapped it on her back without the carrying case. She held up her chin, dried her last few tears and marched out of the cave.

***

Davey led the party. The other boy was named Teddy, and the two girls about twelve or thirteen, were Abigail and Rosalyn. They looked like twins underneath their white bonnets and matching dresses. Solindra plodded along in their footsteps, trusting them to know the way to Ronna. She wasn't even sure where it had been on the map – somewhere downstream from Codic.

Teddy splashed down in the chuckling brook they were following upstream. The water flew up and splattered across the rest of them. Solindra gripped the sancta in her front pocket. After a moment, she pulled it out and tied it to her belt.

"Who's got the list?" she called.

Davey waved. "Just the usual food run, and whatever valuables people want to stash with us."

Solindra's eyebrows shot up. "What, like their diamonds?"

Teddy laughed. "Nope, not when they can swallow those. More like the oil and whiskey, whatever barrels we can roll back."

The vessel eyed the uneven ground. "I hope not."

"I get to be Flame!" Davey yelled from upfront. He threw a handful of dirt at Abigail. Solindra suddenly gripped the rifle's strap at the name.

"No." Teddy crossed his arms. "You were Flame last time. That's not fair."

Abigail grinned and held up some twine. "I'm the Death Spinner and I got you both!" She tagged Davey on the shoulder.

Teddy thumped his chest. "I'm Flame. You can be the Steam Slayer this time, Davey." He pointed at Rosalyn. "She's Ghost, and Solindra gets to be Silvermark 'cause she's got the rifle."

The vessel gripped the rifle's strap tighter across her chest and thought, if you only knew.

"Okay." Rosalyn grinned. "What's the mission this time?"

"To steal and sneak supplies through the battlefield!" Teddy roared. "Only this time, the enemy is using clockwork mines. Steam Slayer, Ghost, you're up."

"Hold on!" Solindra barked. Then she grinned. "I'm Silvermark, so I get to give the orders." The children fell into a line before her. She walked up and down it once, surveying her troops. "Here is our mission: to steal food to get back to our cave base. You should deny this information if captured. The adversary is using clockwork mines, so Steam Slayer, Ghost, it's up to you to find us a safe path to the enemy fortress."

Davey and Rosalyn saluted. They whirled around, fell into a crouch and started to waddle with their eyes on the ground, tapping the ground ahead of them with their knives.

"Watch for animal carcasses; maybe they stepped on some," Davey whispered loudly.

"Or local trails. The locals know not to leave the trail," Rosalyn replied.

"But we'll be sighted on the trail!" Teddy hissed. "I say we burn the whole forest! Show them to respect us!"

"Flame!" Solindra snapped. "Not yet. Not until we have to cover our tracks." She shivered at just how accurate that had been.

Teddy grinned and fell into step behind "Ghost" and "Steam Slayer."

They crouched down and spent the morning squelching through the mud as silently as possible to avoid the make-believe clockwork mines. When the streets of Ronna came into view through the trees, Solindra raised her hand and gestured for everyone to lie flat on the ground.

Rosalyn pointed. "But there's the—"

The vessel pressed her fingers to her lips. She whispered, "Do you think the Hex would walk into a town without studying it first?"

Rosalyn shook her head. "Probably not."

Davey hurled a rock. "Boom! Pow! I got a mine! Everybody duck from the flying dirt!"

"Davey, no!" Solindra snapped. "The *enemy* just saw the mine explosion. They'll come looking. Now, everybody look at the town and tell me what you see. Does it look normal? Watch for at least two minutes before you answer."

She turned her gaze back to the town and bit her lower lip. Of course, her father, Drina and Jing had played these games with her as a child all the time. Now she was playing them with other children. But as her attention swept over the town, she realized what it was to an adult's eye.

Ronna looked complete, not burned out like Consequences. The steam and smoke from a train rose over the town, followed by its whistle several moments later. One boiler tower dominated the center of the town, with pipes leading out of it at almost every direction and height. Billows of smoke were already cranking out of the two factories.

"You kids lived here?" Solindra asked.

Teddy nodded. "Or on some of the farms. Most of us worked in the factories or the farms until our parents said we had to leave for the caves." He dropped his gaze. "I heard some of them got in trouble for it with the law, and well, you know they're hurtin' without the extra hands."

"They did what they thought was best," Solindra replied. "That's what all of us always do." She shaded her eyes and watched the distant figures. They looked to be only half an inch tall from her vantage, trudging out to the fields and their harvesters.

Her upper lip curled. Most of these poor bastards didn't have a damn thing to do with Saturni and the Priory's personal feud.

Large men have even larger shadows. Something else her father had once said. These poor bastards lived and died in those shadows.

Her vision blurred by an attack of tears. She knew she'd seen him last night! She *knew* it hadn't been just a dream.

Abigail nudged her shoulder. "You okay, Miss Solindra? You've got all pale."

Solindra forced a smile. "Yeah. Of course. Everything looks normal."

"Can we still be the Hex?" Davey raised his hand.

"Undercover," she replied. "The Hex used to often pretend to be normal people while sneaking around cities. We'll also walk in on the road."

Rosalyn adjusted her bonnet. "And pretend like we're going to work. We've done this before, Miss Solindra."

The vessel cocked a grin. "Right you are. Lead on then."

The road into the town boasted the grooves of many heavy carts. The dirt drifted up and clung to their boots.

"That's new." Teddy pointed at a sign.

Solindra frowned. It read, "Citizens must check weapons at constable's office. No exceptions! By Law." She adjusted the rifle's strap and shook her head. "Let's just see if they stop me."

The kids glanced up at her nervously.

"Don't worry, I'll stay out of the way while you hustle to get the supplies. You know your way around the town and I don't. Just be sneaky, like the Hex."

"We know," Abigail chirped. "We've done this four, no five, times already. Our parents leave everything ready to go."

Teddy scowled. "Except flour. That wasn't on Miss Elclei's last list. Oh, well, I know where to get that."

The steam whistle of the train rolling out drowned their conversation. Solindra closed her eyes and listened to its song. First the whistle, then the chugging of the engine, and finally the rolling of the wheels along the rails. It wasn't a Killing Train's call, just a normal freight.

They passed the first building and Solindra swung into the narrow space between the train's water tower and the postal office. She sat down on a barrel and hid Silvermark's rifle behind her. "You kids hurry now, so we can get back before dark."

They saluted. Davey's too-long sleeve flew up over his hand and he grinned. The younger boy turned around and trotted in Teddy's footsteps.

The vessel leaned her shoulder against the wall as the four disappeared into the mirthless crowd. She tapped her foot on the brick street and eyed what little of the train depot she could see. Dirt and grime coated its walls, and the tiles and bricks on the floor had been worn with overuse.

She listened and felt the vibrations running through the street below as another engine rolled into the station, just like back at home. She glanced over her shoulder to see another freight train. She heard the whistles of the engineers calling for the hose to be lowered to the steam engine from the water tower. Ahead of her, Codic soldiers marched through the streets between the workers, standing out in their gray uniforms. She kept an eye on the boiler tower with its massive steam-driven clock and waited.

"Silvermark!" Abigail smiled as she and Rosalyn jogged forward, carrying a burlap bag between them that was almost as tall as they were.

Solindra smiled and pressed a finger to her lips.

"Oh, right." The girls giggled. They turned around and scanned the avenue for the boys.

"There's Teddy!" Rosalyn pointed. "But he's running! Oh no, so is Davey."

Solindra's hand immediately swung back for the rifle. She pumped a bullet into the chamber without thinking about it.

"Stop, boy!" A stout man in an apron was chasing the boys. "You didn't show me your papers to buy that!"

Davey wailed. She couldn't hear it, but she could see his mouth open in terror. White flour had spilled across his face from the bag he'd been clutching so tightly to his chest.

Across the way, a Codic soldier raised his pistol at the child. He aimed.

Silvermark's rifle snapped into place on Solindra's shoulder. The soldier's back was to a brick building, outlining his uniform perfectly. She fired first.

The crack of the rifle was the only sound on the street.

His body rebounded off the wall and his shot went wild.

"Run, girls! Don't be seen with me! Tell Elclei I did what I could." She pumped the action again, reloading the chamber.

Solindra advanced away from the children. It amazed her how easy it had been. She'd shot dozens of birds with her father on the mountain, but with a different rifle. This one was so much smoother.

The man in the apron gaped, frozen in mid-step. Davey ran right past her and buried his head into Abigail's arms. Teddy had also stopped so quickly that he'd fallen over, still staring at her. So was everyone else. The entire street had frozen. Solindra was the only thing in motion. The train's final departure whistle growled across the unmoving avenue.

She marched over to the body of the soldier. His head had collapsed in on itself. The bullet had gone in his cheek and out his opposite ear to bury itself in the brick behind him.

With her boot, she traced out a hexagon in the dirt of the road. The dead man's blood smeared into half of the outline.

"Okay, Smith, you and everyone else can try to find me." She raised the silver rifle over her head, and sprinted for the train before the spell broke. She could only hope the children could melt away into the forest. And they could, she told herself, if she kept all eyes on her.

Chapter Twenty

The train rumbled across the landscape, its engineers unaware of their extra passenger poking her head up over the roof of the car. Solindra swung Silvermark's rifle onto her back again and turned to face the fading view of Ronna.

She'd just killed a soldier in public. The next engine to leave that train station would be after her—she'd seen all the interconnecting rails—and she was sure she could make out stacks of smoke and steam firing up from the station. She glanced off to the east and the shelter of the forest there. She could more than likely find her way back to the children's cave.

She bowed her head. The best she could do for them now was not to lead anyone back to them.

She shaded her eyes. Yes, she could see it now. They'd hauled out in the tencar, a tiny engine that could hold a maximum of ten people. But it was faster than this lug.

She frowned and turned her back on the pursuit. She ambulated along the metal roof of the freight car, where she could barely hear her footsteps above wind and rumbling. Ahead was a bridge over a river. Ripples on its surface vibrated along with the bridge as the train started its crossing.

She untied the sancta from her waist. She could boil those soldiers alive when they caught up. Then she would draw another hexagon, and the rumors of the Hex would certainly fly further.

Coldness shook her shoulders and weighed them down. The Hex was her family, well, half of it was. She had to find them. She knew her father had asked that of her.

The tencar was gaining rapidly on the train. The water flashed beneath the train as it chugged along over the narrow, old-fashioned bridge. Soldiers took a few potshots, but all of them pinged off the metal, tens of feet away. But she ducked anyway, sliding down between two of the rolling cars.

Solindra held up the cipher medallion in one hand and hopped backward off the edge of the train.

Steam rose up from the river to meet her and swallowed her completely. The water splashed, but the ripples quickly washed downstream.

She hovered about a foot beneath the surface, surrounded and cushioned by a bubble of vapor. No water had even dampened her hair. It wasn't too large, but with enough air to last a few minutes.

The water made her vision blurry, but she could see the rainbows chasing each other in the heavenly aether bands.

She scratched her ankle absently and glanced down at her boot. Blood still clung to her foot from the man she had killed. She had to laugh, and wondered if she'd had a rifle when she'd met Theo in Valhasse if she would have done the same.

Probably not, she decided. But that was then, and this was now.

Overhead, the tencar flashed by on the bridge. Soldiers standing on the engine mount, each with rifles in one hand, stretched out their other arms as far as possible toward the train.

***

Pearls of sweat shone across Theo's forehead. His heart beat at least twice the pace of Smith's pocket-watch as it counted off each second. He hissed and kept his face and shoulders hunched over the device. He'd had to take off his gloves and he tried to avoid staring at his scarred fingers.

Smith's cane poked him between his shoulders blades again. His index finger shoved the switch forward, spilling quicksilver all over the table.

"Damn!" Theo smacked the small metallic cylinder over into the mercury.

Smith calmly held up the pocket watch in Theo's direction. He waved it back and forth while raising his eyebrows.

The bricoleur closed his eyes and tried to breathe. His nostrils flared like a bull's. He reached for the cylinder and slammed it back into place in front of him. He'd never made a switchpack before, the usual ignition device for most machinery, or with slight modification, most explosives.

They could be stolen off of almost any steam-powered buggy in town. Why would Smith demand that they build their own? Especially these extra-large models.

Theo's fingers danced around the glass bulb with its two exposed wires and dollops of mercury. He pulled up on the string, causing the bulb to tilt. The quicksilver completed the electrical circuit inside.

Sparks popped on the top of the switchpack. A small pillar of flame rose up in the cotton that Theo had stuck there for demonstration.

The bricoleur stepped back and breathed out.

Smith hovered over the table. Finally, he shook his head. "Not enough fire."

"I hate fire." Theo snarled and glared at the Reaper. "This is already bigger than most switchpacks. Let alone homemade ones."

"The flame needs to breathe, Mr. Meilleur." He rapped Theo's scarred knuckles with the cane. "Something of which you didn't understand well at some point."

Theo shoved his hands out toward Smith. "This is Flame's signature."

Smith nodded and pushed forward the burner on the table. "And fire is something you possess, too. But you hate it."

Theo didn't move his heated glare. "I do."

"And so you hate yourself."

"You're as bad as the rest of them."

Smith ignored him. "Tell me, don't you find fire fascinating?"

The bricoleur trembled with both rage and fear. "You... This is it. I'm done. I'm done with this war. I'm done with the Steamscape. I'm out." He whirled around and flew across the room. He raised his hand to open the door.

"You walk out that door and you won't make it two steps down that hall."

Theo waited for that vicious voice to tell him what to do. It always knew how to survive. It had led him here, after all. Then again, it had such a bright, husky, *burning* voice.

Coldness blew in from the door with only the empty, silent corridor beyond.

He dipped his chin to his chest, and then turned to see the cheerful crackle of the flames on the burner. In that instant, he felt a flicker of comforting warmth. He shivered, but in the moment, everything was clear.

He was right. Smith was right. Theo cupped his hands around the fire and gulped. "I think I love the thing that I fear."

"Tsk." Smith frowned. "You just fear power. Fire was power for centuries, and still is in the barbarian lands. Here, it is steam that is stronger than fire."

Theo snapped, "Without the fire, there is no steam."

The Reaper chuckled to himself. "As you've seen, fire is not always required." The cipher medallion clinked on the table beside the burner. Smith's hand hovered over the device.

Then he tucked the sancta back into the folds of his jacket. "Currently, we use steam as a medium to transfer energy. The real trick is bringing the dissolved aether in the water into an energetic frenzy to power our more complex machines. Steam can do it alone, but not nearly as powerfully. But for decades the Priory has known how to ignite the aether itself, but it takes a much bigger spark." He pushed the switchpack toward Theo again. "Hence, make the fire larger."

***

Boras Saturni leaned back in his high-backed chair. Silver and gold plated his office walls. His desk had been polished until it could be used as a mirror.

He stared at the old lithograph on the inside cover of his pocket-watch. The image was cracked and fading. Helen's face and smile had been split in twain because of a wrinkle in the picture. He remembered the original portrait. Infant Adri was somewhere at Helen's feet, but he'd cropped this copy so that his wife's face would fit inside the cover.

He caressed his thumb over her face. "I told you not to go yourself. Last year, I sent the best ten soldiers I had to get you, but they weren't enough. So I sent everything I had and you're still not here with me. Without you, I have nothing."

The lamplight glistened off of platinum candlesticks, just sitting there collecting dust under the expensive electric glow.

He gently slid the cover of the watch closed. "Sometimes, I wish the Hex hadn't vanished," he said into the silence.

"Your wish is granted." Drina uncurled herself from the shadows near the ceiling tiles. She slid down on a silk cord.

"Only half a wish. There's only the three of us." Flame jumped down behind her through the hole they had made. "Seriously, half a wish, folks."

Jing descended last. His metal leg clinked against the metallic floor.

Saturni kicked his chair back and stormed to his feet. He slammed his palm on the emergency bell.

Jing held up a small pair of scissors. "We thought of that, sir. We apologize."

Drina held up her empty hands.

The head of Steampower scowled, but he straightened his shirt and merely glared at them. "You're not here to kill me. I know you, Ms. de Avila, you were never one for excess conversation."

She shook her head silently.

"We want work, Mr. Saturni," Jing said plainly. "Times are tough these days, and with a war back on, our skills are back in demand."

Flame leaned forward on the desk, his knuckles smearing its impeccable polish with grease. "I know you want me dead. But I've already detailed how to kill all the little kings of the board. In fact…" He reached into one of his bandoliers and struck a match.

Drina swatted it out of his hand. "Play nice." She turned back to the steam baron. "And Mr. Saturni always was a crack shot." She nodded to his hand.

Saturni lifted the pistol into view. "Indeed. Mr. Flame is correct, the board did vote in favor of his termination. I told them that they didn't know what they had ordered." He reached down with his other hand and brought up his tobacco pipe. He took a drag and puffed out a smoke ring. "Tell me, whatever happened on that day that you betrayed us? Some of those experiments could have led to the future of steam."

Drina wrinkled her nose. "Adri's infants?"

"The lot of stillborns? No." He puffed up some more smoke, its sweet haze lazing about his beard and face. "The Priory's notes. Those misers were onto something well before the Steam Age." He pointed with his gun. "Now, where's Canon? He's the one who orchestrated burning the Priory's manuals before stealing a baby."

Jing shrugged. "We had commands to go to ground. We followed those orders, Mr. Saturni."

"We did catch up with him eventually," Drina cooed. "Long after we'd gotten his death warrant."

"And what of him?" Saturni drawled.

"I got him." Drina shrugged. "But there was no body left and we didn't think that our word was currency anymore."

"It still isn't," the Steampower head replied crisply.

She raised up her hands again. "Which is why we didn't come back."

"Which begs the question of why now. After all these years."

The Death Spinner opened her mouth, but Jing placed a hand on her shoulder. He said, "Because we need to pay Codic back in blood for recent transgressions. We hear that you've got the war machine to do it, and I bet you'll need someone who isn't afraid to squeeze the trigger at its helm."

Saturni chuckled dryly and leaned back down into his chair. "Yes, we do. But you'll get nowhere near the helm." He sucked on the pipe and set the pistol down on the desk, although within easy reach. Flame watched it like a cat. "The Hex is still currency. I'm sure you know that people are still afraid of you after all these years, which must speak something to the nature of your atrocities." He paused to see the wince around Jing's eyes. He cleared his throat and added, "Or at least to the imaginations of the little folk."

"We need to get to Codic," Flame whined. "I need to set *someone* on fire soon." He was bouncing in place.

"Not in my house, you won't." Saturni frowned. "No, I need you to make some showing to the troops, wave at them, that sort of thing. Mr. Flame, you may set a few prisoners on fire if you need to, but please do it in public, and then only the worst ones."

"Sideshows?" Drina rolled her eyes and sneered.

"Propaganda. Visible demonstration of your skills, and then being with the troops in a very decisive battle. You know the business code, only choose the healthy risks. They have more troops, but we have better machines, so we've chosen a machine's battlefield. You just need to give our boys' morale a kick."

"That's not what we want." Drina pushed off from the desk. "Our payment better be some damned fine information."

Saturni frowned. "Information is what will be kept from you."

Jing narrowed his eyes. "This battle is just a distraction, isn't it? Why else would you publicize the Hex joining it?"

The president of the company flicked a silver letter opener across the desk to the mechanic. "Keep it as a bonus, Mr. Li."

Chapter Twenty-One

Jing twisted the wrench and grunted in satisfaction. Sweat ran together on his forehead in tiny rivers, but he was grinning. He thumped the wrench against the armored shell of the titangle. It had horrifying talons painted on its bottom, so it would look like a swooping bird of prey from above. "This."

Drina raised her eyebrows.

"This feels more like home than that mountain ever did. Newer models, too."

"This is not *why* we signed back up with Saturni." The assassin tossed a glance at Flame, who was lighting matches and tossing them over the side of the platform. Then she turned back to Jing and shrugged. "Although this is how we grew up. You remember the orphan barge. Workers for hire, cheap. Especially for the military."

"Ugh. I don't think that beast could fly faster than a walk." Jing limped around the titangle, eyeing every rivet. "I remember having two legs then. But I suppose if it wasn't for the accident, Mark would've never noticed my mechanical inclination like he did."

"Blood," Drina said. "Not a great hydraulic fluid."

"We survived. And it wasn't just mine."

Her eyes unfocused. "All those dying children. I remember doing the only thing I could to help some of them along." She looked down at her hands, spreading open her fingers.

"They were beyond repair, just like the barge crashing down from the sky."

Flame's grin flickered. "I remember meeting my friend fire for the first time. So magical. It set me free from that box I was in."

"Yeah," Jing sighed. "You were on the barge because you'd murdered your family. That's why you were locked up like that. Mark only rescued you because you weren't afraid of any of what was happening."

"Terrified everyone," Drina remarked.

"Not you," Flame replied.

"You're still terrifying everyone," she murmured, pointing with her eyes at the staring soldiers. They never came closer than fifty feet, but they never faded.

"We don't *know* any of them." Jing set down the wrench. "But they all think they know us."

Drina chuckled. "I could kill one. Then they wouldn't stare so obviously."

Flame smiled. "I like that."

She shook her head. "I think I've gotten old. No practical use for it."

"I don't believe that." The pyromaniac rolled his eyes. "I also can't believe we're ordered to just stay here."

"Orders again," Jing sighed. "That's all we grew up with, on the barge and then in the military. But now, I'm not liking them. I didn't like Mark's orders over the last seventeen years either, apart from one or two things. One or two significant things..." He looked to Drina for help.

Drina stretched. "I thought coming home would be, well, coming home. Back to our old selves. But this doesn't feel right, either."

"Probably because the people that used to give us our orders are at war with each other now." Flame threw another lit match away. "But it's all about money, in'nit?"

"It *never* was about the money," Jing corrected.

"It is now," Flame retorted. "We can only afford honor, integrity and all that shit when we have civilization and that runs on money."

"Steam Slayer better not have heard you say that. Were you asking for a two hour lecture on honor and death and duty while he slowly beat your brain outside your skull?" Drina asked.

Flame stiffened. "He's not here. He probably is living it up killing barbarians. Hell, he's like them enough anyway, thoughts about honor and a good death and those punching gloves with electrical wires sewn into them. But now it's all about getting paid." He shrugged.

A helicopter platform's shadow glided over them. A woman was flying it. Her petticoats and emerald satin dress blew as if in a windstorm. The mountain of cloth was enough so that nothing could have been revealed, even if under attack by a tornado.

The pilot gracefully twirled the platform around and tilted it forward so that the woman could look directly down at the members of the Hex. She thrust one of the levers forward and the platform leveled out to begin a descent.

The skids didn't bounce or screech but gently kissed the ground. As soon as it touched, the pilot killed the engine, but like all platform pilots, had to wait for the dual set of blades beneath it to stop spinning.

Drina shaded her eyes. "That can't be."

"Adri!" Flame straightened up. He spat into his hand and patted his greasy hair.

The steam princess smoothed down her skirts while she waited. Behind her, the soldiers stared in awe. Adri Saturni *and* the Hex.

The blades finally slowed down enough that she could pull the brake lever. They jerked rigid in their tracks. She pushed back from the controls and daintily stepped down from the platform, using the blades as stairs. She pulled her shoulders back, raised her chin and walked over to the Hex. Her parasol snapped open like a pistol shot.

"I had to see this for myself." She looked them up and down. "My little birds had mentioned that you were back, but I thought it was pure propaganda from the board."

Jing looked away. "You hardly look a year older."

Adri laughed. "Thank you, Mr. Li, but flattery failed on me long ago." Her expression faded to a smirk. "I'm sorry to see that you are no longer my father's secret weapon."

Drina frowned. "Do you know what the secret weapon is? You seem to hear of most everything."

Adri laughed again. "No."

"No, you don't? Or no, you won't tell us?"

"Just no, my lady." She twirled the parasol on her shoulder. "I just couldn't believe that if the Hex were back—well, halfway back—that Steampower would advertise you like a new airship. If you don't draw a battle in your direction then I am not the steam princess."

Jing slapped the wrench across his palm. "We're not here for a battle."

"No, you're here for the vessel."

"Where is she?" Drina stepped forward, her hands out of sight.

Adri shook her head. "Not even I know that one. Quite probably dead." Her eyes glowed. "But it worked. Out of all of them, one vessel worked. Truly worked, not just survived. After this war, we can start again." She turned as if to leave, and then called over her shoulder. "And if Ms. Canon is still alive, you'd better hope to find her before I do."

She raised her hand toward the gathering wall of Steampower soldiers and waved. "And don't forget to smile for your audience. I do pray you've learned how to play for the crowd since last we met." She blew a kiss toward the waiting soldiers.

***

Solindra glared at the waiting soldiers. There must have been a score of them, most of them walking behind the engine-cart. Her boots sank lower into the mud and the stream behind her gurgled. She lay flat in the yellowed grass and watched through the stems.

The carriage's water container on the boilerbox was glowing cherry red.

As she watched, they changed from their neat Steampower uniforms into farmer's overalls.

Freezing water coming off the mountains pulled Solindra's attention back to her knees. The water was creeping up the fabric of her clothes and screaming to be noticed. Her chattering teeth might be enough to give her away. She wondered if she were

169

sporting icicles off her boots. The rifle rested against her back, weighing her down. She wished she had it ready to shoot, but she'd barely had time enough to dive to ground.

Presently, one of the soldiers cussed and banged on the overheated engine with a spanner. "Thought this was their finest equipment!"

"Maybe something happened when we unloaded it from the train," another speculated. "It crashed down those last few feet."

"But it worked fine when we fired it up!"

"Get some water," a third voice called. "We need to cool this beast off. I don't think we're gonna make the rendezvous with the others."

Solindra started shaking her head. *No!* she thought. *No, you don't need any water!*

Two of the men trotted over to the stream, several yards away from the vessel. Solindra pressed herself further into the mud and held her breath. She heard them splashing into the creek and filling something metal, like a bowl or a helmet.

Footsteps squelched in the sucking mud and trotted back in the direction of the engine-cart.

Solindra started to exhale.

"Hey. There's something shiny over there."

The vessel cursed, but still didn't move.

The footsteps squelched closer.

I could probably get one shot off if I rolled over now, she mused. But then what?

She heard the metallic click of a rifle's hammer. "Hands up! If you're alive that is. Hey, boys, I got someone!"

She cussed again and raised up her hands, pulling her face up from the mud. She looked up the barrel of a gun to a face that couldn't have been much older than her own. His dark eyes were wide.

She kept eye contact with him while the rest of the soldiers surrounded her. Two of them grabbed her arms and dragged her away from the stream. She left a slimy trail of mud dripping off her clothes and boots.

A man, dressed in a straw hat and overalls, frowned at her with a well-oiled gaze. "Refugee?"

"Perhaps, Major," one of them said.

Solindra shook her head, her teeth grinding together.

He glanced over her shoulder. "No. Not with a cannon like that. Whose side are you on, girl?"

"My own." She kept eye contact.

Another soldier ran his finger down the length of her rifle's barrel. He unhooked the buckle on the strap and pulled it into his hands. "Looks weird." He pumped the action like a shotgun, reloading a fresh bullet and wasting the round already chambered. "Whoops!"

"I thought you'd know how to use a rifle," Solindra snapped.

Several soldiers warily chuckled at the one holding the gun while he fumed at her.

The major's frown deepened. "Not your say, girl. We can't have witnesses and we're traveling too lightly to take prisoners."

She felt her stomach drop. The world seemed to ice over instantly. "I didn't see anything! My face was in the mud the whole time!" She kicked out at one of the men holding her arms and scored a heavy crack on his knee. His grip loosened.

The other soldier stamped down on the back of her calf, and wrenched Solindra to the side. She coughed and gasped, off balance and held in place.

The man she'd kicked leaned forward, his hands on his knees. "What's this?" He reached out to the muddy shape hanging from her belt by a length of twine.

She had the perfect view to watch his entire body tense in one jerk and his mouth twist into a rictus.

He screamed, causing all the other soldiers to jump and raise their own rifles. He started clawing and swatting at his skin. "Swarm! Swarm! Swarm!"

The others stared perplexed at the clear sky, aether bands twinkling in the sunlight.

"Get off me!" The soldier ripped at his arm, peeling off a length flesh with his nails. He gasped like a dying fish. "Kill them all!" The man lunged forward to the engine-cart, still holding the sancta in his hand. "Kill them all!"

"No!" the major thundered. He drew his sidearm.

"Oh no!" The last one holding Solindra yelled and let his grip go. "Get the masks! Get the masks!" He started running.

The soldier with the sancta had retrieved a large metal canister from the cart.

The major raised his arm and fired. The screaming soldier collapsed, but not before he activated the clockwork switch.

Solindra watched as the soldiers' faces blanched and took on the pallor of horror. They started hollering and charging the engine-cart, or just running away.

The dying man hunched back. The gears turned and several metallic darts fired into the sky, trailing smoke.

The vessel hopped backward into the stream. Her ankles sank deep into the black mud, but she didn't notice. She pressed her arms to her chest and lifted a bubble of steam around her, like the one she had used to hide in the river before. She was operating on reflex now. All she could do was stare at the soldiers sprinting.

The darts exploded with three heartfelt pops, and they scattered in the air in three opposite directions before seemingly destroying themselves. The metal pieces fell back to the ground.

Solindra tilted her head. She could barely see anything through the slight haze of the steam.

But she could see enough. The men dropped to their knees, clawing at their throats. It was the same as those bodies in the corridors below Steam Central.

The major managed to crawl the farthest, and stopped moving with his hand against the engine-cart's door.

Solindra's jaw hung open. She turned her gaze back to the soldier who had fired off the canister and saw her cipher medallion still clutched to his chest. His face now sported the grotesque grin of death, leaving his eyes staring off into some other world.

Her steam bubble wavered in a squeak of panic.

Maintain! she screamed to herself. *Don't think about it and just maintain!* She held her breath and tried to remain still.

She didn't know how long she kept the bubble solid. She watched the wind blow through the trees and the movement of the eternal aether bands.

It was getting hard to breathe and she was feeling light headed and faint, but she kept up the bubble.

When she finally fainted, the bubble dissolved as though it was a shawl sliding from her shoulders.

When she awoke a few moments later, she sniffed. Nothing smelled out of place. She tried a few more breaths. Whatever had killed these troops had long since blown away. The chuckling of the brook was the only sound.

The vessel tiptoed around the corpses. She could not look at the face of the man as she pried the sancta loose from his fingers.

She turned away, but then curiosity called from over her shoulder. She pushed open the door of the engine-cart and flinched as it squeaked into the silence. Gasmasks, metallic canisters and more lined the inside of the cart. She took a few of the grenades.

Quickly, she tugged off one of the former soldier's uniforms. It seemed it could fit well enough, and it was better than her own ruined clothing. Some of the boys certainly hadn't been older than she.

Still, she changed on the other side of the carriage, out of sight. After balancing the cap on her head and removing any sign of rank, she stuck her head back inside and snatched up a backpack. She stuffed that with one of the canisters and took a gasmask on an afterthought.

Solindra stepped back and studied the engine-cart. She could put on the mask and set it on fire. She supposed Flame had rubbed off on her after all, just like the other members of the Hex she'd known.

It might explode, but it would destroy whatever those things were, and she had one to take back to Jing.

"Hey!"

Solindra whirled. More soldiers were breaking through the forest. They were mostly out of sight, just blurred shadows.

"You're not supposed to move that during the day. Cover it up!"

"Yes, sir!" She saluted.

The voice paused. "Was that a woman?"

Solindra swung the rifle down into one hand while she threw the backpack over the other shoulder. She rolled some of the other canisters out onto the ground, and heard the expletive shouts behind her. Then she ran across the field and back toward the embrace of the forest.

Chapter Twenty-Two

Solindra's heart raced faster than her feet. Gunshots splintered the branches around her and she heard the bullets singing through the trees ahead. She bunched up her legs and jumped, rolling around the trunk of a tree. With her back pressed against it, she dropped the backpack from her arm. She held her father's rifle to her chest and tried to focus on her breathing.

Tried and failed. Her entire body was shaking. Another bullet thunked into a tree a few feet away.

Now or dead. Her mind shut down. She dropped to her knees, swung around the tree and lined up her shot.

The canister that she'd dropped outside of the engine-cart rocked back with the force of the bullet. The newly-arrived Steampower soldiers screamed and scattered in all directions. Some of them even came straight at her, no longer chasing but fleeing in her direction.

Solindra picked up the backpack and ran. She didn't turn to see if the gas was escaping. Shouts and footsteps followed her. Breaking branches sounded like breaking bones.

She jumped over the edge of the next hill and helplessly bowled down its side. Mark's rifle strap choked her because the gun couldn't bend, but the moment passed as the slide continued.

Coughing, she rolled to her knees at the bottom. Gunfire exploded from the top of the hill and kicked up dried leaves next to her hand.

Solindra pushed herself to her feet, completely forgetting the new aches and stings in her arms and legs.

She didn't dare pause. Her legs twinged and threatened to give out, but she couldn't stop running. She just needed to get a little farther ahead and then, what? Keep running?

Yes, for now.

Solindra pushed through the overgrowth and nearly toppled over a cut bank into a rock-lined river. It was seemingly shallow between the deeper pools created around the boulders, and it was flowing fast.

"Hey! Stop!"

She whirled around to see two Steampower soldiers approaching, their rifles leveled at her chest. She gripped the still-muddy sancta in one palm and held up both her hands. Her own gun and the backpack hung off her arms.

The soldiers stepped forward.

Wind struck up from behind and a blanket of steam suddenly rose up from the river. In seconds, the riverside was covered in the cooling steam.

Solindra dropped. A shot from one of the soldiers whizzed overhead. She held her breath, listening for them to start moving. She rubbed her eyes, trying to clear her vision. It was impossible to see more than a foot away.

A hand reached through the mist and hauled on her shoulder. "Crypter witch!"

She gasped and, in reflex, kicked him in the kneecap. He howled and she wrenched out of his grasp.

"Freddy?" the other soldier called. "Freddy, where are you?" He sounded like he was facing the wrong way.

Solindra rolled backward in the direction of the bank and eased her way between the boulders toward the water. She concentrated and essayed a boot forward. It struck a rock. The water's roar seemed to grow louder in her ears, but she still couldn't see anything.

She hovered her foot over her next step. If she lost her balance here…

She scowled. "I can do better." A disc of steam formed beneath her boot, hovering over the water and solid enough for her to walk on. She made another steam disc, and like a frog hopping across lily pads, she stepped out over the river.

***

The presence was gone. All he had was a void.

Theo rubbed his forehead, trying to coax it out. Through these past horrible years it had told him what to do in order to survive. And now it was gone.

He squared the enlarged switchpack between his hands. It fired off a pillar when he triggered the mercury switch. Smith hadn't shown him with what this would be combined; he had only instructed him to build more. He tried to guess the next link in the concatenation of events that could cause pure aether to ignite.

Aether wasn't even energy itself; it was just something through which energy could be transferred or amplified. Therefore, aether itself could not ignite. Maybe he'd misunderstood something.

He stared at the large switchpack in his hand. These must start up some other engine that affected the fifth element. It might be something far more, well, atomic.

He shook his head. Atoms had been proven over seventy years ago, but he didn't have any idea about what atoms made up aether or what could be done with them. He played with people, not with science like this.

He gripped the switchpack in white knuckles. This was just another step on the path. His goal was to kill Flame. Nothing else mattered. Especially no deals with the Hex.

He just wished that he'd be able to raise his arm with a weapon in hand against the murderer and not freeze up.

In the back of his mind, he hoped that Solindra had fled the country. She didn't deserve Smith. She had a spark, yeah, but it had certainly been no fire.

Theo pushed back his chair and stalked toward the door. Just as he was reaching out his hand, it opened on its own.

Smith tipped his hat from the other side. "Going somewhere, Mr. Meilleur?"

"Yeah, lunch." Theo raised his chin to disguise the crack in his voice.

The Reaper's smile spread like a snake's. "My, what a marvelous idea. I know this fascinating little restaurant none too far from here." He pointed with the tip of the cane. "Let's clean up shop first and make this back into the abandoned apartment it is."

Theo's feet froze to the floor. "Uh. Yes, Mr. Smith."

"Excellent."

They tidied up, or rather, the Reaper watched as Theo stowed all visible signs of their haunting. The bricoleur followed Smith as he moseyed down Redjakel's sparkling avenues and by the buildings that acted as barriers between those boulevards and the noisome alleys and streets in the industrial sections of Steampower's heart.

Smith turned into an alley and pushed open a door halfway down the way. Theo followed and they took seats in a corner booth. A short waitress, probably a few years younger than

Solindra, but with the same red hair, swung by their table. "Beef sandwiches are the house special today, and we've also got stew. Always got stew."

"Just some plain bread for me, Miss Zelia Pressgrove," Smith requested.

The girl's mouth dropped open. "D-do I know you, sir?"

He shook his head. "No, but I always do my research. You have the cleanest kitchen in this quarter of the city and charge less than most of your competitors."

Theo had been equally floored. He crunched his knuckles and tried to loosen his jaw. Zelia offered a half-hearted smile, but still licked her lips. "Uh, yes. Stew and some house wine. Right away."

"Oh my." Smith was gazing at the restaurant's bulletin board. "Fetch me that flyer, boy."

Theo scowled. "Which...?" He saw which one. The bold letters outlining "The Hex" were clearly visible. He plucked it off the wall and dropped it across their table.

The bricoleur gulped.

"Hmm." Smith twisted the paper so that the words were upright. "The Hex resurrected and working fully for Steampower. Interesting indeed." He spun the paper in half-circle back toward Theo. "It looks like we may have a vessel to catch after all."

Theo's eyes slid toward Zelia's long red hair before he could stop himself.

Smith shook his head. "Being a vessel is not her secret. Hers is far more mundane."

"What?"

"Smuggling refugees, in fact. Some of them are hiding in kitchen, cooking our stew, I believe."

How does he know? Theo wondered. He said, "But all those who don't live in Redjakel must report to the camps. Shelter, food, work and all that."

"Yes, that's what they tell you. But that work you so casually mentioned is conscription for the war effort. And one would hate to refuse and be branded a traitor at a time like this."

"How do you find all of this out?"

"The Priory is well funded."

"That doesn't explain how," Theo shot back.

Smith sighed. "Good question. Wrong time."

Theo glared.

"There is always a right time eventually," Smith said and pulled a folding knife from his jacket. He retrieved a small block of wood from his pocket and started to whittle as casually as ever. "As I said before, even a careful man gets careless at some point. The trick is to intercept that point."

"Are you talking about Flame?"

"Perhaps." Smith didn't raise his eyes. Behind him, a shadow rolled up, blocking out the dim light of the alley. "Ah. I'd hoped we would have our meal first. Alas for better days."

Theo stiffened in his seat at the sight of the Steampower soldiers blocking the door. Across the room, Zelia dropped the glass of beer she'd been carrying.

They worked quickly, bursting into the kitchen and opening fire. Voices shouted. Cupboards were kicked open and walls were shot through.

Theo sat motionless, helpless. He saw Zelia casting them a look of iron fury and hatred, all because they had known her name. She probably thought they were the ones who had betrayed her. He tried to shake his head, but couldn't get it to move.

One of the soldiers grabbed her by her flaming hair and dragged her out of the restaurant into the alley. She screamed, and then the bark of a pistol cut her off.

The rest of the refugees' bodies were carted off from the kitchen. The soldiers vanished like a fading thunderstorm.

Theo finally allowed himself to blanch. "Those kids didn't do anything!"

Smith cracked his knuckles. "And that's why they died. That's why I am showing you how to be stronger than they were. Right now, you can have their fate too, if I want it."

"If I want it?"

The Reaper held out his open palms. "Your late crypter friend didn't put up a fight either." He slapped the table. Theo fell limply in his seat, staring at Smith. The Reaper snarled, "Remember, for the moment, you're just the bait. If I don't decide otherwise, you will be fish bait too." He tossed some switchpack wiring across the tabletop. "But you'll be useful in the meantime."

Chapter Twenty-Three

Solindra picked at her uniform. It was a uniform, no mistaking it. She was deep in Codic's territory and wearing a Steampower soldier's garb. She sighed and let her arms hang loosely while she walked. The backpack with the canister in it just grew heavier over time. So did her dad's rifle.

She raised her eyes to the next hill. She didn't have a clue where she was going. She was just walking away from Codic, Adri, those soldiers, everyone.

The sun drew nearer to the horizon and Solindra marched on. The golden solar light sparkled through the aether bands, lighting up millions of twisting rainbows overhead. Solindra ducked her chin and kept walking.

Her stomach growled. She growled right back at it.

Eventually, she rested her weight and the bulk of the backpack against a tree and unshouldered the rifle. It felt like an anchor instead of a gun after her trudge.

She sniffed. Campfire. It was definitely wood burning, but not strong enough to be any danger of a forest fire. She turned her face into the breeze. Her stomach shuddered again as she caught the scent of something cooking along with the smoke.

Her nose dragged her forward. Soon, she came upon a clearing with a floating, but tied down, dirigible not much larger than Pitchstone's emergency dinghy. Its balloon bobbed a little with the breeze and its wood creaked. The airship also had sails folded into frames around the balloon, to better catch the winds.

Several men, at least six of them, bumped shoulders around the cooking fire, trying to stay close to it. No children, Solindra noticed. She realized that she was drooling and wiped her mouth on her sleeve.

How she wished that Jing, Drina and her dad were here! Her knees trembled at the thought of walking down there alone. She didn't have to, but she had no idea where she was. Her stomach groaned loudly.

She patted the cipher medallion on her waist. Nothing for it.

With a sharp whistle, she startled the men at the campfire. They whirled, hands going for their swords and pistols. "Shit!" one of them snarled. "They found us."

"No, no they haven't! Whoever they are." Solindra stepped out of the trees, holding the rifle by the stock over her head. Her other hand was also up. "Can you spare some of what's in the pot? I'm by myself."

She immediately cursed that admission, and then wondered from whom they were hiding. Her stomach finally stopped protesting at that thought.

They leveled several pistols and rifles at her.

She gulped. "I'm not a Steampower soldier. I just stole the uniform. Look, I'm not threatening you and I'm alone."

"What's a girl doin' wearin' a uniform anyway?" The fat one of the group kept her in his rifle sights. None of the guns moved away from her.

"Look, I'm running and hungry. I'm not threatening you or anything."

That resulted in a huddle.

She pointed behind herself. "I can tell you which direction to avoid. There are Steampower men—"

The fat one laughed coldly. "Ain't no Steampower boots in these woods. Not this close to Codic."

She frowned. "Maybe there are, maybe there 'ain't'. Is that a chance you want to take?"

Then she saw it. The shifting of weight from one foot to the next in at least three of the men.

The tall man, with a dark beard and hat, raised his hand and lowered his pistol. "Fine. Lay your rifle up against that tree there and step away from it. Smedly, get the lady some grub."

"Yes, boss." A shorter man with a scar across his hand ducked back toward the fire.

Solindra hesitated. If it were any other rifle, she wouldn't have paused. After a moment, she set it down and took three steps directly in front of it, still holding up her hands. The backpack remained in place against her shoulder blades.

Smedly jogged up but stopped short and held out a bowl of stew at arm's length. Solindra forced a smile and reached forward to grasp the dish. "Thank you."

The scent of the meal nearly overpowered her knees. It had been far too long. She stuck the wooden spoon into the bowl and was in heaven. It burned her tongue, but she didn't mind.

The boss had stepped closer, but was still several yards away. He peered around the vessel at her weapon. "Polishes up nicely. Trade you for it?"

"I'll trade you a bullet from it first," she said without thinking.

The man eased up one hand, the other armed with an old-fashioned muzzle-loading pistol. "Easy now, we're all friends enough here."

Solindra swallowed the last chunk of meat. "Right. It's been dangerous around here lately."

"Oh yes, we know." This time, the boss winked.

She didn't look up, too busy chasing down the last carrot in the bowl. "All that I've seen. Everyone who ain't fighting in this war are the ones suffering for it."

"Yeah." The boss inched toward her. "Come across lots of people heading to Codic."

"No! They can't go there."

The man smiled and took another step. "Why not?"

Solindra shuffled back toward her rifle, just one pace.

"Redjakel and Codic are the only safe places left," he oiled. "Especially with the return of the Hex."

The bowl and spoon fell from the vessel's limp fingers. She blinked several times. "The Hex is back?"

"Half of 'em, they say." The man smirked.

"Where?"

"Territan Badlands. Dramatic scenery for it too, since they brought the bulk of the Steampower army."

The Hex is back. The Badlands. In front of the desert where the Killing Trains roll, Solindra's mind raced, tracing her route across Codic's and Steampower's imaginary line. *The Hex is back.*

Her heart sang at the thought. They had hoisted up a flag so large that she wouldn't be able to not find them.

"It's happening," the boss chuckled. "So that's why everyone's holing up in the nearest capital city. Only safe places left." He started to lean forward. "Even the gentleman who so kindly lent us this boat. Took a whole day of scrubbing to get his brains off the deck."

He lunged.

She stood her ground and grabbed the sancta. As his hands closed in on her neck, she pressed the cipher medallion down into his wrist.

She had a good view of his face. First it froze, then paled and finally colored in green. He threw up his hands. "No, Mama, no! I'll be good! Just don't!" He curled up and crashed down onto the ground.

The others were running up, guns sights bouncing on and off of her with their movements.

Solindra dove back for the rifle and rolled behind the tree trunk. Shots thudded into the wood behind her.

There was no river to save her this time.

Breathing, vision, balance. That's what Drina had taught her in all those games. Take one from them, and earn the other two.

She dug into the backpack. Behind her, footsteps bounced off the trees while the men spread out. She yanked out one of the clockwork grenades, sparked its igniter and hurled it around the trunk in the direction of the boss.

"Grenade!" someone hollered.

The vessel jumped up and sprinted at the anchored airship. That should take care of all three at once. No steady breathing, no vision or balance when they threw themselves to the ground, face-first into the dirt. It exploded.

She threw a second clockwork grenade and pulled one of the knives she'd freed from the Steampower soldiers and leapt onto the anchor. She heard the grenade pop well behind her and amid the spray of shrapnel came at least one horrified wail.

Solindra really wished she had a better idea, but she had only what little opportunity she just stole. With the knife, she started sawing on the anchor's line.

More shots thundered from behind her. She hurled her last grenade.

The explosion stopped the men from shooting long enough for her to finish sawing through the rope. The boat had already been blowing with the wind and now it was set free in its current.

She started to haul herself up the rope, hand over hand. They shot, and a couple bullets struck the hull within a foot of her.

This had been another game on the mountain. Climbing up ropes in between the cliffs had been common enough, and sometimes balancing on ropes strung between some of the heights, although Little Cylinder had only been allowed ones that were two feet above the grass in the Garden.

She climbed now with nothing but the wind around her. More shots and shouts echoed from below, but she could not worry about them.

Her arms burned with effort. The higher she made it up the rope, the higher the ship sailed. She finally was able to kick the hull with her boots. The wind battered the short length of her stolen coat.

The shots sounded almost distant now. She gripped the railing in one hand; the rope had become too tight against the wood to support a higher handhold. She strained to walk her feet up the hull. At last, she pulled herself over the railing, gasping as she collapsed down.

The cipher medallion, rifle and backpack melted off her body, and the vessel slithered down onto the deck.

She suddenly remembered how much she dreaded sky-sailing. Her stomach and hands clenched. She swallowed her most recent meal back down again while it fought to escape.

She'd just climbed up a rope in the air. In the air!

A whimper slipped out of her mouth and she stared ahead unblinkingly.

She laid there shaking for a few minutes while the balloon drifted with the wind and the ship creaked beneath her.

"Get up, Cyl– Solindra. Get up, Sol." She heard her own voice, but she couldn't bring herself to move.

"Move, Sol, or it's only going to get worse."

She managed to uncurl one hand.

"Progress. Good. Now the other one."

Bit by bit she managed to sit upright, trembling every time one of the lines anchoring the balloon to the boat jostled. She wanted to cry, but instead she heard herself say, "Check the boilerbox."

She crawled on her hands and knees to the stern, all the while staring hard at the deck. The coal-fired box was dead. The propeller remained locked in place. She was totally at the wind's mercy.

Next, she checked the water containment. At least that was full. She crawled back to her items and snatched up the sancta. After sliding aft again, she dropped the device into the water.

Almost immediately, steam began to spin the ship's turbine and the propeller lazily started to turn. As the water heated, the blades began to spin with some force.

She pondered steering next, and pulled herself up to her knees, but that was it. She crawled forward to the ship's wheel and all its controls, levers and gauges. It was a fine new ship, even boasting a radar panel. The little square was covered with wires and little metal talismans that showed approximately where other ships and objects were.

She popped open the sailor's drawer at the base of the control panel and pulled out a set of maps, compasses and a sextant. Well, if she knew where she was currently, she could figure out where she was going. The edges of the map fluttered in the wind.

The ship continued to rise. She guessed that it hadn't been weighted for a crew of one. She found the lever with a small plaque reading "Ballonets". She pushed it forward. Hissing like a bag of snakes began to sound overhead. The ballonets full of regular air inside the dirigible were releasing, losing weight, causing the ship to rise faster.

"Damn!" She yanked the lever back toward her guts. The hissing faded to be replaced by the sounds of fans running, pushing the heavier air into the ballonets, and the ship soon started to lower toward the ground.

When the ship was gliding above the treetops, Solindra finally breathed out. She spread the maps out on the deck, weighting them down with the compasses and sextant. She pointed to Codic and followed the river she'd escaped on. Then she had to find the town of Ronna.

She did, and followed the railroad out of the town to the next river, and traced that upstream. She tapped her finger on where she thought she was and checked one of the compasses to see which direction she was going, and whether or not that corresponded with the map.

With a fair wind, she could make the Territan Badlands. She leaned back and frowned. There was no guarantee that the robber's information about the Hex had been correct. Still, it was enough to try.

She pulled herself up to the helm. The steam had built up by now. The wind was at her back in the first bit of solid luck since she'd left Pitchstone. She pulled the lever marked "Sails."

Ropes and pulleys whirred. The sails unfolded on either side of the balloon. She wobbled for balance as the wind punched at them and sped her forward. The bottom of the ship brushed against the trees.

Solindra breathed deeply a few times and vented more air. The ship drifted higher above the shrinking trees. Behind her, all she could see were the taller deciduous trees, but ahead they were starting to fade to shorter trees and hardier pines. She shaded her eyes at the setting sun and tried to make out the horizon.

She turned away from the helm and sat back down, away from the railings and views. She pulled the silver rifle into her lap and stared hard at it. Around her, darkness began to rise with the disappearing sun.

Truth is temporary.

She continued to stare at the engraved rifle. Her steady, safe life certainly had been.

That was what he'd meant. Life changes. Everything anyone knows changes. The truth is a rock, sure, and maybe clinging to it would help her survive the storm, but even rocks eventually weather away.

It was okay to change. Survival meant change. It was okay to be who she needed to be in the moment. Certainly, Cylinder wouldn't have thought about throwing grenades at anyone, but Solindra would, and had.

She wanted to hug the rifle. Her father had certainly changed from the man she'd known from at home. She had never suspected him of being the leader of the Hex. Not once.

There was no permanent anchor to life, she thought. She had tied her foot to the boulder of truth about her dad, and had felt like she was drowning when it had rolled out to sea.

She checked the rifle's load and discovered she was down to two bullets. All she owned in the world was this rifle, two bullets and a stolen sky-ship.

She checked over the railing and espied a dark mass moving portside on the boat. She squinted. The radar's trinkets were all gathering in the corner of the display, rattling together like bones.

Airboats, tanks and ranks of soldiers marched through the forest fast fading to scrublands. The flag of Eliponesia snapped in the wind on tanks, on horseback and even carried by some foot soldiers.

Codic had sent their army.

Solindra kicked the ballonets lever fully backward, trying to hide her airship in night's oncoming embrace.

She took one glance over her shoulder at the proceeding army. "I don't think two bullets will be enough."

Chapter Twenty-Four

Solindra ignored the whine of the whistle; she didn't know its pattern. She picked at the Steampower uniform, walking here amongst all the troops. She ducked her eyes and kept moving. If no one looked too closely…

"Hey!"

She flinched and turned. A sergeant across the way pointed. "Sweetheart, mess tent is that way!" His nostrils flared.

"You'd better hop to it then." She gripped the strap of her rifle and resumed walking, but she heard his rapid footsteps crunching across the rocky soil.

"Who gave you a gun?" The sergeant reached out to snag her shoulder and spin her around. He never got the chance. Instead, he got a rifle butt in his throat.

He dropped to his knees, grabbing at his neck and hacking.

Her shadow spread over him. "I've only got two bullets left, and you're not worth it."

"Not…ladylike!" he wheezed.

She shrugged. "No, but it is very human." Then she leaned down over him. "Point to where the Hex is."

Her motion brought the red sancta in front of the sergeant's nose. She could see him thinking, his forehead creasing and his eyes widening as he wondered if it was what he suspected. He dropped his face, still coughing, and waved a limp hand to the east.

She spun around and walked on.

The vessel hoped he hadn't seen her sweating.

She had attempted to land the stolen airship near, but not too close, to Steampower's army. It had been an ugly walk from there. The Badlands looked pretty in the sunlight with its different colored bands of exposed strata in the light of the moons, but navigating its deceptive heights was hell. Suddenly, the next step would either be two hundred feet high or a thousand feet deep of sandy, crumbling, packed dirt. Or possibly one of the dozens of dead-end canyons that narrowed like funnels.

Finally, the Steampower uniform had come in handy. She'd mixed in easily enough. She had scanned the mass of soldiers. This was Steampower's army, almost all of it. She had left Codic's behind, but not far enough.

Solindra slipped around the tents and decided on the route with the most cover on her way to a miniature plateau.

Her stomach gurgled again.

She gritted her teeth. This time, it would wait. She started toward the helipad-shaped hill, having to dip into an icy stream and climb out the far side. There was no direct route in the landscape's maze. If there was a worse place for an army to gather, she couldn't imagine it.

Finally, she stood at the base of the hill and looked up. Drina was talking and Jing was working on the titangle in the center. Flame was smoking something and staring off at the horizon.

Solindra began to climb up the hill and then froze. What could she say now? The night's wind nipped at the back of her neck, calling her away from the storm she knew was coming.

But she couldn't turn away now. She cupped her mouth. "Drina! Jing!"

The sound of a wrench dropping inside the titangle was the only noise on the mound. She forced her feet to move, but she hadn't made it to the crest when Jing reached down and plucked her up, trying to crush her in a hug.

"Cyl– Solindra!" Drina grabbed her from behind.

Flame waved shyly from around the titangle, and then leaned forward with a leer. "Well, well." He licked his lips.

Drina took a step back to look the young woman over. Her face paled. "That's Mark's rifle!" Even Jing's eyes widened. They both backed away at the sight.

Solindra gulped back her own tears and nodded.

"How did you get that?" the assassin demanded.

"Adri." The vessel shrugged. "She tried to buy me with it."

"Adri." Jing frowned. "She doesn't know where you are."

She could only shrug again. "And I don't know where she is."

Flame checked his fingernails. "I doubt it will stay that way for long. So you made yourselves public to draw the little spark here, and you don't think Adri didn't work that one out too?"

Jing clenched his jaw and shook his head at Flame.

Solindra gasped. "But, but..."

Flame chuckled. "Can't just run away neither. Would look like deserters."

"What's going on?" Solindra's vision whirled between Jing and Drina. "I saw Codic's army—"

"We have scouts and fliers too," Drina said calmly. "We're aware, but this is bad ground to fight on."

Jing blew out a sigh. "This battle is just to draw Codic's attention, but Steampower shouldn't be camping out here tonight with Codic's army drawing close. Alas, they're not listening to us."

"But I saw Codic's forces! They're marching through the night! And this is really Steampower's army? All of it?"

"Couldn't fake it, so they sent the real thing. Saturni has some other plan going on though. Won't tell us, of course."

The young woman's stomach lurched. She swung the backpack off of her shoulders. "I think." She licked her lips. "I think I know." She brushed away the clock from the top of the backpack and revealed the metal canister.

Jing stopped and let out a low whistle. Drina imitated, but watched the mechanic closely for cues. Finally, she asked, "What is it?"

"Gas," Solindra replied. "I saw it kill a dozen men in less than a minute. There are more soldiers with possibly hundreds of these already behind Codic's force."

"And how did you survive if you *saw* it kill them?" Flame rolled his eyes and leaned back against the cool boilerbox of the titangle.

Solindra snapped her fingers. Steam exploded from the box.

Flame rolled away, simpering and poking at the fresh burns across his shoulder. "This was a new shirt, you know."

"Doesn't smell like it."

Jing and Drina exchanged a glance and then looked back at Solindra, wide-eyed. The mechanic drummed his fingers on the canister. "Saturni said he had a plan to attack their economy. This gas wasn't meant for the battle."

Solindra breathed out. "I think I have an idea. Adri knows where the Priory meets. Are they sending the gas there? To take out the whole Priory?"

"Adri probably only saw what they wanted her to see," Jing said. "And they're not Codic's economy."

Drina shook her head. "Can't produce war machines if there's nobody to work the factories."

"I don't understand," Solindra slowly said, a realization dawning but denied.

Flame waggled a finger, new burns forgotten. "People can't spend money if they're dead."

Jing shook his head in disgust. "Gassing the other army, dishonorable, but at least that I can understand. But not Codic and probably Valhasse too. Those civilians didn't choose to be involved, and they sure as hell can't fight back."

Solindra clamped her hands over her ears. But the words echoed around, just as they had inside the children's cave. No wonder those parents had sent them to live in squalor...at least they had a chance to live.

"We have to save them."

Flame hummed to himself and grinned. "You're taking sides, little missy?"

Solindra straightened her shoulders. "I am not fighting for one army or the other, nor for Saturni or the Priory. I'm fighting for those people who didn't have a choice."

The arsonist laughed and clapped his hands. "And what is one lonely crypter going to do about it?"

She narrowed her gray eyes at him.

An orange flash hung in the air like a third moon for an instant. Seconds later, the boom of artillery ricocheted around the badlands. Shattered shouts and colored flares echoed around the Steampower army.

"A battle in this territory at night?" Drina spat. "Codic's got brass balls, I'll give them that."

"I can't think of a worse idea," Jing concurred. "But if they maintain air superiority, then yeah, they'll win."

Her smile curved into a smirk. "But all adds to the extra chaos."

Solindra pressed the stock of her rifle into her shoulder. "They made it here already?"

Small dirt-caked rocks shook loose around them as more artillery echoed around the crevasses.

Flame held up his hands and smiled. "And the skies rained down the fires of hell." He stretched his face toward the aether bands. "They'll be expecting us to make an entrance."

"We'll be fashionably late," Drina snapped.

"I'd rather make an exit." Jing placed his hand on Solindra's shoulder.

She pushed off his hand. "We're not leaving, but I'm not fighting for the Saturnis!"

Flame swaggered closer. "Battle's begun and you're in a Steampower uniform. I'm sure you'll have an excuse to pick a side as soon as some Codic lad shoots at you. Maybe he kills Jing. He's a big enough target."

"That's enough, Flame," Jing grumbled.

Solindra turned to see dozens of soldiers gathering at the bottom of mound, both terrified and hopeful. Their black uniforms disappeared into the dark night, but their faces shone like gathering stars.

"It's never enough, Ghost." Flame smiled and raised his hands. "Good men, do not fear. We have a plan."

"We do?" Solindra hissed.

"Well, *I* do." He winked at her. She immediately started to swing the rifle off her shoulder.

"We need to go," Drina said. "Before Adri—"

Flame whistled. "Little late for that, Death." He hooked an arm around the vessel's throat, pinning the rifle uselessly to her chest.

"Adri made me a better deal than the Hex ever could." He yanked Solindra toward the door of the titangle. "Amazing. I get paid twice for the same kidnapping job."

"You used to be loyal," Jing snarled, advancing.

Flame laughed. "Yeah, when the Hex used to actually exist."

Drina started to slip around to the side. Ghost stepped up directly in front of them, like a personal lunar eclipse.

But Flame knew this tactic and he just backed up to the open maw of the aircraft. "Not today. We're just going to fly out of here."

"Not this time, Flame." Solindra kicked his shin with the back of her heel. She ducked forward, which dragged the barrel of the rifle over her shoulder and along Flame's chest. Her finger squeezed the trigger.

Flame recoiled from the shot, grabbing at his armpit underneath his bandoliers. He withdrew bloody fingers.

Solindra spun around and smashed her foot against his chest, knocking him off the hill. She pumped the rifle's action and pointed it down at the careening arsonist. Fire outlined the air around her.

Shadow and fire crossed overhead. A dirigible, raining flames and piceous oil from its guts, started its descent over the hill. Overhead, the skies lit up enough to see Codic's biplanes flying in on the horizon. Rotating crank guns spat their deadly bullets and the air seemed to rumble and sizzle at their approach.

Chapter Twenty-Five

Dive!

Theo slapped his hands over the back of his neck and plummeted forward. Dirt shot up into his nose, blocking his nasal cavities, forcing him to breathe through his mouth. The sharp curves of the crevasses had muted the whine of the biplane's engine. It roared up and over the cliff behind him.

Theo rolled over and couldn't help but grin. The impacts of the battle were shaking the entirety of the badlands, but he had to smile.

That sweet, dark voice was back, telling him how to survive. It was more than a spark – it was a tower of flame. Always alert, always burning. He wasn't lost anymore. He had his anchor.

Theo wiped his sweaty forehead, smudging dirt across it. He stared up at the sky, stealing a moment of peace. The moons were late in rising tonight, but the coiling, ever-changing pulses from the aether bands illuminated the badlands just enough. He watched the curling hues forever in motion, lighting the ground beneath his hands for just a few seconds.

Theo pushed himself up on his elbows and twisted his neck around. He saw everything. Flame holding Solindra hostage and then stumbling away from her, clutching his armpit and crashing down the slope. The overhead dirigible tilted intentionally toward the earth as it vomited streams of fire onto the hill.

His mouth dried. He clawed his way forward on the ground. He hadn't come this far just to see it end. Not like this.

The rain of fire moved off the mound and into the scattering herd of Steampower soldiers who had been crowded at its base.

A black Steampower biplane twirled in the air overhead and dived at the dirigible, shredding the balloon with its bullets. The light from the plane's rotating guns seared into Theo's eyes. He just stared, watching men trying to outrun death and the flames on their own clothing.

He could see the desperation etched across the dirigible's crew as they sought to dump their endless stream of fire while they went down. And then he saw nothing but fire as a spark caught the gas in their balloon.

The fireball disappeared into a slender canyon.

Theo's jaw hung loosely. He rubbed his eyes. He'd come to find the Hex. They had been his only hope.

Fires started to fade away with nothing to burn, leaving on blackened dirt tumbling down the hill's sides.

"What can I do now?"

He stared limply at the blackened mound and its titangle. Its exterior had melted and the paint had curled completely off. The door kicked open and two women stumbled out. Jing followed them.

Theo rubbed his eyes again and a laugh exploded from somewhere inside. He pushed himself up to his feet and half-slid, half-ran down an embankment toward hill where the Hex and Solindra stood. Shouting, he waved his hands above his head, but his voice was lost in the chaos.

He bounced his shoulder off of a Steampower soldier and rolled into a knot of them. His fists snapped up; he'd learned to box from a carnival champion long ago. But these soldiers' eyes were elsewhere.

The ships raining fire dragged his gaze upward. He wasn't armed, nor was he wearing a Codic uniform. He pushed through some Steampower soldiers, hustling to their own stations and orders.

The bricoleur tripped over a body. At least he thought it was a body, until it groaned.

Theo stared down at Flame. An explosion boomed like thunder several yards away, but he didn't hear it.

Flame's eyes sprang open, the whites starkly contrasting with the dirt and blood that stained everything else about him. Theo's hands clenched for weapons he didn't have.

There he was, wounded and sprawled out. Blood seeped through the crisscrossing bandoliers onto his grenades and pistols.

Theo looked around for a weapon. He definitely had his choice with Flame's bandoliers in reach. But how much time would that waste when seconds were suddenly worth hours? He spat and spun on his heel, poised to run. "There are bigger things than you!"

***

Solindra shouldered her rifle and aimed. She didn't move much, but the next fire-bearing ship was twisting into the wind and starting to hover. Her father could probably have managed a trick shot that both pierced that balloon and ricocheted off the metal to cause a spark. She, however, narrowed her gaze on the pilot. Her finger hovered over the trigger.

The rifle went slack in her hands and she pointed it at the ground. She needed to be sure for her last bullet.

She jerked the firearm back up against her shoulder as someone charged straight up the mound, waving his hands.

"Theo!"

Drina rose up behind her like a shadow. The vessel spun to see the assassin's arm back in mid-throw and the flash of light off a blade.

193

She didn't have time to shout. Theo skidded to a stop and held up his hands. Drina's hand shot forward.

Solindra brought the rifle's barrel up and smashed it into her arm. The knife flew away behind them, bouncing off the titangle with a metallic clang.

"Drina, no!"

"You don't know what he did." Another throwing knife appeared in the Death Spinner's hand.

"Wait!" Theo shouted, still holding up his hands. "I was wrong, but that's not important right now! We're all going to die."

"No, just you." Drina lifted up the new blade.

"Smith is going to explode Redjakel. The whole city. With an aether bomb."

The knife didn't move. "Go on."

"What's an aether bomb?" Solindra breathed.

Jing came up behind them, carrying the titangle's broken door as a shield. "A discussion for a safer place. Death, we can take care of him after he talks."

Solindra shook her head. "But what about Codic? Steampower will attack them."

Theo inched up the hill and stopped just short of its crest. He put his hands on his knees and panted. "I'm sorry. I'm sorry. I didn't know what kind of demon Smith was."

"I'm not saying that we're better demons." Drina smiled tightly.

Theo, still gasping, shook his head. "Maybe. I don't know. But Redjakel needs the Hex. Please. All that aether stored underground. There's more."

The ground rumbled underneath their boots as if in an earthquake. Overhead, a Steampower plane buzzed twenty feet off the ground and pulled up. Two Codic planes chased it. From below, Steampower bullets seared into the sky after the fighters.

But Codic had ten men and ten aircraft for every one of Steampower's shiny armaments. A Codic biplane with its rotating gun swooped out of the sky and screamed toward the solitary Steampower biplane, its gun spitting.

The planes twisted around each other and spun up and over the nearest dirigible. Fire spilled over the airship's side, ending the lives of a score of Steampower soldiers below.

Codic commanded the air, and Steampower had terrible terrain in which to shoot into the sky. They scattered like ants through an unknown maze, only managing the occasional pot shot.

Jing spat. "This was a bluff. Battle was to be real, but Codic got here before Steampower was ready."

Theo's hands slackened at his side. "But what about Redjakel and Codic? What can we do? All of those people in both cities never caused this war."

Drina shrugged. "Which one do we have a better chance at succeeding at saving?"

"Neither," Jing snorted.

Solindra planted the rifle on the ground. "Redjakel."

"You sure?" the mechanic prompted.

She nodded. "Codic stands a better chance against men than the people of Redjakel do against the crypters."

She lurched at the sight of the pale faces of the Steampower soldiers still around the mound. Most of them were haggard and detached, but the worst ones were the hopeful countenances that kept staring up at them, waiting.

Drina remarked, "We can't do anything anyway. We're not a flood by ourselves."

Jing surveyed the badlands. "Battle's already over. They're just not done dying yet. Better to just hide because Codic is in no mood for prisoners."

Solindra slung the rifle over her shoulder and stared down at her boots. "I wish…No, we have to go."

She mouthed, "Forgive us."

She didn't want to look, but was helpless against staring back at those few hopeful faces. Boys her own age. When the Hex turned away, she could see they knew they were abandoned, betrayed to this hell by the company and by the Hex, their patron saints.

Another explosion rocked the far base of the mound, vanishing the hopeless faces in dirt and fire. Solindra turned away and let gravity pull her down the slope, her boots skidding on the rocky ground.

Jing pointed. "We've got our own ground transportation hidden away, just for us. Horses, but they'll cover more ground in the badlands than an engine could."

Solindra stopped. "Wait. Where's Flame?"

"What? Why?" Theo demanded.

"He's Adri's knight, and I won't be her pawn. We have to—"

A hand reached out from the mouth of a shadow-filled hollow and jerked her hair back. "I'm right here, darlin'." Flame pulled her back another step and jammed a clockwork grenade into her mouth. "Thanks for askin'."

Jing and Drina brought up their guns.

"No, no." Flame jabbed his finger into Solindra's shoulder.

"Flame…" the assassin growled.

He chuckled. "What do you want me to say? The Hex has been done for years."

Theo struck a fistful of matches against the coarse soil and held them up in front of Flame's face.

The arsonist's eyes glazed over at the glow.

Theo smiled benevolently and stepped forward. He launched the handful of burning matches up toward the sky. Most of them blew out immediately, but several kept alight through their arcs.

Solindra jerked her weight forward. Flame's grip tightened like a constrictor's. Theo lunged, snatching one of the flares out of Flame's bandoliers, ripping one of the bands off completely. He struck the flare alight against the rock and held it to Flame's back. His clothes, already so saturated with oil, took up the fire.

The pyromaniac's face seemed to melt. He dropped his grip on the vessel and started to claw at his back, spinning in rapid circles as the flames climbed higher. "Not fair, man, not fair!"

Theo kicked him hard in the chest back into the crevasse. Meanwhile, Solindra spat the grenade into her hand. Theo snatched it up without dropping his rhythm, pulled its trigger and hurled it after Flame.

It was the first of many explosions from the items on Flame's remaining bandolier.

Chapter Twenty-Six

The light from the diamond moon sprinkled through the aether bands, invisible now but for their ever-changing colors. The other moon was but a glowing crescent. If not for the jewel moon, the ground would have been a living prism in the lights of the aether colors. The wind picked up, lifting fallen leaves into the rainbow hues. Off the bark of a tree. Off the puddles in the mud.

Off the flank of a cantering horse as it passed through the shadows. The rhythm of its hooves disturbed the still of midnight.

Three more horses followed in its wake.

Solindra furtively tried to massage her hindquarters. She'd never even ridden a horse before this. The rifle bounced along with its stride and knocked against the back of her skull again. There had to be a better way to carry that too.

She groaned and tried not to imagine the leathery calluses forming on her posterior. The mental image faded to be replaced by those hapless soldiers on the battlefield again. Or the image of those regular people in Codic, also left to die.

Jing called over. "Sit up, Sol, our ride ain't over yet." His gaze softened, as if he were reading her mind.

Theo growled, "We grew up being told the Hex could do everything. Be anywhere."

"We were six people," the mechanic replied, looking ahead. "Best we can do now is stay our course because it's already too late to turn back."

"Couldn't we telegraph Codic?" Solindra burst.

"Who would believe it?" Drina rolled her eyes. "We don't have any contacts in Codic's civic government anymore."

"But…we're the Hex."

"Anyone could claim to be the Hex on telegraph. Many used to, actually. That's why we used code."

Jing's brow narrowed. "Would anyone still have that code?"

"Doubtful."

Solindra slouched down into the saddle. "But we could try?"

Drina and Jing exchanged a glance. He said, "We'll try if we find a telegraph. Hope someone can get the word out. But we can't risk telephone or radio."

"Rather worry about this aether bomb," Drina muttered, "because I've never heard of such a device before." She cast a look over to the mechanic.

"It was an idea." Jing shrugged. "But the theory always failed in trial. It would take a crypter to get it to work."

The only sound was the drumbeat of the hooves.

"Or a supposedly ancient order of crypters?" Theo suggested.

"I know, kid," Jing replied.

Solindra scowled. "No, because crypters direct the aether. The aether then moves the steam. At least I think. I'm certainly no expert."

"Transfer of energy," Jing said. "Aether moves energy through it, so in theory, with enough aether…" He swallowed. "This will be bad."

"That's what Smith said." Theo leaned back in his saddle to look at the mechanic.

"But it only works with steam!" Solindra protested. "I've seen that."

"To start, but with an enormous supply of aether and a chain reaction—" Jing broke off. "Such an amount of aether shouldn't even be possible to get. You'd have to have ships harvesting it for years from the bands, at altitudes where your hands turn black from the cold and you can't even breathe. Not even the crypters can do that, not that I know of." He looked back at the bricoleur.

Theo shook his head. "Don't ask me. I didn't get to see any of it. But I remember that pure aether." He shivered, thinking back to that moment where he'd thought he'd followed Merlina into the alley. Then he slouched forward. She couldn't have been there. Smith had seen to that.

His grip tightened on his reins. At least Flame had never pretended to be on his side.

"Redjakel should be in sight by dawn." Drina leaned forward and tapped her horse's flanks with her heels. They charged onward through the glowing silvery light of the diamond moon.

"If it's still there," Theo muttered as he dug his own heels down. "Hyah!"

***

The city stood. Golden sunlight reflected off the brass of Steam Central's skyscraper. Solindra patted her mount's neck as the animal grazed on the grass at their feet.

"It looks so peaceful from here," the vessel said.

"I don't think we've ever been in so much danger," Jing murmured.

Drina shrugged. "We can ride away. We don't have to do this."

Solindra set her jaw. "No. We left the soldiers and we left the people of Codic. We're all Eliponesians. We're not leaving the people of Redjakel. Not unless they have their hands stained by their own actions."

Jing leaned away from her. "Meaning?"

"If you see Saturni or Adri, shoot them."

Drina nudged the vessel. "Of course, by saving everyone – on the off chance we succeed anyway – we save those two too."

"A bullet is more personal anyway."

The Death Spinner blinked. "That sounded like Silvermark."

Jing patted the assassin's shoulder. "Alas, Solindra's no longer our little Cylinder."

Solindra ignored them. "Theo, your turn. Where is Smith?"

The bricoleur frowned. "I can show you where he last was."

"You'd best do better than that."

"Yes, ma'am." He almost saluted sarcastically, but held himself steady. The others were right. This was a new person, not the girl he'd met before. He lifted his foot into the stirrup and hesitated to swing his other leg over. Was this new person worth endangering his life for?

He slid into the saddle and gathered up the reins. Why not? He'd killed Flame and now had no idea what to do with the life he still had. "What's our plan, Sol?"

"Stop this aether bomb."

Jing grunted. "I don't want to mess around with it while the Reaper's there. I'd rather just break his fingers so they can't work the bomb's triggers."

"I vote we avoid Smith," Drina said. "Or I can deal with him while you three blow yourselves up trying to be noble."

"Right, Death." Jing rolled his dark eyes.

"We might not run into him at all." Solindra stared ahead at the city in the growing dawn. She could see differences now. Refugee tents dotted the plain in front of the city. All the roads were now blocked with wooden barricades. As they trotted nearer, she could see that not all of them were manned. She guessed it was because most of their army had gone off to war, and then wondered if they had beaten the news of the battle here.

They unsaddled the horses and turned them loose as they neared the city. They slinked wide around in the shadows and approached a barricaded avenue. The hasty construction had led to an uneven wall.

Solindra slung the rifle over her back and started to climb without a word. Drina followed her up like a spider, quickly overtaking the younger woman. Theo came after. Jing's metal prosthesis forced him to climb slowly, using his muscled arms and one leg. The steampowered leg hung like a dead weight.

Warning bells started screaming as they descended to the street. They froze, watching and listening. But no one seemed to converge on them. In fact, they didn't see anyone at all.

"What's going on?" Theo cocked his head into the wind. "That's code! They're signaling in telegraph code."

Both Solindra and Jing held up their hands for silence.

The bell tolled: - .... --- ..- .... .- -. -.. ... -.. .. .- -.. -.-. --- -.. .. -.-. .--. .-. . ... -.. . -. .- -.. .- -.. ... --.- ..- .- .-. . .-.-.- ... - -- .--. .--. .-. .-.. .- -. . .... --. .- ... . .-.. .- -.. ... .--. . . -.-. .... .. -.-. --- -. -.. - --- .-. .-- .... . .-. . .- .--. .--. .- .-. . -. - .-.. -.- -- --- ... - --- ..-. - .... . -.-. .. - -.-- .... .- -.. --. .- - .... . .-. . -.. - .... --- ..- ... .- -. -.. ... .- .-. . -.. . .- -.. -- .- -.-- -... . . ...- . -. .... .- .-.. ..-. - .... . .--. --- .--. ..- .-.. .- - .. --- -. --- ..-. - .... . -.-. .. - -.-- .. ... .- - .-.. . .- ... - .-- --- ..- -. -.. . -.. .-.-.-

They waited in stillness and darkness for the bell to sing its verses. Tears started to slide down Solindra's cheeks.

Drina shrugged. "I got Codic."

"Shh!" Jing shook his head stiffly for silence. Even his lips were tight.

Solindra pressed her hands to her ears. "That's it. It looks like Steampower won."

"No." Theo mashed his fist into his other open palm. "They don't have an army left. What happened? I couldn't pick that up."

Jing dropped his chest. "I can't..."

Drina looked between Solindra and Jing. She crossed her arms. "Can it be worse than our imaginations?"

Solindra nodded and bit her lip.

Jing pressed his eyes closed. "Steampower gassed President LaBier's speech, where apparently most of the city had gathered. Thousands are dead, maybe even half the population of the city is at least wounded. LaBier's condition or whereabouts remain unknown."

"We knew this would happen," Drina whispered.

Solindra gasped. "We're all from the same country. The people haven't forgotten that. How? How could they?"

Theo took her hand. "Then let's do what we can here."

Solindra nodded.

He dropped her hand and led them through alleys. They remained in the shadows. Away from the open areas and the glow of the Light District, the winds stole the warmth from the city. Their boots crunched over discarded gears and other trash.

"This one." Theo rapped his knuckles softly on metal side of the warehouse and listened. Nothing moved from inside. "They pumped the aether into the underground here. I saw Smith fiddling with it when we dropped off the switchpacks."

"Switchpacks?" Solindra whispered.

"Shh!" Theo waved his hand behind his head, pressing his ear up against the door.

"Over at least a year," Jing mused. "Nobody would notice dirigible balloons coming in for repairs in this district, I bet. Maybe they—"

"Shh!" Theo hissed again.

Drina raised an eyebrow and a knife behind the boy's head.

Jing and Solindra shook their heads.

Theo turned around to a sweetly smiling assassin with her hands behind her back. He shook off whatever thought he had at her expression. "It's quiet. Probably the best we're going to get."

"I don't like it," Solindra whispered. "Too quiet, you know?"

"This is where the aether is. They can't possibly have moved it."

Drina purred, "And you said this was the only supply they had left?"

Theo nodded. "But I think it's the bigger one."

"Then that's more than enough to cripple Redjakel permanently," Jing murmured.

Solindra swallowed. "All those people." She shook herself free from her horrifying daydreams and pulled on the sliding door. "Let's do this."

Jing pushed open the door just enough for them to slip inside. "This would be a good time to spring the trap." Beside him, Drina nodded.

"Trap, Mr. Li?"

A match flared in the gloom of the warehouse as Smith lit a lantern. He smirked in the growing light. "There is no trap. Traps require illusion or misdirection. This is only reality."

Solindra froze, trembling. Smith was here! She tried to flex her hands, but they were suddenly numb.

Theo stumbled back toward the door. "I didn't know. I didn't know! You said you would leave it empty."

"Yes, but I was lying, Mr. Meilleur. In fact, I even told you that you were bait and still you didn't puzzle this together."

Drina whirled on Theo, slamming him against the wall. He started to gasp, but felt a prick against his skin. A single drop of blood stained her stiletto.

"Ms. Death, please. He's nothing but my unwitting errand boy. You wouldn't kill the bootblack, would you?"

Drina never looked away from Theo's terrified eyes. "I have before."

"I am not surprised, or frightened, by that admission." He twiddled his mustache. "Now I can destroy the vessel and Redjakel together."

"I'm innocent." Theo closed his eyes and then an icy sensation chilled his spine and blood. He couldn't pray to the Hex. He had no one left. He didn't know any other patron saints.

"He is." Smith's glass cane echoed as he tapped it against the concrete floor while he stood. "Remember, innocence is synonymous with ignorance." He snapped his gaze over to Solindra. "And you, thing, don't you dare point that shiny toy at me."

Her fingers fumbled her grip on her father's rifle. She had it halfway up to her shoulder. She knew he wasn't armed; she knew she could shoot him. But she just couldn't make herself stop being numb long enough to just do it. It was like touching a stove when she knew it was cold, but she'd felt that heat before and couldn't bring herself to risk the burn.

A few feet away, Drina winked at Theo. She spun and launched the stiletto at Smith.

He parried with his cane, but the knife still managed to graze his forearm, opening a small slice. The Death Spinner shot off two more knives. The Reaper charged Solindra, bringing his cane up like a sword.

Jing held up his fists and stood in Smith's path. He caught the cane in both hands, and he and Smith grappled for a moment. The blue sancta swung in between the two men, suspended on a chain around the Reaper's neck.

Smith grinned and gritted his teeth at the same time. "It seems I have the advantage."

Jing jerked up his metal knee into Smith's thigh. The Reaper hardly flinched. Then Jing smirked.

The gunshot echoed like thunder inside the metal walls of the warehouse. Jing's knee smoked as the barrel retracted back inside its casing.

Smith's face contorted. Jing breathed out and started to relax his grip.

The Reaper's face twisted into a grin. Jing looked down. The bullet was rapidly spinning in place, trapped in a cloud of steam in front of Smith's stomach. Steam pulled from the moisture of the blood across Smith's arm.

Smith's pupils suddenly dilated and the bullet shot back at Jing. The prosthetic kneecap sparked and exploded into scrap metal. The mechanic stumbled back with the force of the shot, a surprised expression widening across his face.

The Reaper spun and put his foot down in front of Solindra.

She tried to straighten and swing the rifle between herself and Smith. He raised the cane over her chest, pointed end aimed at her heart.

Solindra thrust out with the rifle butt, the fastest move possible from her lopsided position. It slammed into Smith's thigh.

He staggered back half a step. She spun the rifle around so that the barrel pointed toward his head. It wasn't aimed, not with the fight. The barrel's end bobbed and swayed, but couldn't find its target.

Theo bowled himself shoulder first into the Reaper and knocked both of them back. Drina had circled around and dropped a thick silken cord around Smith's neck.

Where Smith no longer was. The silk hissed through the empty air.

The Reaper whirled the cane around in front of him like a stave.

On the table behind him, a telephone bell started to ring.

Smith scowled. "Excuse me, the Gentlemen require my services."

He slammed the point of his cane into Drina's side, spun around behind Theo and, in the second of chaos, retreated from the fight.

He trotted over to the table and ignored the ringing telephone. He lowered his hands to the typewriter, wired into the floor, and his fingers tapped out, "Truth."

Drina hesitated and glanced back at Jing. She stepped between Solindra and Smith.

Gears started to click and whirl along the wall. The structure rumbled and fissures crackled into existence along the wall. Sections of metal sheeting fell away to reveal that an entire wall of the warehouse was clockwork.

Theo held his hands over his head as chunks of twisted metal rained down. Jing tried to limp away from the wall, but his broken prosthesis held him in place.

Drina and Solindra lunged forward. The vessel aimed the rifle, but the Death Spinner was two steps ahead and in her line of sight.

"Truth will win." Smith raised his hand to the wall.

Drina thrust with two knives. One swept wide across the top of Smith's chest, drawing his gaze while the other plunged straight toward his gut.

The Reaper batted away the first knife with the cane.

He grabbed her wrist with his other hand. His thumb dug into a pressure point and her hand slackened involuntarily. With his thumb, he flipped the thin stiletto back toward her.

Drina's face pinched with anguish as the knife pushed into her chest against her ribs. She gasped.

Smith shoved her away and whirled to face the others.

And he stopped. Solindra was only three feet away with her rifle barrel at his chest.

Smith held the glass cane across his chest.

Her last bullet boomed as it spiraled out of the barrel. The glass cane shattered underneath the bullet, and the round bit deep into Smith's heart. His cipher medallion swung over the bullet hole, but it was too late.

Smith's eyes widened. He slumped forward and his knees buckled. Then he collapsed face-first onto the concrete floor.

Solindra exhaled and lowered her rifle. It felt ten times heavier now.

Jing wheezed and pointed. The clockwork wall was spinning faster. Several of Theo's large switchpacks fired into life with pillars of flame along the wall.

Aether bands creeped up the wall as slivers of the element started to escape the underground storage. Automatic pulleys retracted well covers and crackling glass bulbs rose up from the floor. Pumps were pushing the aether into the glass.

"Chain reaction," Theo gasped. "What can we do? Is there anything we can do?"

Jing shook his head. "Aether itself can't explode." He tried to lift his metal leg, but the joints wouldn't move inside of it.

Solindra dropped the rifle and landed in front of him. She turned to Drina, who was pressing a hand against her bleeding breast.

The assassin heaved for breath. "I'm okay enough for now. We have to run."

Jing shook his head again. "Can't outrun this."

"Then stop it before the aether ignites!" Theo screamed. "You're Ghost! You're the Hex! You can do anything."

"Never went up against the Priory," Drina gasped.

"Aether can't ignite," Solindra said, staring into the middle distance. "It's not energy. It's the medium through which energy is transferred. It reacts with everything else."

A gear snapped and wheeled off the wall, twisted and smoking. The entire wall seemed to bulge and waver like a mirage.

"Too late." Theo smeared the sweat across his face. "Too late."

Aether bands spiraled up in the air and curled their tendrils toward them. Solindra tried to walk toward the wall, but the bulge no longer seemed to be in the same world.

"Can't stop it!" Jing cupped his hands to be heard above the sounds of machinery.

The entire wall twisted and rose away from the floor. Chunks of concrete rumbled to the base. Rebar and steampipes hung uselessly into the empty air. Switchpack fires burned.

"It's the fuel!" Solindra screamed. "The aether is just converting everything to energy, and that's what will destroy

Redjakel! Everything in Redjakel will be converted into pure energy."

Another automated switchpack flared to life.

"Can't stop it, the fire's already burning." Solindra started to hammer the rifle butt against the concrete floor. "Release the aether! Get the fuel away from the fire."

More aether spiraled into the machine hovering over the ground, feeding the frenzy.

"Make holes! It can't destroy the city if there's no aether to make the transformation from matter to pure energy, so make holes!"

"What with?" Theo spun around, looking for anything. His hands fumbled for the thermite bombs he had grabbed from Flame's bandolier.

Jing snatched up one of them from Theo's slick fingers and tried to lurch forward, dragging his metal leg behind him.

Solindra slid into place alongside the mechanic's leg. She pressed her red sancta against it. Steam from the sweat rising from their skin coalesced into a cloud around his metal knee. Jing moved it, and the metal squeaked, but it worked.

She rose, her uniform blowing in the winds. "Release the aether."

The wall was hovering fifteen feet now and spinning slowly. The gears whirled as if spun by tornadoes. Behind it, a cogwheel started to curve unnaturally and glow, then it disappeared into a burst of white light. The building shook at the small burst, and a shockwave pushed them to the ground.

Theo, staring at the machine the entire time, handed each of them a thermite container.

"Oh, Flame." Drina smiled at the small magnesium switchpack on top of the device.

They limped into a circle. One by one they met each other's eyes and set the devices on the concrete floor. They lit the thermite's switchpacks and stepped back in unison.

More items started to spin within the field of the machine. Aether tendrils encircled them and more white bursts flared and shook the entire world around them. They ate through the floor and the distant wall, beginning to convert the very matter into energy.

The burning thermite canisters melted through the floor. Aether bands, lighting up in their rainbow hues, began to seep up through the holes. At first they were only as wide as a fist, but they expanded as the fifth element began to escape.

"Is that enough?" Drina asked. The aether still caught in the chain reaction was eating away at the wall and buildings beyond, carried with the wind.

Solindra pulled out her sancta. The colorful aether swirled around her hands, answering her call without the intervention of steam. It spun faster and faster. She dropped her hands to the concrete and the aether streams followed, spiking through the floor like a meteor shower.

It blasted apart the center of the concrete and glass floor, sending fragments flying in all directions. Aether started to rise while cracks spread out across the floor in all directions.

"Run!" Theo bellowed.

Solindra turned but her gaze stuck on Smith's body. The glass cane was shattered. The floor beneath his body was vaporizing.

Theo held back for just a second. He pulled the old coin out from around his neck and lifted it over his head. He tossed it down onto the floor ahead of him and into the rising tide of aether. He watched it dissolve into a flash of light and send out its own thunderclap.

Then he turned and ran for the warehouse door after the others.

They sprinted down the alley and into the avenues, and vanished into the fleeing crowds. Behind them, the rising explosion ate through the pieces of the buildings where it touched, vanishing them into light. But the flashes grew smaller with each passing moment, as the aether drifted away from the warehouses, swirling as it rose to join its brothers and sisters in the sky.

Chapter Twenty-Seven

"Codic with no city. Steampower with no army."

Solindra stood apart from the wall and the shadow where the others waited. She looked between the shining pillars of Steam Central and its surrounding skyscrapers, to the warehouse district.

Even the aether bomb's failed destruction wasn't too apparent from this short distance. Not against the gritty, whirling machine of people that kept Steam Central's lights glowing. She watched the sun setting, coming to earth in between the two worlds that shared one city.

Drina, Jing and Theo weren't watching. Jing leaned against a walking staff while he fiddled with his leg with his free hand.

Drina shook her head. "I still think Codic has the advantage here."

Jing frowned. "They're without a lot of their leadership. Still no word on LaBier."

Solindra turned away from the setting sun, putting it at her back. The golden and orange rays reflected on the silver rifle. "Priory's intact, if they were hiding."

Theo shrugged. "Hard to say on that. We don't know. All we do know is that this isn't over." He snorted. "No more Smith, but what about Adri? Or more Reapers? Which side do we go after? There's no end in sight to this."

Solindra shook her head. "We're all Eliponesian. We are still one nation. We're suffering the same."

He dusted imaginary dirt from his shirt. "Really, Sol? How are four people going to put a nation back together?"

"It doesn't take much to start an avalanche." She swung the rifle over her shoulder. "Maybe we should start by rescuing Helen Saturni." She leveled her gray eyes with his. "Theo, you're the new Flame. We still need a spy and fighter."

Jing pushed himself away from the wall and leaned on his walking staff. "Solindra, do you honestly want to do this?" He and Drina exchanged a glance.

The vessel nodded firmly. "I will not stand by while people who live on the wrong side of an imaginary line are killed for other men's bounties."

"We can teach you." The mechanic pressed his lips together. "Their peace will only exist if we do our jobs well, and they'll never know."

She nodded again.

Drina put a hand on the younger woman's shoulder. She wheezed and tipped forward. Then she straightened. "Upfront, we are telling you that you will have to do things to protect these people that will haunt you for all your life."

Solindra looked down into the pillars of steam rising up from the city below. "I'm already haunted." She started walking.

Nearby, steam drifted out from the pipes that disappeared into its depths. Machinery played its own deep, rhythmic music from inside the buildings. But along the edge of the alley, where the vapor drifted, a few blue and purple steamflowers opened their petals.

"This is what you wanted, Dad," the vessel whispered to the flowers.

"What was that?" Jing prompted.

"I need to send a message. Everywhere. All at once."

"Won't be easy," he said.

"Yes, but you're Ghost."

She looked at each of them: Jing, Drina and Theo. "Ghost, the Death Spinner and Flame." She dropped her gaze to a puddle, shiny with spilled oil but still enough like a mirror. "And I am Silvermark."

***

Adri smoothed the lace of her white dress in one fluid motion as she turned away from the giant mirror at the head of the board room. She dipped a hand into her handbag, but didn't retrieve anything immediately. A glow seemed to surround her, as the sunlight bounced off her dress and mixed with the glimmer from the diamond moon through the window.

In the mirror, she watched behind her as Boras Saturni slammed his hand against the conference table again. "Unacceptable losses!"

A board member raised his index finger. "But they left most of our equipment intact, and we can always get more uniforms. Heavens know there are more than enough people in the city without much to do. Give them a job, a leg up."

"Hmm. There might be a food shortage next year though," mused a second man, "since those people aren't farming now."

"That's a problem for next year, John," corrected a third. "Also, our tractors should be in mass production by then. Harvesting so much that we won't hardly need farmers."

"Gentlemen," Saturni's voice creaked from the head of the table. He barely glanced over as Adri stepped up beside him, hand still in her purse. "Our immediate objectives have always been to usher in a smarter, economical age against the antiquated government, and to rescue my wife."

"Why?" Adri asked crisply. The room seemed to dim at her voice, except for the fading sunlight radiating off her dress. "You raised your daughter just fine, didn't you?"

Saturni opened his mouth, but the steam princess had pulled the bag away from her hand, revealing a revolver.

She shot her father through his ear and pushed the body away from his chair before it could fall over. She smoothed her skirt with her free hand and took her seat.

The board inhaled collectively.

A speaker with a beard as wide as his hat roared to his feet. "Ms. Saturni, how dare you? We are important men who are the leaders of this country—"

A second gunshot exploded in the chamber. The speaker's body slouched forward across the table.

Adri placed the smoking pistol onto the table. "A bullet kills each of you equally. And I can always find more uniforms for this table."

Several other men had their mouths open in protest and rage. Then jaws clicked shut. Gazes wavered and fell.

She purred into the gathering silence, "Since you made yourselves little kings and put the law into the paws of this board, I have done nothing illegal. Not unless one of you speaks out against me." She held up the smoking gun. "No? No one? Good." She straightened her shoulders and leaned forward. "Now, gentlemen, to business. We must finish this war that my dear, late father began. I have a plan to kill the Priory and steal the rest of their secrets. This will work wonders for profit with their information in pocket."

"What about the Hex?" a chair asked, and hid his face behind his gloved hands. "People are drawing that blasted symbol everywhere."

"Yes, we must tell everyone how they abandoned our troops in battle." Adri smiled viciously. "In order to win this war and conquer the hearts of all our citizens, we must dismiss their beacon of false hope first. We will destroy the Hex."

The board member named John swallowed. "Um. Excuse me, Ms. Saturni?" He stuck his hands under the table to hide their shaking. "We learned about Flame's demise. But, um, what could the two remaining rogue soldiers do?"

As if on cue, the telegraph machine, wired directly to a mechanical typewriter, began to hum. The keys punched out the ghost message.

We are the voices in the darkness. We are the riders on the storm. We are the Hex, and to those who visited these atrocities on our land, we'll be hunting you.

When the keys fell back down into silence, Adri ripped the page away from the spool. She slid it across the conference table. "Let me put it like this. You're either on my side or theirs, and I don't think they like you very much."

***

Down in the streets of Valhasse, tiny strips of telegraph paper were circling faster than dust devils. Many of the grime-smeared workers were cheering. A few older men and women who remembered the Hex were in tears. Others had just gone home or to their tents and barricaded themselves inside.

An urgent whistle down in the train yards squealed to no pattern. The heavy train cars rocked with the power of the mob behind it. The cattle train had been fitted to hold people instead, another Killing Train was ready to ride the rails. Only the people had stolen the rails out from underneath it.

First one car toppled on its side, suddenly useless to the world. The two linked cars on either side hung halfway on, halfway tipped into the air. Then, like a swarm of ants, the rioters began to take apart the Killing Train bit by bit.

***

The Hex's message had gotten through. The train yards in Redjakel crumbled under the weight of the mob. A steam whistle coughed out one last alarm and went dead.

Across the blocks and avenues, in a less mutinous part of town, a man limped into a hotel. He sidestepped a pair of arguing teenagers.

211

The older one tried to yank the telegraph tape from the other's hands. "Don't get caught with this. Steampower will hang you for it!"

"Oh, yeah? Are they going to hang everyone? The Hex is back! Ain't nobody gonna fu—"

The older one tried to cram a fist into the other's mouth. "Shut up! Shut up! Shut up!"

The man drew his jacket tighter over his chest and limped to the counter.

The manager of the hotel pulled out his guestbook. "Bit of trouble, sir?" He pointed to the bloodstains on the newcomer's shirt.

The man scowled, but then forced a tight grin. "Indeed."

"Such trouble out tonight! I hope it stays away from those of us who just keep our heads down and—"

"Pardon me, sir," the man interrupted. "I just need to know if you've a room for rent."

"I do. Name please, sir?"

The man straightened. "Martin Coxwell, Esquire."

Once up in his private room, Coxwell listened against the tiny window. He could hear the roar from the warehouse district and the train yards, but it was just a beast in the distance. He removed his jacket to reveal a blue cipher medallion hanging by a small chain around his neck.

And a hole over his heart. In fact, a hole clear through his chest cavity. Candlelight shone visibly through the cavity. The top half of his heart was missing, and in its place steam glimmered in the meager light. Tiny, insubstantial gears pumped blood in and out of the organ in veins and arteries composed of steam. The clockwork heart continued its beat.

www.ingramcontent.com/pod-product-compliance
Lightning Source LLC
Chambersburg PA
CBHW071159260626
47162CB00003B/1101